My Kind of Guy

Paddy Bostock

A Wings ePress, Inc.
Political Fantasy Novel

Wings ePress, Inc.

Edited by: Jeanne Smith
Copy Edited by: Christie Kraemer
Executive Editor: Jeanne Smith
Cover Artist: Trisha FitzGerald-Jung

All rights reserved

Wings ePress Books
www.wingsepress.com

Copyright © 2020 by: Paddy Bostock
ISBN-13: 978-1-61309-578-2
ISBN-10: 1-61309-578-3

Published In the United States Of America

Wings ePress Inc.
3000 N. Rock Road
Newton, KS 67114

Dedication

To Cindy—MY kind of guy.

* * *

One

Ex-MI6 agent Mervyn Iain Vincent, MIV of MIVI, as he used to joke before taking early retirement, was in the glum-going-on-grumpy mood he'd been nursing for the past several years, during which the world around him had so radically changed since his post-1989 Berlin days when the hope of fresh starts was in the air. The arrival of the state-assets-thieving madman in the Kremlin had been hard enough to bear, but since 2016 there had been an apparently Moscow-sponsored madman in the White House too. *And,* misery of miseries, there was yet another newly installed at 10 Downing Street. With this triad of gung-ho socio/psychopaths in charge of countries, and others doing their populist damnedest to emulate them across Asia, South America and Europe, it seemed to Mervyn the efforts he had made to maintain the world's equilibrium were headed down the tubes fast. Not to mention humans were about to become extinct because of the unchecked global warming none of the socio/psychos gave a fuck about. No wonder he was glum-going-on-grumpy. A surprise, he reckoned, he hadn't lost his marbles altogether and jumped in the Thames with a lead-stuffed lifebuoy.

Mind you, on this particular day, he was also glum-going-on-grumpy because his cherished Morris Minor Traveller had a flat tyre and an equally flat battery, his roof was leaking, and his washing machine had taken to dirtying more clothes than it cleaned. Yes, he should have taken more care of these things, stitches in time saving nine and all that, but preoccupation with global politics, and the extinction of the human race had pretty much taken his eye off such mundane balls.

Also, early in that same morning, and despite the numbers he regularly added to his British Telecom personal blacklist, he had received *three* scam calls from Bangladeshis called respectively "John," "Percival," and "Ronald," all in their different ways claiming his life would become a living hell unless he immediately gave them the details of his credit and debit cards. He cut them off before they'd got a sentence out, of course, having learnt from experience "John" would tell him his computer connection had been "compromised with malware" and would be discontinued in the next twenty-four hours unless... "Percival" would claim to be a policeman about to jail him for fraud unless...and "Ronald," posing as an Australian animal welfare official, would give him the sad news of his Visa card having been eaten and subsequently excreted by a homeless kangaroo and would be no longer therefore be valid unless...

What, Mervyn reflected increasingly, was the world coming to with such scam artists rife, and tweeting nutcases in charge of politics? These days he only paid shopkeepers in cash, never bought anything on the Internet, rarely used his hated smartphone, and only skimmed the news on his computer every two or three days in case it told him of novel and worse horrors. Pretty much these days he lived in a state of anxious purdah.

No wonder when his precious and practically antique landline phone rang for a fourth time and a voice introducing itself as Lizzie Leah said, "I've just lost my husband, Doctor Vincent, and..." Mervyn toyed with such replies as: "That was careless of you," before hanging up and throwing the phone through the—conveniently open—window of his study.

Even as an *ex*-MIVI agent maladjusted to the twenty-first century, however, Mervyn had lost none of the secret agent skills that had kept him out of harm's way in situations which would have left James Bond baffled and facing the prospect of a bad guy's Luger between his eyes. It was the naming that was the giveaway. Scammers only ever addressed their scammees as "you" on their phishing trips because they didn't *know* your name, only your phone number. "*You* are about be blown up by an unexploded World War Two bomb under your house unless... *you* will be eaten up by a newly discovered strain of cancer endemic in *your* part of the country unless...*you* will be arrested on the charge of falsifying incriminating police evidence unless...

But this one had given her full name and addressed him as Doctor Vincent, thereby evincing knowledge of both his name *and* his title—Mervyn held an ancient Oxford doctorate in forensic anthropology. Instead of advising Lizzie to go and stick her head up a cow's bottom therefore, he said, "And how may I be of assistance, Miss Leah?"

Which was when Lizzie said she hoped Mervyn, in his role as private eye, might be able to help her in finding her missing husband. That was Mervyn's part-time job since quitting MI6, private eye, just the odd case taken here and there to distract his mind as far as possible from the horrors of these dark days.

"Tomorrow work for you?" asked Lizzie.

"Yes, that should be okay," Mervyn replied, ostensibly checking the diary he didn't have.

~ * ~

The following morning in his tiny two-up-two-down cottage on the western fringe of Wimbledon Common, Mervyn awoke to a blue sky. Which astonished him and marginally improved his mood. Despite it being mid-June, the previous week had consisted of persistent yellowish grey skies, wind, wind, wind, rain, rain, and more rain, all of which he took to be clear signs of the climate change that would exterminate him, or if not *him* at least all those of future generations.

"Wow," he said to Suzie, the Battersea rescue Heinz 57 London Terrier who slept at the foot of his bed. "*Sun!*"

"Raaf, raaf," said Suzie, turning over, peering through the window and wagging her tail.

"Nice day for the race, eh? By which, Suzie, I'm thinking the *human* race, not a horse race."

"Raaf, raaf, *RAAF*," said Suzie, oblivious to the joke but enthusing anyway because Master was.

Seeing as they both turned out to be Wimbledonians, Mervyn had arranged to meet Lizzie at a pub called The Hand in Hand, a stone's throw along the path that led from his house past Cannizaro Park. She would have to come a little further than him from South Wimbledon, but hadn't minded.

"The walk'll do me good," she'd said in her broad Scouse. "Bit of peace and quiet up your end of the woods, eh?"

Which was true enough, and precisely why Mervyn had chosen to live as far from the madding crowd as possible. Every day he walked the Common with Suzie for at least two hours. Same route most days, but Mervyn didn't care. The odd chat with another dog owner or horse rider, a cup of coffee and an egg sandwich at The Windmill café, then back home chatting to trees along the way. Nuts, he reckoned most folk would thank him, but Mervyn didn't care; trees were his friends. In his book they were a sight more intelligent than most people and always outlived them unless chopped down to make way for roads or high-speed railways thereby depriving the planet of the very oxygen it needed to prevent humans from becoming extinct. Mercifully, nobody had yet come up with a scheme to drive a motorway through Wimbledon Common, which Mervyn reckoned gave him a marginally better chance of survival, at least in the short term.

It was an abbreviated version of the walk he and Suzie took on this day, finishing up at The Hand in Hand where, while sitting outside so he could smoke, he was looking forward to a pint or two of Young's Special while he waited for Lizzie, who had said he would recognize her from the outfit she'd be wearing.

"Just look for the bits of red," she'd said.

And sure enough, as Mervyn and Suzie made their way through the gate, there she was. The "bits of red" had been an understatement though. The woman of maybe late thirties sitting at one of the tables was decked out in *all* red: red trainers, red leggings and a red silk shirt bearing, over her left breast, the Liver Bird crest of Liverpool Football Club. Her hair was *also* red. And not the dyed kind Mervyn saw and loathed on much younger women whenever he went shopping in town. Genuine, luxuriant, and down over her shoulders, it reminded him of a girl called Bärbel he known back in his late cold war Berlin days. She was sipping at a half-full sleever of Mervyn's own favourite tipple.

"Lizzie Leah. You Mervyn?" she said, standing and reaching out her right hand while the other held onto the lead of a large hairy Lurcher called Jürgen, who practically pulled her over, so keen was he to meet Suzie.

There followed the usual entanglement of leads and an embarrassing moment when Jürgen tried to shag Suzie even though he'd been snipped. Not that Suzie seemed to mind, even though she too was short of her reproductive equipment.

"Yuh-yes," Mervyn managed to mutter as he and Lizzie struggled to restrain their lusty dogs.

"*Naughty* Jürgen," said Lizzie, dragging him backwards and in so doing knocking over her half-full glass.

"Ooops," said Mervyn, thinking "*Jürgen?*"

~ * ~

It wasn't until Suzie and Jürgen had been disentangled, given doggie treats, and tied to opposite ends of the table that Mervyn and Lizzie finally managed the handshake.

"Sorry about that...still reckons he's got the balls for it," said Lizzie, as Mervyn righted her glass and offered to have it replenished while he went inside to have filled the tankard in his name kept behind the bar.

"Funny name for a dog, Jürgen. He a German?" he said on returning and placing the drinks carefully on the tabletop.

Lizzie laughed. "Not a footie fan, eh?"

"Nuh-no." It was a long time since Mervyn had shared conversation with any woman, let alone one as alluring as Lizzie, and even then not about football.

"So you won't have heard of Kloppo then."

"Nuh-no."

Lizzie shook her head sadly and pointed at her Liver Bird badge. "Only the best manager we ever had since Bill Shankly. Only the coach who just won us the European Champions League cup. He's a German. Jürgen Klopp."

"Oh. Which is why your dog's call—"

"Clever deduction, Mister Private Eye."

Reckoning this was as good a moment as any to get down to business, Mervyn said, "Part *time* private eye, just the odd case here and there to keep my hand in. And while we're on the subject, may I ask how you found my name? Your call came as a bit of a bolt from the blue."

Lizzie took out a pouch of Golden Virginia and inside it a packet of green Rizla papers. "Mind if I smoke?" she asked in a way suggesting she was going to smoke even if Mervyn did mind.

"Not at all. Perhaps while you're at it, you could...?" he said, arching an eyebrow.

"Roll you one too? My pleasure, love. A fatty or a thinny?"

Mervyn smiled for the first time he could remember since a golfer on the Common's fairway had hit another golfer on the head with his ball after a sliced bunker shot. "Fatty, if that's okay."

"A-Okay," said Lizzie, expertly twiddling the tobacco between a thumb and an index finger. "Fatty coming up. Oh, and your name. Googled you on my phone, didn't I?"

"But I've never put my name *on* the Internet. I'm more of a word-of-mouth type."

"Well, someone *else* must have, a satisfied customer maybe? Came up under Missing Persons Detectives. You know what the Internet's like these days. Nothing private anymore."

"Even *eyes*," said Mervyn with more animus than he'd intended. A dedicated identity protector from way back was Doctor MIV MIVI. Then it had been a prerequisite for the job, now it was simply a longing for anonymity—and, of course, protection from hackers and scammers.

But Lizzie just laughed, handed over the fatty, and took to rolling her own, a medium thinny. "Need a light?"

"Thanks, I've got my own. And look, to get back on track here, your reason for calling, the reason for this meeting was your lost husband. Should we not perhaps think about that?"

"Raaf, raaf," said Jürgen, having chewed through his restraints and now making for Suzie again.

"Oh, for fuck's *sake*, Jürgie," said Lizzie, caught in mid-roll-up.

Mervyn came to the rescue by tying him up again, patting his head, and saying, "*Genug Hündchen.*"

"Thanks," said Lizzie, finally lighting her cigarette. "What was that you said to him?"

"Enough, doggie."

"In?"

"His own language. German."

"Wow. One of them cunning linguists, are you?"

Mervyn blushed, fidgeted, and smiled obliquely.

"Sorry, didn't mean to embarrass you."

"No need to be. I just have a smattering of a few European languages, that's all. They were necessary to my old job. But look, Miss Leah, is it not about time you told me about this husband of yours, the one you lost?"

"Ah, right, *him*. And it's Lizzie."

"*Lizzie*. Although it doesn't sound as though you're overly worried by his loss. I assume he's not dead."

"Not so far as I know. And you're right...I couldn't give a shit about losing the knobhead."

"Right."

"Except he owes me money, five hundred quid."

"Ah," said Mervyn, swigging down a third of his pint of Young's Special with one hand and jotting a note into his PI notepad with the other. "Usual story," said the scribble.

"And perhaps you could describe the manner of his loss, Lizzie, the moment you realised he was gone. A phone call, a message under your pillow?"

Lizzie shook her lustrous red locks. "No, nothing like that. Me and Leo, that's his name...Leo, were out walking the dog over the other side of the Common by the windmill. He was dawdling behind me checking his phone, and when I looked round to tell him to hurry up, he'd—"

"Gone," said Mervyn, renowned in his Secret Service days for such intuitive deductions.

Lizzie was amazed. "Yeah. Poof, just like that."

"And you went back to check?"

"Sure. Thought he might've been caught short and was doing a wee or something, so I looked under all the trees, but nothing."

"Mysterious."

"You're right about that. Wanna know what I think? He couldn't stand the idea of Liverpool beating his lot in the Champions League final so he did a runner, that's what."

"'His lot' being?"

"Spurs."

"That would be Tottenham *Hot*spurs."

"So you *do* know something about footie. Anyhow, that's my idea. Either that or he was taken by aliens, Wombles maybe. Remember them from the old telly show, *The Wombles of Wimbledon Common*? Maybe they've got him locked away in their underground grotto."

Mervyn smiled obliquely again, nodded, and jotted in his notebook, "clearly barking."

Nonetheless, he said, "Interesting. Now listen, why don't we have a bite to eat? They do a nice Shepherds' Pie here. Then perhaps we could take a stroll back to my office where you can give me a few more details of this Leo, a photo you might have, that sort of thing.

"So you'll take the case?"

"Consider me hired." After all, Mervyn had no other cases on at the moment and the disappearance of a person into thin air had a certain allure to it. Also, he liked the woman's pizzazz, barmy though her theories might be. A bit more of that might help lift at least a smidgeon of his current gloom.

"*Woweeee*," said Lizzie starting to hum extracts from "Walk On," the anthem of Liverpool FC's famed Spion Kop.

Two

Letting Jürgen and Suzie off their leads in the vindicated hope they would take more interest in trying to catch rabbits than having sex with each other, Mervyn and Lizzie took their time ambling back to his little cottage. It was finally an undilutedly sunny day and they wanted to make the most of it. Along the way, he explained he worked from home, hence the "office," and apologised in advance for the mess Lizzie would find there.

"Not much of a DIY fan. All fingers and thumbs, I am, more likely to break stuff than fix it. Give me a can of paint and more of it'll end up on me than on any wall. Plus, I like things where I can find them. They seem to get lost in cupboards."

Lizzie laughed her infectious laugh. "Don't worry, love. I'm not the tidiest person in the world myself. Housewife...I...am...*not*."

"What *do* you do?"

"Drive a bus. You might have seen me around the place."

It was Mervyn's turn to chuckle. For the first time for a very long time. "Actually no. Matter of fact, I've *never* seen a lady bus driver."

"*Woman* bus driver," Lizzie corrected.

"Sorry. Bit slow on the uptake with the old PC, I'm afraid."

"No worries. We learn something new every day, right?"

"Indeed. And Jürgen? What happens to him when you're out on the bus?" asked Mervyn, who worked from home and rarely needed to leave Suzie.

"He comes with me. Wouldn't have taken the job otherwise. Sits behind me on one of the handicapped seats and licks all the customers when they get on. They love him. Favourite bus from Wimbledon to Clapham and back, mine is. You'll have to come for a ride one day."

"With pleasure."

"And you? Always been a PI, have you?"

"Actually no."

"So what then?"

Normally, Mervyn told nobody about his past employment. MI6 forbade it what with official secrets and everything. On the other hand, he'd been out of the service going on ten years, so...

"I was a spy."

"Woweee. Like James *Bond*?"

"Sort of. But you shouldn't believe all you see in the movies. It not exactly as though I look like Sean Connery or Daniel Craig, is it?"

Lizzie took a step back, shrugged, and joke-pouted. "You look O-*kay*, though."

"Anyway, anyway, enough about me," Mervyn was saying as, mercifully from his point of view, they reached the gate to the overgrown front garden of the little house that would have benefited from several coats of paint—of the same colour.

"After you, welcome to my humble abode," said Mervyn, semi-bowing thespianly, and gesturing Lizzie through with an outstretched palm.

Having failed to catch any rabbits, Jürgen and Suzie followed them with their tails between their legs. On the other hand, Suzie knew where the biscuits were kept so she reckoned that would cheer up her new best friend.

~ * ~

"So, a cup of tea perhaps?" said Mervyn, as Lizzie surveyed the chaos of the kitchen and, through its window, the wilderness at the rear of the house. Noticing, Mervyn outlined his philosophy of gardening, namely what he termed "unspoiled natural luxuriance" which sounded to Lizzie more like an excuse for idleness than a proper philosophy, but she didn't say so.

"Plants and trees are living things and shouldn't be interfered with," Mervyn was saying. "Nothing I dislike more than prissy little gardens with sculpted beds and flowers that get changed every season to suit the current fashion. Leave 'em alone and let 'em grow is my view."

Lizzie smiled. "And the…?" she said, eyeing clumps of nameless growths sprouting from the ankle-high lawn and elsewhere.

"Weeds?"

"Yes."

"I like my weeds. Some have very delicate flowers. Plus, they are of course important for attracting bees and other insects which might otherwise become extinct even before we humans do."

"Uh-huh. A Greenie then, are you?"

"And proud of it. *Now*, how about that cup of tea? Won't take me a second to find a clean cup," said Mervyn, ferreting about amongst a pile of semi-washed crockery on the draining board. "Milk and two sugars?"

"Black and no sugar, thanks."

"Russian style, eh?"

"No, just black and no sugar."

"Okay." Mervyn was beginning to sense an, albeit amused, hint of disapproval from his guest. For which he couldn't blame her. He wasn't used to visitors, that was all. "Coming right up. Just got to find the kettle. Why don't you sit yourself down somewhere and make yourself comfortable? Afterwards we'll go to my study in the other room and get down to business."

Lizzie tutted faux critically as she sat herself down on a wicker chair behind a pile of newspapers and books on an ancient table while Mervyn scurried about finding tea bags. God alone knew how he managed to cook his dinners, she reflected; p'raps that's why he was so thin. She'd said he looked okay after the James Bond reference, but the truth of the matter was he looked a lot like a beanpole that could do with a few hot dinners inside him, as her mother up in Bootle would have said. And *this* was the bloke she'd hired to find Leo. Okay, he could speak a few lingos and might once have been a spy, but...

Mind you, once the rigmarole of the tepid tea was over and they moved to his "study," things began to look up a bit. Not that the study was any tidier than the kitchen or the garden. Piles of papers on the floor, shelves creaking with dusty books, a brimming ashtray on the desk, and...so...on. But once Doctor Mervyn Vincent sat himself down behind his computer and took to speed-playing the keyboard like a pro pianist, Lizzie relaxed a little. Maybe the guy was just an absent-minded brainbox of the kind she'd heard of but never so far met in the flesh.

"Soo, Lizzie, pull up a pew and let's sort out a few things. First off, I'd like to be clear about your reason for hiring me rather than going to the police. Surely they have a missing persons' procedure."

Lizzie pulled, or rather dragged up the suggested pew—another wicker chair, this one with a ratty cushion on—and sat opposite Mervyn. "I tried, but they reckoned I was nuts. I think it was the 'poof, just like that, he was gone' that did it. Plus, they didn't seem all that impressed about my footie theory."

"Or the aliens, particularly the Wombles?"

"No. Also they said there were thousands of missing persons around London and, what with the cuts and everything, they had no chance of finding them all. So it was a case of don't call us we'll call you."

"And they haven't?"

"Fat chance."

"Okay," said Mervyn, typing super-fast into the file he'd created entitled: Lizzie.

"Also, just to be absolutely clear, you told me this Leo was your husband so I'm assuming his second name is Leah like yours."

Lizzie fidgeted a bit and scrutinized her long, red-lacquered fingernails.

"*Missus* Leah? Can I make that assumption?"

Lizzie sucked in her lower lip and bit it before replying.

"No. His name's McGuire, but mine isn't. We weren't actually married, you see, so he wasn't legally my husband."

Mervyn raised an interrogative eyebrow.

Lizzie shrugged. "He made me use the name McGuire when I was with him, that's all. I was to call him husband and he'd call me wife. It was a game he liked to play. Said it was more fun than just boyfriend and girlfriend. You'll think I'm stupid now, won't you? Some saddo lonely old dumb bitch."

"Not at all. I don't make value judgements of that kind. Not my job," said Mervyn, tapping "gigolo?" into the Leo side of his file. "And your birth name *is* Leah? Sorry to be pernickety."

"L-E-A-H."

"Good, fine. And can we be *sure* Leo's real name is McGuire?"

"That's what he told me."

"And you believed him."

"Why wouldn't I?"

"Quite, quite. And how long had you known this Leo McGuire before he vanished?"

"Six months, nine months maybe. I wasn't counting."

"Uh-huh," said Mervyn continuing to type. "And do you have a recent photo of him I could use?"

"Not one he gave me. Said he didn't carry pictures, wasn't his style. But there is this," said Lizzie taken a phone from her bag. "Took it myself when he was busy doing something else."

"Perhaps you could pass the phone over?" Mervyn stood and held out a hand across the table.

"It's a bit of a weird shot."

"I'm sure it'll be fine," said Mervyn as Lizzie did as requested.

Transferring the photo to his new file, Mervyn glimpsed briefly the image of a square jawed, blue-eyed man with fashionable three-day stubble and black hair faintly streaked with grey. It *was* indeed a bit weird as Lizzie had said it would be, seeing as she'd taken it from behind while Leo preened in a wall mirror. But at least it offered two views of his head, one from behind, the other the front.

"And he didn't notice you taking it?"

"If he did, he never said. Too busy looking at himself, I expect. He liked doing that. Not a lot to go on, is it? Mind if I smoke? It's making me nervous all this." Lizzie took out the roll-up equipment again.

"Go right ahead. And make me another fatty too, if you would be so kind. We won't be long now before we call it a day. I don't suppose he told you what he did for a living."

"Salesman," said Lizzie in mid roll-up.

"Of?"

"He never said. Just that he travelled a lot. Often abroad, although he never told me where."

Mervyn nodded. Fitted the gigolo image all right. He wondered how many more women this Leo had on his books. A "wife" in every port of call, most likely. With the flimsy information Lizzie had given him though, tracing the creep wasn't going to be a stroll in the park.

"Nothing else you can tell me about him? Medical conditions? Habits? Family background?"

"Sorry, love, can't help you there either," Lizzie was saying when, bored with being ignored for so long, Jürgen took to pawing her arm.

"Down, Jürgie, *down*." she told him to little avail because this was the sign Jürgen needed to pee, a sign with which Mervyn was all too familiar from Suzie.

"He can do it in the garden if he wants. It'll do the weeds good."

"No, look, Doctor Vincent, I reckon we'll be going home now. I know I haven't been much help, but—"

"Fine, fine. Okay. If I think of anything else, I have your number. It's been a pleasure meeting you, Miss Leah, and I hope very much we'll be seeing each other again soon. If I find anything, I'll certainly be in touch and—"

But Lizzie Leah was already out of her seat and heading back to the front door with Jürgen at her heels.

"Mmm," mused Mervyn. "First so chatty, now so keen to go."

But he guessed that was women for you. At least in his experience, which he had to admit was limited. There had been Bärbel in Berlin, Chantal in Paris, and Melinda in New York, but that was about the size of it.

Three

With his mind pre-occupied by global extinction and mendacious buffoons in critical power positions, Mervyn Vincent rarely slept well. And if he did nod off peacefully for an hour or two, he would soon be awoken by the recurring nightmare in which all the wheels of his Morris Minor Traveller fall off simultaneously as he is negotiating an Alpine hairpin bend and he plummets down a mountainside into a river in which he drowns. Either that or it is the one in which his house is being invaded at four-fifteen a.m. by the very lying buffoons he loathes and hordes of their masked populist/fascist supporters, all armed with scimitars and set to chop off his head. There were other versions of course, but the subtext was always the same: Mervyn dies badly. Which he reckoned was at the very least unfair. Had not Freud said dreams were about death *and* sex? Well, sorry to disappoint you, Sigmund, but no sex for Mervyn Vincent.

And so it was on the night after his interview with Lizzie Leah. Okay, so there had been a couple of *very* brief interludes of him and Lizzie lying improbably naked on a Caribbean beach, but they were fast obliterated by Lizzie morphing into Leo, who bit his dick off. It was at this point in the dream, at four forty-eight by the bedside clock, that Mervyn awoke thrashing as per usual, and poor old Suzie was kicked off the bed again. Mind you, used to the experience, she didn't complain. Just wandered back to her doggie bed in the corner and dozed off until peace was restored by Master smoking a cigarette, lying back down, and waiting for the next horror show to hit.

Only *this* time it was different. This time Master sat bolt upright, said, "Eureka," and scuttled off downstairs mumbling.

"Raaf," mumbled Suzie, the heavy eyelids closing again.

And what was it that caused this sudden change of nocturnal behaviour? The Lizzie episode was the initial prompt, but much more important was the epiphany to which this led, the sudden unexplained knowledge of just who the Leo biting Mervyn's dick off *was*. An eidetic memory can be a very useful tool, especially when it works even in dreams. Hence the eureka before the downstairs rush to the computer to check out the suspicion of to whom the face seen from front and back in the mirror photo belonged. Leon Devine, Mervyn reckoned, the rookie agent drummed out of MI6 for "behaviour contravening all rules of the service and endangering national security." The scandal had happened only months after Mervyn himself had quit and would surely be recorded in the top-secret file to which he, as a respected alumnus, still had access.

And sure enough, when he logged in, there was the report of the Cambridge-educated son of an English father and Russian mother whose initially starry career had been abruptly terminated as the result of not only his serial womanizing—MI6 happily turned a blind eye to such things—but much more critically his loose tongue and the suspicion of unauthorized intelligence leaks all across the globe. When last heard of, the report continued, Devine had gone rogue, peddling secrets—and arms—to the highest bidders, including those in Russia and the Middle East. And there at the top of the report was the very... same...face Mervyn had seen that afternoon on Lizzie's phone, a little younger and with no grey in the hair, but the same ice-blue eyes and the same square jaw. And if he'd crossed yet another red line, this time with one or another of his dissatisfied and less tolerant clients, it was perfectly possible Lizzie was right and he *had* vanished poof without trace. A quick squirt of Sarin or some such by a counter-agent, then whisked off to the boot of a waiting car and hey presto.

It was a theory all right, one he would need to check out with his old boss ASAP in case she had any info.

~ * ~

In one sense, both Lizzie and Mervyn were right in their conclusions about Leo's disappearance. It *had* happened "poof just like that," only for a different reason than the doings of Liverpool FC or Wombles, although the alien intervention idea carried an ironic truth. One minute on the walk with Lizzie he'd been scrolling through his messages wondering which of the Mrs McGuires he might visit next when, bammo, the phone rang and an American voice said, "Job done. Get the hell outta Dodge double quick time." There followed a brief instruction as to where the limo would be waiting and then silence.

And so it was that Leon Devine had made a rapid U-turn, done a runner to the Windmill car park and hopped into the back seat of the limo waiting to take him post haste to Heathrow. There it had merely been a matter of bypassing the procedures suffered by the regular prole passengers—showing passports, stripping, having flashlights shone up their bottoms, all that type of thing—and heading straight to the VIP airstrip where the Gulfstream was waiting to blast him across the Atlantic to a similar JFK facility. Thereafter, another limo would speed him to the Fifth Avenue apartment of Hal Schornstein, one of the prime movers in the loony incumbent's 2020 presidential re-election campaign and, along with his counterpart in the Kremlin, *agent provocateur* in chief for the continuance and growth of populist unrest throughout Europe.

Wearing a back-to-front baseball cap bearing the logo America First, Hal had greeted Leon with a bear hug and a glass of bourbon.

"Great seein' ya again, Leo McGuire. Wunnerful job."

"Glad you liked it," said Leon, who was also glad about the million-dollar payment he'd been promised on successful completion of the gig. It would sit nicely with the other millions of dollars earned from the Russians, Middle-Eastern oil-rich sheiks, and others for similar outings. One thing he was proud of was covering his tracks. He'd learnt his lessons well during his brief time at MI6.

"Tonight you sleep here," Hal continued, "then tomorrow and tomorrow and the tomorrow after that till we call again, you keep your head down and *way* outta sight, okay?"

"No problemo." Leon would be happy enough to re-connect with the Mrs McGuire who lived in a trailer parked amongst the redwoods near Muir Woods only an hour's drive from San Francisco.

"Atta boy. No phone except the one we give you. No Facebook or Googlin' or any of that shit, deal?"

"Deal."

"Great. So good working with you again. Guess you must've been kinda tied up in Yurp all during the Brexit bullshit."

Dropping onto a white sofa, sipping his bourbon, and gazing out at views across Manhattan, Leon said, "Yeah, that's been fun. Brexiteer Brits need imagined enemies so I help provide them. Germans are their favourites."

"You got the lingos, huh?"

"Some." Because of his parentage, Leon was bilingual in English and Russian, although he also had fluent French and German plus smatterings of Italian, Dutch, and Spanish. Cambridge had been good to him in that regard. Not because it taught the spoken form of those languages particularly well, spending far more time on translation and literature than it did on language, but there had always been the vacations. "Now look, Hal, I am a tad bushed what with the flight over and everything. Mind if I get my head down for a bit?"

"Walk this way," said Hal, showing Leon to the bedroom he always used in NYC, the one with the four-poster, the en-suite stained-glass bathroom, the red leather armchairs, the well-stocked bar, and the TV with six thousand channels. "Sleep tight and don't let the bed bugs bite," he added closing the door behind him.

Leon didn't sleep immediately though. Glad to be free of Hal, he topped up the bourbon, settled into an armchair and turned on the TV already set to Fox News. On it, the president was waxing lyrical yet *again* about his only state visit to the UK where he had been hosted by

Mister and Missus Queen who had liked him *very* much. As had the Prince of Wales—Wales the country *not* "Whales" the fish as the fake news slimeballs had been taunting him with after a Tweet mistype. And then there had been the hundreds of thousands of waving fans down on the streets as he flew over in his helicopter. They had just *lurved* him. No mention was made of airborne being the only way the president was allowed to travel between castles because Downing Street, the police, and the Foreign Office feared his feet touching the ground could get him killed, which it was felt would be bad for diplomatic relations between the UK and the US.

"No protesters in sight any place. That's the special relationship we got going with my kinda guys," he prated until Leon had had enough and switched over to the soccer channel, on which David Beckham was boasting about his new team Inter Miami.

"Some ponce," Leon muttered, switching Beckham off too.

Better by far it would be for Leon to be out of the game for a while hidden away quietly in Muir Woods re-charging the batteries. But if another job came his way meantime, well off he would go again. Money was money. And it wasn't as if the *only* phone he'd have with him would be Hal's. How dumb could the guy be?

~ * ~

Mervyn met his old boss Dame Margery Middleton, "Double M" as she called herself for fun, at her club behind Park Lane.

"Better than in the bally office," she'd told Mervyn when he called for an appointment. "Too many distractions there. I'll bring whatever we have on Devine with me. Most of it's in my head anyway. And we can have ourselves a bite to eat. Hope that suits."

It was fine with Mervyn, who had been by no means enamoured with the prospect of a trip to his old stomping ground at Vauxhall Cross. There were too many familiar faces there; too many catch-up conversations he wouldn't want to have. Okay, Margery's was a women-only club, but male visitors were tolerated as long as they behaved themselves, so...

"I'll leave a note at the downstairs desk. All you'll need is the code word I'll give you, some ID, and bingo," she'd reassured him. "I have my own little private space where they also do a decent lunch."

Which proved accurate to a T as always with Margery, who hadn't reached her exalted position in a male world by ever being caught out on detail. Once having given her code word and flashed his passport, Mervyn was ushered up to a somewhat larger than "little" private space on the third floor where his ex-boss, looking as trim as ever, was waiting for him with a pen poised over *The Times* crossword.

"Hey ho, MIVI," she greeted him. "Stuck on sixteen down. Any idea what the solution to "Battle gear?" might be? You were always something of a cruciverbalist as I recall."

"Any letters so far?"

"First one's a B, then there's an L, a C, a V, an H, and an M a bit further along. Ends in a T. Two words, fifteen letters altogether."

"Balaclava Helmet?" Mervyn ventured.

"Spot on, old chap. Spot *on*," said Margery, jotting in the answer and putting the paper to one side on an escritoire. "Now then, to lunch. What's it to be? They do a rather jolly steak and kidney pudding with frites and peas. How would that suit? Haven't become a veggie or anything since we last met, have you?"

Fine was how it suited Mervyn, particularly as accompaniment it came with what Double M termed "a more than decent Beaujolais." As they munched and sipped, she got straight down to business, explaining The Circus didn't have all that much accurate information about Devine's most recent activities because of more pressing matters and staffing shortages.

"That's austerity for you," she complained. "Bally government at more sixes and sevens than a barrel load of chimps over the Brexit bollocks, but *very* nifty when it comes to trimming budgets. The armed forces are moaning, the coppers are whingeing…the hospitals, the schools, the whole damn country being told to economize 'cos there's no more cash in the kitty and books have to be balanced. And *still* the clown in Downing Street rides high in the polls. It makes one wonder how, does it not?"

"Precisely because he's the nation's top Brexit-monger executing the 'will of the people' on their behalf. Or so he parrots *ad infinitum*."

"True enough, even though he's an Eton and Oxford toff who knows nothing of ordinary lives. All the thumb-sucking, cross-eyed, brain-dead, lefty Opposition had to do was *say* they wanted to remain Europeans and it would all have been a different story."

"A sad case of the hard right and the hard left for once coming together over something, ma'am, namely xenophobia. And, as you always used to remind us, the 'might haves,' 'should haves,' and 'would haves' don't count. What's done is done, so let's keep our eyes focused on the now."

Margery laughed. "A wise woman I must have been."

"Indeed so, ma'am.'"

"*Any*how, the current mayhem aside, what we *do* know is Devine appears to have had fingers in all manner of pies in all manner of places. As our report showed, they were mainly the marketing of sometimes already past-their-sell-by-date secrets and weapons. Where he got those from we can only guess, but the smart money was on both the Yanks and the Ruskies."

"Mmm," Mervyn mused, forking the succulent morsel of steak and kidney he'd kept until last.

"What seems rather *more* interesting, however, is the suspicion of his rabble-rousing contribution to debates across Europe and elsewhere where alt-right populist figures were up for election and especially when immigration was on the agenda. Always blame 'the other,' that sort of thing, then stress the glories of nationhood and sovereignty. Germany, as you may know, is at this moment at a particularly awkward juncture in that regard. As, of course is the dear old UK, or what will be left of it once Scotland and Wales get their independence, and Northern Ireland becomes re-unified with the South."

Mervyn shook his head. "Just sad little England all on its own again after all these centuries."

"Quite. Seen through other eyes, however, as the sceptred isle in a silver sea with its happy breed of men, as the bard ironically put it."

"The same tripe that tipped the balance for the Brexit peddlers. And this was the sort of stuff Devine would be putting across?"

"Apparently yes, and with much vitriol. Always under a different alias, of course, although McGuire appears to be one of his favourites."

"Ah, *that* one."

"You know it already?"

Which was when Mervyn explained his recent encounter with Lizzie Leah, at which Double M winced.

"Poor girl."

"I had him down as no more than a gigolo at first, but after what you've told me..."

Margery poured them both another shot of the more than decent Beaujolais. "*Any*way, in addition to the speeches, beneath the surface there appear to have been hefty bungs to back up the rhetoric. To the Brit Conservative and Brexit Parties, Germany's *Alternative für Deutschland*, and France's National Rally, for example. Never verified because of the subterfuge involved, but it seems probable. And we reckon *huge* chunks of moolah swapped hands."

"Their source?"

Margery shrugged. "We're not sure, but Washington and Moscow again look the likeliest players."

"The new axis of evil."

"Quite. Both want to split the EU back into a bunch of easily manipulable nation states. Nothing the Yanks and the Ruskies want *less* than a unified and self-confident rival continent of Europe. Too hard to handle."

"High stakes then?"

"The highest. And you have to remember, given Devine's mummy and daddy, he will have had easy access to both the US and Russia."

"Fill me in, ma'am, would you?"

"His mother Svetlana, which, by the way, means 'luminescent' in Russian, was a mere secretary in Gorbachev's Kremlin, but jumped ship *very* successfully wßhen the oligarchs took over and rose to a senior position of some sort. That's how she met and married Sir Montmorency Devine. Less is known of her after that except she moved to the UK and gave birth to Leon."

"In?"

"Eighty-five. There's also a younger sister called Taya, both of them educated at the poshest of posh boarding schools so Mama and Papa could get on with their busy lives. Ever come into contact with Sir Monty, did you?"

"No."

"Ex-Foreign Office. Back and forth with Svetlana in tow to both the States and Russia for one reason or another from the eighties till he threw in the towel in twenty-ten."

"And evidence of *them* having played the same sorts of games as their son?"

"Not that we know of. Certainly they were well connected in both countries, but perhaps there weren't as many opportunities as there have been since twenty-sixteen. Bit of a watershed that was."

"True enough."

"Anyway, these days they're both paddling their boats from a mansion somewhere near Henley-on-Thames, so far as we know out of the game. I'll give you their number should you deem a visit necessary," said Margery, checking her watch.

"Thanks."

"And *that*, my old friend, is pretty much all I can tell you on the Leon Devine front. If anything new comes up, you'll be the first to know. Meanwhile I'm going to have to love you and leave you. Duty calls and so on. Hope you liked your lunch."

"Very much. Many thanks for it. And by the by, before you go, you have no objection to my sharing the Leon info with Lizzie Leah?"

"None at all. She is your client, after all. And should he be back in touch with her we may need her help in tracking him down. She may also need our protection."

"Quite."

"So then, that about wraps it up. Toodle pip," said Double M, springing from her chair on her athlete's legs and heading to the door.

It was a sadder but wiser Mervyn Vincent who finished off the more than decent Beaujolais and took the stairs to the street where he climbed into the pre-paid cab that would take him back to the western fringes of Wimbledon Common. What, he wondered along the way, had he got himself involved in? Another fine mess by the sound of things, but one a lot less funny than anything Laurel and Hardy got up to.

Four

Despite Double M having expressed no objection to Mervyn sharing information on Leon with Lizzie Leah, Mervyn mulled over the wisdom of so doing for a day or two before contacting her. Yes, she was his client and had a right to know. And yes, there may come a day when she would need protection from a person apparently up to his neck in international intrigue. What if he again sought refuge with her in South Wimbledon, for example? On the other hand, Mervyn didn't want to alarm her or disturb what seemed an otherwise quiet and blameless life. In the last analysis, he concluded, the decision would depend on his assessment of her reliability when it came to both her nervous disposition and her readiness to be sworn to absolute secrecy. After all, loose lips could famously sink ships. Furthermore, he had little to go on except the one meeting during which she had been open on the one hand and yet, oddly closed on the other, vide her sudden departure from his house. Also, from what little he knew of them, apart from being a bunch of thick-skinned comedians, Liverpudlians could also be gasbags. The whole thing was a bit of a toss-up, which in the end Mervyn resolved by persuading himself he was overthinking a situation that might be better determined by instinct.

"When in doubt trust the id and screw the ego, eh Suzie?" he said to Miss Heinz 57, who was currently chewing a Bonio in her downstairs bed.

"Raaf, *raaf*," she replied as a firm believer in nasal intuition.

And so it was that, reassured by canine wisdom, which he tended to trust more than its human equivalent, Mervyn picked up the phone.

"Yeah, that'd be great," Lizzie replied to the invitation to another meet-up at The Hand in Hand. "Me and Jürgie're off this afternoon and haven't had our walkies yet, so…"

"Excellent."

"Any progress with the case?"

"I'll tell you when I see you. Say around two?"

"Two's fine."

"Looking forward to it." Mervyn surprised himself by finding he *was*, and, hard though he tried to deny it after hanging up, not just for professional reasons.

"Tricky beast, Mister Id," he muttered, tying his shoelaces.

"Raaf, raaf," Suzie agreed, recognising the shoelace routine, discarding the Bonio and springing from her bed, tail wagging as she awaited her lead being found in the chaotic cupboard marked "Suzie's Stuff."

~ * ~

Leon Devine enjoyed the Gulfstream trip to San Francisco International. Never did he tire of the superstar inboard treatment he got on those planes, the regular flow of top-of-the-range champagnes that came with a click of the finger from his La-Z-Boy lounger and the in-flight porn, both of which came at no extra cost. Not that *he* was paying, of course. The bosses picked up *that* tab. Sooo much better life was now he had become his own master rather than running around at the behest of some fucking government agency with all its tight-arsed rules and regulations. Okay, they'd taught him some trade skills, but that was about the size of it, so they could go screw themselves. Now he could market him*self* in the wondrous beauty of the *free* market, no questions asked. Carry his *own* metaphorical gun and blow away the guys he knew for sure deserved it. It was, to Leon Devine's mind, rather like being in what he thought of as heaven. Not that he was religious. What was it Bertrand Russell had said? A person might as well worship a teapot in the sky as God, something like that. And how right he was. Money, on the other hand, was well worth worshipping because it bought you the things you wanted, turned *you* into the god.

Leon lay back on his lounger and relished the power. When he arrived in Frisco, he'd rent himself the biggest, newest, fastest Mercedes Sports on the market and head up to Muir Woods and his latest American Mrs McGuire whom he'd already texted the witty message: Norwich—Nickers Off Ready When I Come Home. Okay there was a K missing, but who gave a shit for spelling? Not the president of the wonderful U.S. of A, that was for sure. And if the master tweeter could get away with it, so could Leon Devine—oops, Leo McGuire.

"Duh," he said as the Gulfstream glided down to private airstrip three. "Mustn't ever make *that* mistake in public."

~ * ~

Unlike the day of Mervyn's first meeting with Lizzie Leah, Wimbledon was not bathed in sunlight for the second...quite the opposite. Although the temperature was in the mid-twenties, the sky was a leaden ochre, and the air so laden with humidity, pollen, and pollution, he feared the date of his extinction to be rapidly approaching. So far had his already low blood pressure plummeted he had been barely able to put one foot in front of the other on the way to The Hand in Hand and joined-up thought was just as much of a challenge. Even the normally perky Suzie was loping along behind rather than sprinting hither and thither sniffing things.

Lizzie noticed when he plonked himself down sighing at the courtyard table at which she was sitting, dressed today in blue jeans and a white T rather than the all-red Liverpool FC number. The hair was still red, though.

"All right, love, are you? Looking a bit peaky," she said. "Green around the gills, like."

"It's this bloody weather. Call it global warming, call it climate change, call it anything you want. Just let's not pretend *nothing*'s happening to the atmosphere as the extermination deniers say so they can go on burning as many fossil fuels as they want, claiming it's all our fault for wanting the products they sell."

"Tell you what, you just sit yourself down and look after Suzie and Jürgie while I go and fetch us some drinks. There's nothing a nice pint of Young's Special can't fix."

Mervyn smiled. He couldn't help it.

"That would be very kind. The next one's on me. Meanwhile, I'll roll us the cigarettes, okay?"

"Smashing. Then you'll be right as rain."

And Lizzie was spot on in her prognosis. *Some* panacea her prescription was. By the time Mervyn had downed half his pint and smoked one of his fatty roll-ups, he was, if not a *new* man, at least a much less grumpy one.

"Ahhhh, that's better, Miss Leah. Sometimes I think alcohol and nicotine are far healthier substances to ingest than what passes for air."

"Dead right, love. And it's Lizzie remember? None of this 'Miss Leah' stuff."

"Sorry, *Lizzie*."

"Now then, on the phone you said you had things to tell me about Leo. Feel up to it now?"

"Sure, of course. Right after I've bought us a refill each. Okay if I leave Suzie with you? Jürgen doesn't look all that interested in sex today."

Lizzie peered down at the Lurcher sprawled at her feet and laughed. "He *is* a bit dopey. Maybe it's the weather like you were saying."

"Perhaps we should buy the dogs some Young's too."

Lizzie was still chuckling when Mervyn returned with the drinks and two packets of cheese and onion crisps. Her chirpy mood dissolved pretty quickly however, once he outlined what he had learnt from Margery Middleton about Leon Devine aka Leo McGuire.

"Huh-holy kuh-Christ," she spluttered through a mega exhalation of Golden Virginia. "You muh-mean I've been luh-living with a duh-dangerous fucking *criminal*?"

Mervyn reached out a hand, took one of hers and held it.

"Given the outbreak in contemporary politics of what once would have been termed criminality, Lizzie, it is difficult to judge just *how* dangerous your Mister Devine has been or how many laws he has broken. My informant was non-specific in that regard. Just let us say he seems to be something of a maverick who is playing fast and loose with the old rules."

"Like the madman in the wuh-White House?" said Lizzie, calming a little.

"Using him as a model like many others, no doubt. But there's no need for you to be alarmed, although it's just as well you came to me when you did. We, that means my old pals at MI6 and I, will always be here to help, so there's nothing to fear."

Looking over her shoulder despite Mervyn's reassurance, Lizzie freed her hand, slugged down the remainder of her second pint of Young's and took to rolling another cigarette.

"You mean I'll have a copper outside the door every day and night?"

"No, nothing so obvious. But we will instal at your home a special buzzer you can press should you suspect anything untoward and police will be there within five minutes. Should Devine contact you, we will need to know as soon as possible in order to apprehend him for questioning on certain matters of national security."

"Bloody hell. As bad as that."

"Afraid so. Now, if you wouldn't mind, I'd be grateful for your assessment of his behaviour towards you. I know that may been difficult given the nature of your relationship, and I have no wish to pry into what may need to remain private, but I need to get a feel for the person."

"Sod privacy, he was a bastard," said Lizzie, lighting the fresh roll-up and handing another to Mervyn. "Mind you, my mother always said I had a weakness for bastards. Bit of a history of them I have."

Mervyn nodded and said he was sorry. "And with Devine was there ever violence?"

Lizzie hung her head. "Not physical, more mental. Eat this, don't eat that, wear this, don't wear that...know what I mean?"

"I can guess. But he never actually hurt you?"

"Like I said, not physically."

"And the sex?" asked Mervyn uncomfortably. "Sorry, but I have to ask."

"What there was of it, which wasn't much. But he was always the one in charge and that didn't do my head any good either."

"I see. No respecter of women or their rights then?"

"No respecter of *any*body's rights except his own. Question *those* and you were in for a right mouthful. Master of the sodding universe, he reckoned he was. And I bought it. All *my* fault. Ma was right about the bastards. Gave the son of a bitch the five hundred quid too, didn't I?"

Mervyn lit the roll-up. "Don't blame yourself, Lizzie. We all make mistakes. They're hard-wired in humans. And he never said anything about his job, how he made his living?"

"Only what I told you, salesman of some sort. Travelled a lot. You reckon he's got other women like me in different places?"

"It's possible. Sorry, but I can't lie."

"And children?"

"I have no idea. One hopes not, for their sakes."

"Hold my hand again, Doctor Vincent. I think I'm going to cry."

"Mervyn. You Lizzie, me Mervyn," said Mervyn, which at least raised the vestige of a smile.

"*Mervyn*. And you'll still take my case? Even though you must see me as a bit of a sad bitch?"

"Wild horses couldn't dissuade me. With your help, together we'll catch the..."

"Bastard!"

"Quite. Now, how about I freshen our glasses again? Then, lousy though the weather is, I suggest we take a stroll across the Common with the dogs. Young's Special may be a helpful antidote to all manner of ills, but so is Mother Nature. I never told you how I like talking to the trees, did I? Many of them were here before us and will be here when we're gone, but still we humans think we're so important."

Lizzie shook out her red locks over her shoulders and managed a laugh. "Some nutter *you* must be."

"Certifiable, Lizzie. Cert…if…i…able."

"My kind of bloke."

Five

In his Fifth Avenue apartment, Hal Schornstein was on a mega-secure line to a Russian "friend," Sergei Figov who, in the name of Billy Eccles, was currently airbnb-ing a two-bed apartment in Primrose Hill North West London while its owners used the money to swan around Saint-Tropez liked they owned the place.

Hal kicked off the conversation with, "The McGuire guy done good, huh Sergy?"

"*Billy*," whispered Sergei, just in case the line wasn't as mega-secure as it was meant to be.

"Huh?"

"The London name?"

"Ah hah. Okey dokey, 'Billy.' Anyways, like I was saying, our boy done good."

"Efficient," Sergei conceded.

"No comeback over there?"

"Nothing. All is quiet. Accidents will happen, no?"

"Right on. So our guy's gonna win?"

"It looks so."

Hal and Sergei were referring to the cycling crash that had befallen Nigel Redfern, Liberal candidate in the up-coming parliamentary bi-election for the seat of Battersea, who had been running the alt-right Brexiteer candidate neck to neck until his mishap.

"No way they'll find some new pinko to fill his shoes?"

"Too late for that. Liberal votes will be counted, but they will not win anyhow."

"How so? Redfern was coming close, right?"

"*Da*. But there was a big drop in support when voters also found out in one of our newspapers the man had a criminal record and six love children with three different women, two of them black and one Asian."

"McGuire did that too?" said Hal.

"The media leak plus a bot on the Internet."

"Wow, that *plus* the accident." Hal was referring back to the way Leon had sprung out from a clump of bushes while Redfern was pedaling around Hyde Park and thrust a thick wooden stick through his front wheel spokes, causing him to be catapulted across the handlebars, land on his head, and be rushed off to hospital unconscious when a fellow cyclist dialled 999. By which time Leon was long gone. If the guy became a zombie, so the guy became a zombie. Liberals *were* zombies anyway, as recently pointed out by the psycho in the Kremlin. In any case, the bloke should have been wearing a helmet.

"He is a clever man. Speaks nice Russian, too. This I like."

"Worth every dime. So our guy's all set?"

"Other parties nowhere. You know how it is since we got our guy into Downing Street."

Actually Hal didn't, because he didn't give a good goddam for British politics or any others apart from American. Okay, push came to shove, Russian. But, hey, over there they didn't have to worry about freakin' democracy. Opposition guys and gals just got slung in the slammer till the "elections" were over. Which was the way America should be headed. Which was the way Yurp would be headed too, if Hal Schornstein had anything to do with it. Only a matter of time till the good guys came out tops all over, he figured.

"O*okay*, Sergy…"

"*Billy*."

"'Billy,' until next time. You're outta London soon, am I right?"

"Tomorrow."

"To?"

"Munich."

"Where you may be meeting up with friend McGuire again only under a different name. This time around it's Norman Farrago. A little job we have for him there, too."

"Would be a pleasure. My kind of guy, whatever name he calls himself."

"Ours too," said Hal, cutting the call and heading to the TV to see what Fox News was saying about their favourite president's latest forays against impeachment.

~ * ~

After calling Sir Montmorency and Lady Svetlana Devine on the number Double M had given him, and finding they wouldn't be averse to a visit, Mervyn set out for Henley-on-Thames with Suzie in his newly fixed Morris Minor Traveller.

"C'mon, old pal, you can make it," he encouraged the ancient, dark blue, wood-panelled station wagon, which coughed, spluttered and died a few times before gurgling into something resembling life.

"*There* now, that's better," he said, patting the steering wheel. "You'll *like* it once we get going."

"Blub, blub, blub, blurg" said Maurice, which was what Mervyn imaginatively called the car he had inherited from his father. No satnav, a radio that received only two channels, a heater that scarcely worked until the outside temperature was at least twenty degrees, and a top speed of fifty-five miles per hour. But Mervyn didn't care. To him, Maurice *was* his dead father and he took solace from sitting in the same driver's seat and operating the same old temperamental pedals. If, as was normally the case, he was beeped, honked and sworn at by other motorists even in the slow lane, well *tant pis*—or "tant piss" as Mervyn liked to pronounce it.

And so it was, under yet another yellow sky and with extinction looming large in his mind, that Mervyn hit the highway with an AA road map open on the passenger seat beside him. He could have used his phone for directions, but disliked mobiles on principle and particularly disliked the Americanized voice of the GPS woman who barked "No, no, *no,* asshole! I said take a *right,*" when he took a left, then added, "Jesus pleasus, now we're fuckin' *lost.*" For going on eighty years his father had found his way around this country—and most of Europe—without such interference. And if Henry Iain Vincent could, so could his son.

Unsurprisingly, the trip took a little longer than it would have done in the kind of car Leon Devine was currently blasting around Californian highways, but Mervyn didn't mind. Took coffee and comfort breaks whenever he felt like it, chatted amicably with the vintage car connoisseurs who admired Maurice outside the cafés, and arrived at the Devine mansion only marginally *cum tempore*, which in any case he—and Maurice—reckoned to be the polite way to arrive anywhere.

"Doctor Mervyn Vincent," he replied to the voice that barked out at him when he pressed the bell at the gates.

"Spell it for me," demanded The Voice.

Mervyn sighed but did as requested.

"Correct," said The Voice.

Mervyn rolled his eyes. Still, at least he'd got his name right.

"State your business," hissed The Voice.

"Visitor."

"Oh, for Gawd's sake, that's *obvious. Reason* for the visit?"

"To speak to Sir and Lady Devine about their son, Leon, as agreed."

Silence while The Voice checked its diary or memory bank or whatever.

"Right, okay, welcome, come on in," said Sir Montmorency Devine, aka The Voice. "Can't be too careful these days, dontcha know," he added as the iron gates with the brass spikes on top slowly swung open to reveal the beginnings of a conifer, oak, and elm-lined driveway leading to the mansion.

Maurice sighed and did one of his characteristic wheel wobbles when required to go farther than he reckoned any journey should take.

"C'mon, old chap," said Mervyn. "You've been a fine fellow so far. Just a *little* bit farther."

"Blurg," said Maurice, but at least responded to his accelerator being squeezed for the little bit farther that turned out to be a *lot* farther than he'd been counting on. Miles and miles, it seemed to him, of bloody foliage—plus an artificial lake—until he finally deposited Master outside the front door of the sort of house Bluebeard might have built for his weekend getaways. Gargoyles, turrets, the whole nine yards.

"Mister Vincent, I presume," said Sir Montmorency from its portals when Mervyn staggered out with a sleepy Suzie in tow, patting Maurice's bonnet in thanks for his travails as he went.

"*Doctor* Vincent, as it happens," said Mervyn.

"Ah hah," said Sir Montmorency, squinting disdainfully at Maurice. Blue-eyed and square jawed like his son, he was dressed in a red redingote over green leather jodhpurs and spit shined blue riding boots. "Walk this way, would you? Lady Devine is waiting inside and the tea's going cold."

So much for *cum tempore* politesse, but Mervyn walked this way anyway.

~ * ~

Into a circular hallway he walked. Then up a spiral staircase and into a Victoriana decorated lounge twice the total square meterage of his entire house with beige walls, brown hardwood flooring, huge gilt-framed Stubbs-type horse paintings, and, also in beige, several four-seater couches with green velour cushions. The room was roughly the size of an average aircraft hangar, both ends sporting floor-to-ceiling French windows, the front one of which overlooked the entrance driveway, and the rear one a tennis court appearing tiny against the lands that stretched away behind it. Mervyn didn't like it.

"Over here," Sir Montmorency ordered, steering him to the tennis-court end where sat a round mahogany table and four high-backed, bow-legged, green cushioned chairs, one of which was occupied by a statuesque, chestnut-haired woman who stood and dipped her head marginally in recognition of their visitor. Mervyn assumed her to be

Lady Devine, which was proved correct when she offered a hand, said "Svetlana," then sat back down again. Mervyn already felt sorry for her.

"Molly had to re-heat the tea," her husband complained, gesturing at what was either an ornate samovar or a faux ornate teapot placed at the centre of the table along with a plate of nondescript biscuits that might have been chocolate Hobnobs. The boat had evidently *not* been pushed out in welcome to Mervyn.

He assumed Molly to be the maid, dressed in all black hovering behind Svetlana Lady Devine's chair and was again proven right when Sir Montmorency commanded her first to pour the tea into the white porcelain cups then dismissed her with, "That'll be all for now, Molly. Back to your quarters."

So off she scuttled, taking with her Mervyn's unspoken sympathy. Also Suzie's, the dog who reckoned that was no way to treat a human. She'd only been allowed upstairs on the strict understanding she wouldn't piss on the floor, which Mervyn had ensured by letting her piss on portal's doorstep while Devine wasn't looking.

"So," said the very evident Master of the House when the three of them were settled in their bow-legged Victorian chairs. "The reason for your visit is exactly? Some sort of private investigator you said you were on the phone. And this has what precisely to do with our son, Leon?"

"As I also said on the phone, although perhaps you weren't listening, the small matter of the five hundred pounds owed to my client."

"Whose name is?"

"Confidential."

Sir Montmorency glowered while sipping his tea. "Whether male or female you will however be at liberty to divulge."

"Female."

In Svetlana's glance Mervyn saw both recognition and pain. He also wondered about the purple/yellow discoloration beneath her left eye. A riding accident perhaps?

"An*other* bitch," said Sir Montmorency. "Poor old Leon, his damn life's been blighted by them. Is that not so, Sveta?"

"*Da*," said his wife. Unconvincingly.

"Poor chap," Devine continued before launching into a five-minute paean singing the praises of a blameless son who had been head boy at Charterhouse where he had excelled at both sports and all academic subjects, been welcomed with open arms at Cambridge, where he had obtained a blue from captaining the rugger team, had taken a leading role in the debating society, and also been elected President of Tory students before graduating in Classics with First Class Honours. After which entry to the Secret Services had been a breeze.

"Could've become Prime Minister if he'd entered politics," averred his father. "But instead his bent was international relations, at which he, of course, again shone. Not so, Sveta?"

"*Da.*"

"Only to find his talents ignored by his superiors, hence his decision to leave. With great regret from Vauxhall House, needless to say."

Mervyn nodded as sympathetically as he was able throughout this diatribe then, when it was over, said, "And the bitches?"

"Always pulled him down. They *always* were his weakness. Why *can't* a woman be more like a man, for Gawd's sake? How *many* times has my hand gone into my pocket to rescue him from one female fix or another, eh Sveta?"

"*Da*," said Svetlana Lady Devine, rising from her bandy-legged Victorian chair, opening the French window onto the balcony, and firing up what to Mervyn looked a lot like a black Sobranie. How he would have liked to follow her and cadge one for himself. But he was left with her husband who was still ranting about the injustices meted out to the son he hadn't seen for almost five years, although from the occasional tweet he'd heard the boy was doing *wonderful* business for a mega-successful international company.

Devine delved into the pocket of his jodhpurs. "So listen here, Mister Private Investigator, if five hundred quid will shut the latest bitch up, take this," he said riffling through a bunch of fresh fifty-pound notes and selecting ten of them.

So Mervyn did. It would be at least some recompense for Lizzie. Clearly there was little else to be gleaned from this miserable household.

"Now, *if* you don't mind, piss awf out of my house, take your dog with you, and never come back," said Sir Montmorency, springing from his bow-legged Victorian chair, upsetting the mahogany table and its contents and pointing at the door leading back down the spiral staircase.

"With the greatest pleasure," said Mervyn, winking at Suzie who, while Devine was still trying to right the table, pissed on his foot.

Climbing back into Maurice Minor for the journey home, Mervyn looked back up at the Devine mansion. And there, now on the balcony overlooking the forecourt and with a fresh Sobranie in her hand, stood Svetlana.

She waved sadly and Mervyn waved back.

Six

Leon Devine just *lurved* America, which he had visited most of, in either his old MI6 role or since then as a freelancer. What he liked most was its chintzy brashness and go-getting can-do attitude by comparison with stuck-up-its-arse Little England. If it said it was going to put a man on the moon, it *put* a man on the moon even if the whole deal had been no more than the Hollywood mock-up some said it was. Even if it *were*, it was a damn good mock-up. And okay, a lot of The American Dream was no more than that, a fantasy also created by the moviemakers. Pushing back frontiers, black hats and white hats, all manner of crude crap, but Leon bought into it anyway. Soo much more fun than the grandiose horseshit embedded in the public school and Cambridge education at which he'd excelled then had rapidly seen through. Ditto his father's poncey Foreign Office bollocks. No, no, America was the country for Leon Devine all right, a place where greed was acknowledged to be good and money was out in the open speaking volumes. And after the wonderful events of 2016, it had just got better. What a guy the new president was! And of course, the architect of his success until he was arbitrarily fired, Steve Bannon, whom Leon had once met at an alt-right rally. From whom he'd learnt so much of his current trade, particularly the importance of understanding that lies can be just as impressive as truths, especially if backed up by mind-numbing algorithms, memes, and slogans.

There were the occasional hiccups in his love affair with America, though, like the one he was currently experiencing on Highway 1 just south of Mendocino where he'd been pulled over in his Merc open-top sports by speed cops.

It was Officer Jimmy Duval who leaned down right in Leon's face and said, "You know how fast you were travelling, sir?"

"Fast," Leon admitted.

"Ninety-two point six miles per hour."

"*That* fast?"

"That fast. You know the limit is fifty-five, right?"

"So slow?" said Leon in his best posh-Brit-overseas voice, which in his experience always worked wonders. Why Americans retained such a peculiar awe for original speakers of their language he had no idea. But they did. Maybe they thought they were related to the queen. Americans could also be very simplistic people, but who the fuck cared if it worked?

"License please."

Leon sighed, scrabbled in the glove compartment and handed over the Martin Entwhistle one, which Jimmy and his colleague Bret Hansum scanned before Jimmy passed it back.

"You over on vacation, Mart?" said Bret.

"Yes, absolutely. Just *lov*ing the wonderful scenery. *Terri*bly sorry for putting the old foot down. Promise never to do it again. Fifty-five, you say?"

"Fifty-five," Jimmy confirmed.

"I'll set the auto-pilot to that," said Leon, fiddling with a dial beneath the steering wheel. "*There* now," he added when the operation was over.

"We oughta give you a ticket, you know that, Mart," said Bret.

"I do, truly I do. But..."

"This one time we ain't gonna." Jimmy waved an admonitory finger under Leon's nose. "In the innerest of good relations, okay. I got family in Birmingham."

"Alabama?" said Leon, going for local knowledge further to grease the wheels.

"Birmingham, *England*. Now get the fuck outta here."

"With the greatest pleasure, and thanks *so* much."

But by then, Jimmy and Bret were back in their cruiser shrugging and palming air.

"Phew, that was a close one," muttered Leon, tuning the radio to 4U Classic Rock, twisting the steering wheel and heading—slowly—back to Muir Woods where the California Mrs McGuire would be waiting in her trailer with his dinner.

Tomorrow would be a new day, one on which he expected to hear from Hal back in NYC with the new mission.

~ * ~

In a temperature of forty-two degrees ignited by the freak heat wave causing havoc throughout Europe, Georg Büchner was dripping buckets onto a bench in Munich's *Englisher Garten* as he tried to put the final touches to his plans for an *Alternative für Deutschland* youth rally the following weekend at Bayern-München's stadium, the Allianz Arena.

"*Scheiße Mensch*," he muttered, squeezing the sweat from his sodden handkerchief while wondering if Munich had been such a good choice of venue after all. But, as far as he knew, it was also sweltering in Hamburg and all other points north, west and east, so...

And despite the weather, which Georg denied was the result of climate change, he knew the ancient *Freistadt München* to be the best option in any case. Better history of demands for independence it had, as did the whole state of Bavaria which had been home for so long to protests of nationhood, and therefore its right to freedom from both the Federal Republic of Germany and now, of course, the European Union. Hitler had loved the place. Furthermore, Georg needed a location reasonably close to Austria. And Italy, whose Northern League had for so long fostered the very policies AFD preached and had only recently spawned a new far-right Prime Minister bent on "modernizing" the place. Also, not very far from Rome and despite local opposition, Steve Bannon was still trying to establish his alt-right academy at the Trisulti monastery on the slopes of Mont Ernici. And more power to his elbow, especially given the resignation and upcoming departure of Chancellor Merkel. And, of course, the UK's Brexit, which was the *very* scenario the AFD needed as a backdrop for *its* demands for the *"Volk"* of the *"Vaterland"* with its eerie echoes of "America First" aimed at the poor neglected rednecks and hillbillies. And indeed, the Kremlin psycho's interesting comment in an interview with the British *Financial Times* that the whole liberal idea was now "obsolete." Given its anti-immigrant, anti-Semitic, and basically anti-everything-else-*other* stance that fitted soo well with the AFD's vision for Germany, far too fucking hot though it might be, Munich was the right town all right.

"Anyway," thought Georg. "The venue's already been announced, the tickets sold, the media alerted, so too late to change all that just because of a little sunshine."

Plus, he had some pretty shit-hot speakers lined up. Bannon had said he was too busy, but the guys and gals from France, Italy, Poland and Hungary looked like proper firebrands. Plus, there was the Brit guy with his fluent German, the one slated to tell of the joys of Brexit. *He* could turn out to be the star of the show. What was his name again?

It wasn't until Georg pulled out his phone and connected with his American/Russian contact Sergei Figov on another mega-secure number to ensure the booking had been made that he discovered it to be Norman Farrago.

"Not Leo Muck-something?"

"No Georg. Know the guy you're thinking of and, trust me, this is the same one. Only the name is different. You know the biz."

"Yeah, yeah, sure," said Georg, not wishing to cut a poor figure with an agent as influential as Figov.

"He'll be with you tomorrow or the next day. That suit?"

"*Wunderbar,*" said Georg, killing the call and pulling a fresh handkerchief from another pocket.

~ * ~

Wandering around a suddenly overheated Cannizaro Park in a T-shirt and jeans with Suzie panting along at his heels, Mervyn

Vincent was beginning to wonder if he should drop the Leon Devine case. After all, he had from Devine Snr the five hundred pounds to give Lizzie Leah, so effectively the job was done. It wasn't as though Lizzie had said she wanted the bloke found for any other reason. Neither had his parents shown any interest in his reappearance. And, if Margery Middleton were right and he was in some way involved in alt-right politics, so what? It wasn't as though that constituted criminal activity, especially not in the current political climate, otherwise Steve Bannon and the nutjobs in the White House and Downing Street would be in jail already. Effectively therefore, Mervyn would have no case to pass along to either MI6 or the police and would be made to look foolish if he tried. If Leon were proven to have been involved in something acceptably unlawful like participation in a Kremlin-ordered poisoning, for example, he might have tried his luck. But even then, the government could only huff and puff while the Kremlin waved away all such accusations as the work of unknown "criminals." On the gigolo front, sexual harassment, imprisonment or extortion might have worked, but Mervyn had no evidence of that either. All in all he was pretty much up a gum tree. About the unfortunate accident that had befallen Nigel Redfern in the neighbouring Battersea constituency bi-election he had heard, and Devine's involvement in it would have been perfect, even though Redfern had pretty much recovered apart from a persistent headache. But neither Mervyn nor anybody else had any evidence of foul play, let alone by Leon, so *that* event remained in the realms of the "would haves," and "might haves" of the conditional perfect's cloud cuckoo land.

"Bugger," he muttered, finding himself at the portals of The Hand in Hand and, recognising the table at which he and Lizzie had sat on two occasions, feeling a, for him, unusual sense of absence.

Nonetheless, into the pub he went, telling Suzie to wait for him at the door where he could keep an eye on her. Having heard of dog thieves in the area, Mervyn never took any chances. Who would want to steal a Heinz 57 mutt he didn't know, but he wasn't taking the risk.

"Pint of the usual in your mug, Mervyn?" said landlord Sean O'Casey.

"If you please, Sean. Works wonders for all known ailments, I'm told."

Sean laughed. "Fancy fronting that on an advert for the pub? You and your mug—'mug' as in *face* like—on a big poster down in town?"

"For a small fee, Sean, I'm all yours."

"Deal. This one's on the house." Sean passed over the brimming pint of Young's Special

"Raaf, raaf," Suzie only semi-barked because of the pervasive heat.

"With Suzie in your arms, of course," said Sean, moving along the bar to serve another local called Molly Anderson who'd had eyes for Mervyn for some time and only wished he would notice.

Mervyn shook his head and smiled as he took the mug and headed back outside, smoothing Suzie's ruff on the way and thinking, "Thank whatever god's on duty today for the ordinary things in life. Where would we be without them?"

Even better it would be if Lizzie were there with him, he couldn't help reflecting as he took out his tobacco pouch and papers, but a person couldn't have everything. Maybe tomorrow he would call and tell her about the five hundred pounds.

That was when his phone took to trilling in his pocket and, when he swiped the screen to accept the call, a voice said, "Doctor Vincent? Doctor Mervyn Vincent?"

"Speaking."

"This is Taya Devine. I need to talk to you."

When Mervyn asked how she'd got his number, Taya came clean. "My mother gave it to me. Found it on The Boss's phone."

"The boss being your father, I assume."

"From your recent visit."

"Exactly."

"And why did she not call herself?"

Silence down the line.

"Miss Devine?"

"You may not have noticed, but my mother is under certain..."

"Restrictions?"

"Yes. But this is not the time to explain those. Could we perhaps meet? I think it could be of mutual benefit. There is more you should know about my brother."

"You are aware of my position where he is concerned?"

"Yes. My mother and I are in regular touch despite those restrictions you spoke of."

"Well, I was rather thinking it was case closed where Leon was concerned but I suppose..."

"I would be immensely grateful, Doctor Vincent."

"Right-ho then. Just tell me where and when."

"How would Regent's Park suit? It's close to my work."

"Fine."

"At lunchtime tomorrow? Say one o'clock at the Broad Walk Café?"

"Okay, tomorrow should be manageable," said Mervyn, ending the call and reflecting it had been some time since he'd been up in town. Suzie would like it too. She hadn't travelled on buses or trains in months, and Mervyn would let them take the strain this time instead of poor old Maurice.

"Mmm," he mused, sipping at his Young's Special. "Just when you think one box is shut, another one opens."

Seven

Once Mervyn had bought the coffees and the toasted New Yorker paninis while Taya looked after Suzie and they had settled themselves at a metal table outside in the shade, Mervyn asked the obvious question.

"So why exactly are you so keen to speak to me, Miss Devine?"

"Mother said you looked the kind person who might help us…"

"With?"

"Leon."

Mervyn nodded. "I see."

"He was the reason for your visit, wasn't he?"

"Yes."

"And as I said on the phone, she couldn't do it herself, so…"

"It had to be you," said Mervyn, admiring the attitude of this late-twenties woman in her white trouser suit with the red blouse. A hint of the father and brother in the face, but otherwise a younger version of Svetlana, who must have been a stunner when young. "By the way, before we go any further, may I ask what you do for a living? You said you worked close by."

Taya shrugged. "I'm a teacher of Russian at The University of Westminster. The old Regent's Street Polytechnic, thereafter The Poly of Central London."

"Now a uni*ver*sity?"

"More's the pity. The whole ideology of the old poly lost, but what can you do? Modern times, eh? Money, money, money from the new business model and students paying lifetime mortgage loan amounts for qualifications that will never get them jobs."

"Sadly." Mervyn sympathized, himself a graduate of The London School of Economics in the days when it still opened its doors to as many homegrown students as it did to those from overseas who paid through the nose for the privilege.

"*Any*way, down to business, the reason for this meeting."

"As I said...Leon."

"In what regard?" said Mervyn, keen not to show his cards until he knew what game was being played. "You will, I suppose, know I was only employed to seek reimbursement for a certain sum my client had lent your brother."

"Yes. In the name of Leo McGuire, no doubt."

Mervyn sipped at his coffee. So *that* much she knew.

"I don't believe the name was mentioned during my meeting with your parents, Miss Devine."

"Taya."

"*Taya*. So one must assume you are aware of his activities using that soubriquet."

"Yes, I have been for some years, Doctor Vincent."

"Mervyn."

"*Mervyn*. Let us not beat around too many bushes, shall we? I don't know how much else you know about my brother or what other interests you have in him, and I shall not ask, okay?"

Mervyn nodded appreciatively. "Deal."

"My reason for calling this meeting was simply to tell *you* what *I* know of his history in case it helps with his current problem. I'm scared for him and hope you may be able to help. Are you up for that?"

Mervyn swallowed a hunk of New Yorker. "I could be. Quite *what* I can do I can't be sure, but let's just say Vincent is willing."

Taya smiled and thanked him.

And so it was Mervyn learned how, hating his father but wanting to live up to his illustrious image, and loving his mother but kept at a distance from her by Sir Montmorency, his little sister was the only one since childhood in whom Leon had ever been able to confide.

"Since school, where he was bullied," she said, "he has had problems with women. Somehow, he could just never get close to them. Between the two of us, I even sometimes wondered if he might be gay. Anyway, whichever way he swung, my theory always was that was why he adopted the role of macho super-stud who cannot guarantee a long-term relationship, and how the string of Mrs McGuires came to be littered all over the place. It's not that he hates them or treats them cruelly, they are merely living metaphors for his virility."

"And there were no male relationships?"

"Not that I know of. And I *would* know."

"I'm sorry. Sexual matters can be a tad awkward, can't they?"

"Well put, Mister Litotes."

Mervyn managed a smile. "Mind if I smoke?" he said, pushing his New Yorker to one side and pulling out his roll-up equipment.

Taya took from her handbag a pack of her mother's black Sobranies. "Fancy trying one of these?"

"With great pleasure. It's been a long time."

When they were both puffing happily, causing other customers to waft hands under their noses—did *no*body smoke anymore?—Mervyn asked how his problems with women had impinged on Leon's life apart from just the relationships themselves.

"With a vengeance. The macho image had to be maintained at all times, you see, hence the fast cars, fast planes, whole fast lifestyle. *And* the fast money to go with it."

"And he has admitted these things to you?"

"Not in so many words, but the subtext is always clear. 'Look at me, little sis. What a success I am.' It shines through all his texts and emails."

Mervyn wondered if this were the moment to introduce politics into the equation but Taya was way ahead of him.

"That's why he loves the world's new populist power mongers so much. *Any*body who can flout the law, cock a snook at convention so openly and nonetheless succeed, although the whole performance is shot through with lies. *They* are his heroes. Populism is his bible, the one he preaches wherever he can get paid for it. Which is in many places, so he tells me. And gets paid handsomely. Private jets wherever he goes."

Mervyn nodded. "He told my client and your father he was an international salesman. Now I know of what. And who would have paid for this luxury treatment?"

"He's never been explicit, but from the hints, I'd say Washington DC, possibly with a splash of Moscow."

Puffing at his Sobranie, Mervyn raised an eyebrow. "Interesting. Interesting in*deed*. So, Taya, perhaps you might explain how precisely you think I might be of help? Before you do, however, perhaps you should be aware of *my* background until I undertook the current occasional spot of private eyeing."

Which was when Mervyn outlined the ties he retained with MI6 and spoke of the recent re-connection with his old boss there who had suspected much of what Taya had just confirmed.

"You don't mind if I share our conversation with her? She's a very fair-minded sort."

"Not at all," said Taya. "Wow, MI6, eh? And you think *she* could be got on board?"

"In what regard?"

"Helping Leon out of his current problems."

"That would rather depend on what sort of help you have in mind, Taya."

"I'm coming to that. Perhaps we could freshen our coffees before I do?"

"With pleasure," said Mervyn, picking up the cups and heading back inside the café.

~ * ~

Had the Muir Woods Mrs McGuire not shot him in the foot, Leon Devine would have been on the Gulfstream heading for the Munich job Hal Schornstein had called him about sooner, instead of wasting time lying bandaged in a bed at the Saint Francis Memorial Hospital on Hyde Street, San Francisco. But you know how it is with the Second Amendment to the American constitution, how it entitles folks to bear arms and shoot each other whenever they see fit. Which, judging by the statistics, is often and has become an even more regular pastime since the psycho in the White House cosied up to the National Rifle Association, thereby coming good on one of his election promises to the hillbilly and redneck constituency who he reckoned to be his kind of guys. "Shoot any fucker you want...except *me*," he tweeted them, thinking that was funny.

Anyway, so it was that, perfectly legally, the Muir Woods Mrs McGuire—real name Connie Horowitz—kept in her trailer a Glock 19.9mm lady pistol, a Model 70 Featherweight hunting rifle, and a Remington 870 shotgun, figuring a woman living alone in a trailer out in the middle of nowhere needed protection. Plus, she knew how to use all three weapons, regularly wandering the woods tracking illegal wildlife hunters with one or the other of her guns. Connie didn't hold with killing animals. Not that she killed their hunters either, but she sure scared the shit out of them such that, these days, the wildlife was pretty much totally protected. This wasn't the sort of Mrs McGuire Leon should have been messing with, therefore, but given the insights into his character provided by his sister to Mervyn Vincent, *precisely* the kind he would most wish to impress. And the reason Connie shot him in the—left—foot when he finally returned to the trailer at twilight when the dinner she'd prepared had already gone cold? Was she didn't believe a word of the "pulled over by speed cops" narrative he spun on his return, reckoning it "a pissy antsy lie" before accusing him of having other Mrs McGuires "further down this road and a whole lot of other roads."

"Deny it, asshole," she'd hissed at the door to the trailer.

Leon was taken aback by this accusation, of course he was, but barely blinked as he adopted his best Hugh Grant voice and said, "Dahling, *dahling,* how on *earth* could you *possibly* suggest such a thing? You are the light of my life, my one and only true love. I swear it by all that's holy. I…"

Connie was unimpressed. "Bullshit. So, how come when your phone rang and I answered it…?

"My *phone*? You *can't* have answered my phone. I always carry my phone with me, *dahling*. I couldn't exist without it. Look." Leon pulled the latest, flashiest phone on the market from his Levi's back pocket.

"And the spare? The backup? The one you left on my bedside table?"

Hiatus while Leon yoga breathed and Connie debated which foot to shoot him in. She'd have preferred to shoot him through the heart or the dick as poetic justice, but figured she might just get arrested for doing so and had thus decided on a foot. That would hurt like fuck, hopefully hobble him, and could be explained away as a freak accident if the cops came calling.

"The call was just some Visa card scam," Connie coolly explained while Leon took to sweating and his blue eyes to swiveling. "But hey, guess what happened when I accidentally pressed the wrong shutdown button?"

"Bitch, my phone is *my* business. Those numbers are private. You had no right to…"

"And it hit your Favorites list?" Connie continued undeterred. "The one with eighteen other Mrs McGuires in it, some here in the States, some in the UK, some in France and Germany, others in Italy? With one of the dames stateside I had an inneresting chat. All it took was a description and…"

Leon pulled at his square jaw, sucked in his upper lip, bit on it, and decided a runner back to the Merc Sports would be his best option. But foreseeing such a reaction, Connie Horowitz was faster on the draw than Annie Oakley as from behind her back came the Glock 19.9 and the bullet severed two of Leon's toes, causing him to scream and slump forwards into her arms, giving her the opportunity to whack him over the head with the butt of the pistol for good measure, and then to dump him on the dusty ground outside the trailer.

Having wiped the gun of her prints and placed it in Leon's hand, she then she called 911, screamed hysterically, claimed her Brit lover had been horsing around with her pistol and accidentally shot himself in the foot banging his head on the steps of her trailer as he fell and needed immediate assistance. How *sorry* she would be if he bled out, and so on…Hence the fast response unit from the Muir Woods paramedic ambulance service which, wah-wah-wahs blaring and blue lights flashing, delivered Leon Devine to Saint Francis Memorial Hospital minus two toes but out of mortal danger.

Back at her trailer, after a homemade pizza and to the accompaniment of several glasses of California Troublemaker red wine, Connie Horowitz had several more conversations with other Mrs McGuires in places as disparate as Houston, Texas, the Garden District of New Orleans, Brooklyn NYC, Belmont in Boston, Pensacola, Florida and Spokane in Washington State. There were others elsewhere but, tired, Connie called it a night with a Mrs McGuire in Wimbledon, England who she really liked. Such a great accent! Just like George in The Beatles.

Just as well, once he'd taken Hal Schornstein's call, billed his massive hospital charges to the US State Department, discharged himself on crutches from Saint Francis Memorial, and limped onto the Gulfstream, that Leon Devine had no immediate plans to return to America or the UK. No siree, too damn dangerous. Points south in Italy would be more interesting destinations after the Munich gig. And hey, he reflected on the plane, the cripple image could be a pretty useful one for *that* occasion, nothing better to whip up a crowd than a little fake heroism in the face of a malevolent universe jam full of enemies of the people. Better still, it wouldn't even need to be fake. Maybe he'd blame the injury on a Muslim immigrant. Yeah, that's what he would do. *Nice thinking, Leon.*

Eight

Mervyn Vincent wasn't at his best when dealing with weeping women. His northern Presbyterian ancestry with its surfeit of stiff upper lips hadn't prepared him for it. Okay, he'd escaped from Yorkshire to London as quickly as possible, but even there, he hadn't been able to handle extreme emotion with the same aplomb as some of his southern-born fellow LSE students. And of course his MI6 training had done nothing to contribute to his dealings with a sex historically deemed the weaker, but who were required to be even tougher than the blokes if they were to make it as secret agents. Big girls didn't cry and that was that and, without any particular evidence, Mervyn had come to believe it was into such a category that Lizzie Leah fell. They bred 'em tough in Liverpool, didn't they? If you didn't laugh, you cried and so on.

But the call he'd received from Lizzie the previous morning at four a.m.—not the *best* of times for Mervyn's focus—had debunked that assumption. Most of what Lizzie blubbered at him down the line he'd been barely able to understand, although he'd done his best with "I'm so sorries" and "dearie mes." The core message, however, he'd been able to decipher, namely that another Mrs McGuire, an American one, had phoned her and blown Leon Devine's cover forever. Which was interesting despite the angst it was causing Lizzie and why he'd agreed to meet her again at The Hand in Hand later the same morning.

Unsure of how to greet an un-made-up, un-coiffed, dishevelled person with swollen eyes dressed in a tatty green tracksuit slumped across their usual table and looking nothing like the flamboyant, all-red person he'd first met there, Mervyn merely sat and said, "Hi, Lizzie, it's me."

"'Lo," was all Lizzie could manage from between her splayed out arms.

At her feet, Jürgen was looking equally gloomy. Probably it had been a hard day's night for him too. He paid no attention at all to Suzie, even when she tried to kiss him better. Just rolled over onto his other side.

"A pint of the cure-all Young's Special?" said Mervyn, going for levity.

"If you want."

"Okay, dokey. Back in a mo. Keep an eye on Suzie while I'm gone, would you?"

"Nnnn," said Lizzie, which Mervyn took for a yes.

Astonished he was when, returning with the drinks, he found her sitting bolt upright on her seat thumping both fists on the tabletop in a furious tattoo. As if weeping woman weren't difficult enough to cope with, what was Mervyn supposed to do with a simultaneously weeping *and* cursing woman shrieking, "Fuck, fuck, *FUCK,*" at the top of her croaky voice, apart from anything else in public? Heads were already turning.

"Um, Lizzie? I've got your drink. *And* a packet of cheese and onion crisps."

"Grrrrr," Lizzie snarled.

This wasn't going at all well. Probably best not to mention what he'd learnt of Leon from his sister *just* yet, Mervyn reckoned. But then, to his relief and amazement, she stopped screaming "fuck," ran a hand through her tousled red hair, relaxed her shoulders and, in a relatively calm voice said, "Sorry, Merv. But that *bastard,* eh?"

"Indeed," said Mervyn, still uncertain of the ground rules to this behaviour, first the weeping, then the fury, then the apology. "And you had no idea of...?" he added with fingers firmly crossed.

"All the other Missus fucking McGuires? No, none. I'd wondered, hadn't I, but..."

"Still it must have come as a bit of shock," said the Mister Litotes of Taya's designation.

Astonishingly, Lizzie laughed. "It did. Only you know what? Me and Connie, that's the California Missus McGuire's real name, had quite a long chat. To be honest, I felt a bit sorry for her. Until she told me how she'd shot the bugger in the foot, then I felt real proud of her. Shot...him...in...the...*foot*," she chortled, blatting at her cheeks.

"Raaf, *raaf*," said Jürgen, getting back on four legs and licking her leg.

"Took two toes off. Good for Connie, that's what I reckon. Pity she didn't shoot his balls off."

Mervyn reflexively crossed his legs. "Brave woman. Mind you, Americans appear to shoot each other quite a lot. It's the gun laws over there, you know."

"*Anyway*, me and Connie're gonna keep in touch. At least I made a friend out of all this. Also, we said we'd contact all the other Missus McGuires and put them in the picture. Form a club, like, so they'll be ready with the next time he comes calling on his gammy foot. Me, I'm gonna find a way of running him over with my bus."

Lizzie chortled some more.

"It's a plan, I suppose," said Mervyn, super-relieved now he had firm evidence of how Lizzie had at least seen the upside of this turbulent situation but unwilling fully to condone the murder-by-bus idea. "Fancy a crisp?"

"Ta." Lizzie took a handful, crammed them into her mouth, chewed hard, then washed down the lot with a hefty swig at her Young's Special. "You know what me and Connie might also do?"

"No, do tell."

"Start an international charity society for women in gigolo danger. Put it on Instagram or Facebook or Twitter or whatever. Tell 'em the signs to look for, give advice, all that."

"Like how to shoot the blokes' toes off and run them over with buses?" said Mervyn, hoping the irony would work.

And it did. Lizzie shrugged. "Well, maybe not *that* extreme, maybe just how to spot them in the first place. Know what I mean? And make fucking sure not to get involved."

"Great idea, Lizzie."

"I'm full of good ideas, love."

"Raaf, raaf," said Jürgen, planting both forepaws on Lizzie's shoulders and licking her right ear.

Mervyn smiled. "That's the way to go. And if I can help out with the computer work at all, just let me know."

"Not just a pretty face then, Mister?"

Mervyn blushed. "Another pint of the magic brew and more crisps?"

Lizzie slid over her empty glass. "It's my go really, but if you're offering."

And so it was that, for reasons still beyond Mervyn's ken, an apparently delicate situation reached a calm, indeed positive, outcome. Nonetheless, he still didn't reckon it propitious *enough* to outline to Lizzie Taya's explanation of her brother's macho sexuality problems, let alone her proposal to rehabilitate him philosophically, "turn" him as MI6 would have it, and employ his oratorical skills to defuse and downplay the very populist agendas he had been disseminating with such profitable abandon. That would be for another occasion and would, in any case, require the approval of Dame Margery Middleton, but it would have to come soon because the Munich event Taya had earmarked as a suitable intervention point was only days away. Always assuming Leon would make it on his damaged foot. But Mervyn reckoned he would. In his reading, Devine would turn up come hell or high water full complement of toes or no full complement. It would be a question of pride, of advantage even.

~ * ~

As previously, Mervyn met Dame Margery at her club behind Park Lane with Taya's plans for Leon Devine and found her in the grumpy-going-on-foul mood that had afflicted her on a daily basis since the appointment of the new Tory leader and hence the new prime minister.

"Bally buffoon," she said over another lunch of steak and kidney pudding with frites and peas. Double M nurtured a long list of buffoons, mainly men, which was why Mervyn asked for clarification.

Margery vengefully forked a kidney. "The one in bally Downing Street."

"Ah, *that* one."

"The same. You may or may not know, Mervyn, that I was an undergrad at Oxford around the time the bounder was there too. Not at *my* college, of course."

"Which was?"

"Somerville, which was still for gals only in my day. Didn't go co-ed till the mid-nineties. Anyway, *any*way, that's all history. But you will, of course, have heard of the Bullingdon Club."

Mervyn nodded and poured them both a second glass of the more-than-decent Beaujolais. Dame Margery looked as though she needed it.

"Of which the buffoon in question was a prominent member. As indeed was the appalling Cameron whose asinine decision to call the referendum on EU membership to satisfy the hard-right Tory bigots triggered the fractured mess the country is currently in, *two* male chauvinist pigs from the *same* posh-boys-only club wreaking havoc on an entire nation. Do you have *any* idea what those Bullingdonians got up to at Oxford?"

"Rape and pillage as I understand it."

"Precisely, sexism and vandalism. Rampaging about smashing anything that got in their way and with sex workers provided on demand. And all because they were very, very rich and very, very privileged, which they reckoned entitled them to do anything they bally well wanted. And *this* is the psychopath currently infesting Number Ten after being elected by Tory grandees fearing the total demise of their party if they didn't choose him above people with actual human qualifications."

"*Posh* populists, eh?"

"Indeed. Well put, Mervyn. Let us never forget the unholy alliance between the super-rich extreme right and the super-poor extreme left when it came to Brexit."

"The same game that swung the 2016 US presidential election."

"Precisely. The same game Hitler played after the Versailles reparations treaty, the Wall Street crash of nineteen twenty-nine, and the thirties depression. In recent times, echoed by the banking fiasco of two-thousand-and-eight and the subsequent austerity here and all across Europe. And who was to blame?"

Mervyn nodded. "The other. Jews for Hitler, Mexicans and Muslims for the White House, Europeans for the buffoon and his Brexiteers."

Dame Margery hung her head, desultorily forked a frite and sighed.

"Spot on. Which was the very reason the United Nations, the World Bank, and the European Union were created after World War Two. To make sure history would not repeat itself in the way it just has. But now in Downing Street we have the very gung-ho buffoon who styles himself as Winston Churchill and would be happy to fight any war the madman in the White House might start. A poodle for a PM, that's what we have. *Any*way, look, that wasn't why you called this meeting, was it? Sorry for the blether. Just needed to get it off my chest, that's all."

"No problem, ma'am. I perfectly see your objections and, in fact, share them. In the light of which I have a little project in which you might be interested. Nothing so revolutionary as overnight radically to change the heinous path we are currently on, but perhaps sufficient to give rise to a little thought."

"Shoot," said Dame Margery.

So it was that Mervyn outlined the likely sponsorship Leon was receiving from Washington and Moscow for his current populist activities, at which Double M hoisted the same sort of interested eyebrow as Mervyn when Taya had passed on her suspicions to him.

"Mmm, as we had suspected. And the source of this information?"

So Mervyn told her and then asked if she might be interested.

"Very. Is there more?"

"Indeed there is." Mervyn went to explain the plan for her brother as outlined by Taya Devine and wonder if MI6 might like to get involved at all.

"As I said, there's no guarantee it would move mountains or change the course of history. But it might create a few shock ripples, particularly if accompanied by extensive Internet coverage and, who knows, render your Downing Street populist buffoon's life a little less cosy. There's nothing narcissists like less than critical competition. Tends to disconnect the few neurons they're able to deploy and cause them to loose off even more self-justifying hyperbole on Twitter."

Dame Margery sipped at her more than decent Beaujolais, nodded and shrugged, thereby giving away nothing. It was another three sips at the red before she said, "And the role of my guys and gals in all of this would be?"

"Provision of resources essentially, computer stuff on the hardware side, possibly a little psycho backup on the human. Re-admitting Devine back into the MI6 fold might help, although the initial approaches would come from Taya and me. And, should she be willing, Lizzie Leah."

"Lizzie...?"

"Leah. The Liverpool woman whose case I took in the first instance, the one whose troubles kicked off this whole business. I told you about that."

"Ah, yes. And how and where precisely would you be intending to broach the matter with friend Devine?"

"By attending a speaking date he is scheduled for in Munich."

"About which you know how?"

"By him confiding all his secrets in his sister."

"I see. And at this event you would...?"

"Confront him with some potentially distressing news in regard to the women he has kept around the world who, by the way, may now be seeking revenge for his gigolo activities. One, an American, has already shot off two of his toes."

Dame Margery first snickered then guffawed into her more than decent Beaujolais glass, almost knocking it over. "Served the bugger right. I'd have shot his balls off."

"That's what Lizzie said."

"A gal after my own heart. And after this confrontation?"

"Offer him help in exchange for certain favours that could, in any case, be in his long-term interest."

"And if he refuses and does a runner?"

"Pretty unlikely with two toes missing, but if he tries then more persuasive methods may be required. You may or may not remember, ma'am, that during my time with The Circus I was half decent at karate."

"Indeed I do, with a black belt if memory serves. Kept it up, have you?"

"Sufficiently, although even so, a little sedation may be required. But we'll face that eventuality when we come to it."

"Then what? Lock him up somewhere and brainwash him?"

"Ma'am, I haven't yet worked out the details. Just let's say we'll take everything one step at a time and be prepared."

"Like a good boy scout."

"Indeed," said Mervyn, prodding at the steak and kidney pudding that was going cold. "What I *do* need before any moves are made, however, is your seal of approval. A no from you now and all deals are off, hence this meeting."

"And after we've protected him from the vicious women he's violated and adjusted his political credos, we unleash him on an unsuspecting world saying precisely the opposite of what he was saying before?"

Mervyn smiled. "I like the 'we.'"

Dame Margery chuckled. "I tell you what, Mervyn, you and your lady friends bring the boy back to London in one piece, and my lot will do what we can to help. How's that?"

"Perfect, ma'am. Many thanks."

"Could we perhaps also tutor him in a few disparaging remarks about the buffoon in Downing Street?"

"Shouldn't be a problem."

"Oh, and by the by, do we tell Sir Monty and his Russian lady anything of this?"

"Not a dicky bird. Taya has already insisted on that."

"An interesting gal, this Taya, and indeed the Liverpudlian woman. I should be glad to meet both of them."

"No problem. Could be arranged, I'm sure."

And with that, Doctor Mervyn Vincent and Dame Margery Middleton set aside their chilly steak and kidney puddings with equally tired frites and peas but did justice to the remaining more than decent Beaujolais before calling cabs to take them to Vauxhall Bridge in Double M's case and in Mervyn's Waterloo Station for the train back to Wimbledon.

Nine

Having phoned both women to check their gastronomic tastes and outline the result of his meeting with Dame Margery, the same evening Mervyn treated Taya Devine and Lizzie Leah to dinner at a dog friendly Italian restaurant called *L'Ultima Cena* near Clapham Common. Time being of the essence as the Munich gig approached, it was a matter of some urgency that he got his team together and he was relieved to find both Taya and Lizzie available. From her flat in Putney it took Taya no time at all to pedal the three miles on her bike while, to Mervyn's amusement, he, Jürgen and Suzie were driven to the eatery by Lizzie in a single-decker bus with a Not In Service sign at the front. She left it with a special London Transport Priority Parking badge right outside the restaurant.

"Wouldn't want to get a ticket, would we?" she said, eyeing the cyclist chaining her bike to a lamppost who looked over her shoulder, gawped at the bus, then recognized Mervyn and briefly waved.

"Won't be a minute," she said, as Lizzie took a longer look at the woman's blue eyes and frowned slightly.

Prior to the dinner date, Mervyn had told Taya on the phone of Lizzie's relationship with Leon, said he was hoping to bring her with him as she was his client who deserved to be kept in the picture and may be of help in their enterprise. He had also told Lizzie who Taya was and it was only after some reassurance she had accepted the invitation. And clearly from her expression, there were still some reservations. Introductions by him were clearly in order and it was a mildly nervous Mervyn who just hoped they would go smoothly.

He was, however, saved such potential embarrassment by Taya who, once she had completed the bike chaining, straightened her back, walked over to Lizzie with her hand outthrust and said, "Hi, there. You must be Lizzie Leah. I'm Taya Devine, the sister of the man you knew as Leo McGuire."

Mervyn held his breath as Lizzie's eyes widened and an ominous flush spread across her cheeks.

"As I said, Taya's a friend, she..." he started but was again pre-empted, this time by Taya abandoning the handshake idea, taking a quivering Lizzie in a full embrace, and saying, "I am *so* sorry for what my brother did to you and to all the other women, believe me. I am a woman too, and I know how you must have suffered. Now I am here to help. *If* you will allow me."

"Raaf, raaf," said Jürgen whose lead Mervyn had picked up after Lizzie dropped it.

Lizzie swallowed back tears, looked accusingly at Mervyn for a second, then turned back to Taya. "Nuh-not like brother like sister then?" she mumbled.

Taya broke the embrace and took a step back. "Different kettle of cod altogether, sweetheart, trust me. But, look, if you feel you simply *can't*, let's call the whole thing off."

Lizzie managed a smile. "Like in potato, potahto, tomato, tomahto." Lizzie was a fan of Fred Astaire and Ginger Rogers.

Mervyn grinned too. Pronunciation wasn't the only factor in the vast social gap that divided the two women. Trust Liverpool Lizzie to make the joke. He was also pleased to see Taya pick up on the situation.

"Or the rain in Spain stays mainly in the plain," she countered in a very fair stab at a Scouse accent.

"Think you got *that* one upside down and back to front, girl," said Lizzie, taking back Jürgen's lead from Mervyn. "But never mind, I reckon we can work it out. Life is very short and there's no good wasting time, right?"

"Raaf raaf," said Suzie.

"Tell you what," said Mervyn. "Now the introductions are over, why don't we go inside? *L'Ultima Cena* has a nice little barroom we might frequent before we get down to serious eating. I have a pre-ordered bottle of Montepulciano d'Abruzzo awaiting us."

Lizzie shook her head. "Not for me, love. Not when I'm driving. Don't wanna lose me licence, do I? Also, before we go in, what does Lultimah Chainy mean in English?"

"The Last Supper." Taya spoke fluent Italian, French, and German, as well as her quasi-native Russian.

"And do let us hope it won't be," said Mervyn as he led Suzie inside. Jürgen, Lizzie, and Taya followed, the two women holding hands which, checking behind him, Mervyn took as a very good sign.

"*Buona sera*, Matteo," he greeted The Last Supper's owner, a one-time operative in SISMI, Italy's military intelligence and security service until 2007.

~ * ~

Walking awkwardly on a crutch, and with his right foot bound in a shin-high orthopaedic white boot, Norman Farrago, aka Leon Devine, deplaned at Munich International Airport early evening to be greeted on the tarmac by Georg Büchner.

"Something wrong with your foot?" asked the German (in German).

"Skiing accident," Leon explained (also in German).

Büchner looked dubious. "In *this* weather?" he said, lifting a palm at the thirty-five degree heat as if weighing it.

"Timberline glacier, Mount Hood, Oregon. All-year-round pistes," replied Leon, who'd done his homework before leaving the US. Fat chance he was going to admit to some woman having shot off two of his toes, which would soon need replacing with prosthetic ones. Neither did he mention the cowardly attack by a Muslim immigrant scenario. That killer line he was keeping up his sleeve for the gig performance.

Büchner shrugged and nodded at the waiting midnight blue BMW X7 SUV with its engine idling. "If you say so. Can you make it to the car?"

"Sure, no problemo."

But Leon turned the occasion into an injured hero-type problemo anyway, with a lot of theatrical limping while Georg strolled along beside him, one arm outstretched just in case of a fall. "Bit of a bump in the snow, was there?" he said.

Leon pointed down at his white boot. "*Child*. Had to swerve to miss a fucking child, then the skis got twisted and I double-somersaulted before landing on one foot—*this* one and whammo, crunch, ouch."

That's how good Leon's German was. And how developed his imagination, given he'd never skied in his life.

Büchner raised an eyebrow. "Shame. "Kid okay was he?"

"*She*. And yes, she was A-Okay. They gave me a medal for missing her."

"Bit of a hero then, are you?" said Büchner as they finally reached the waiting Beemer with its back doors open.

"Goes with the turf." Leon threw his crutch in ahead of him and hobbled inside the big car with a deep sigh while Büchner instructed the driver to take them to the Bayerischer Hof hotel on the Promenadeplatz and not to spare the horses. Horst Schneider obliged, covering the forty traffic-heavy city kilometers in just under an hour.

"You reckon we could eat soon? I'm starved," said Leon once he and Georg had taken the elevator to his room.

"Downstairs in the restaurant or room service?"

"Room service. We'll have stuff to discuss, and we don't need folk listening in, do we?"

"I guess not," said Büchner, picking up the phone and listening to the auto-menu. "*Schweinebraten mit Spätzle* (roast pork with noodles)?" he called over his shoulder.

"Perfect. And a bottle of something local, red for preference."

"A *Spätburgunder* suit?"

Leon was no wine expert but liked to pretend he was. "I suppose it'll have to suffice. Meanwhile, I'll just freshen up," he said, throwing his crutch onto the four-poster and hobbling into the bathroom to deodorize himself, leaving Büchner to wait for the food and drink.

"Bit of a tosser," Büchner muttered to himself, preparing a table by the window. "Let's hope his speeches are better than his behaviour."

Mind you, once the pair got down to munching on their pork and noodles and slugging back the excellent *Spätburgunder*, Büchner's fears on the speech front were quickly assuaged. Not only did Farrago's oratorical German sound fully up to scratch as he produced a few edited samples including regular inclusions of *Volk* and *Vaterland* with occasional Hitleresque salutes, but the content was spot on, too. Down the list of *Alternative für Deutschland*'s favourite policies he went as to the manner born—racism, Islamophobia, anti-Semitism, xenophobia generally, anti-gay, anti-feminist, anti-European Union, pro-conscription *und so weiter und so fort...*

Büchner smiled and ordered up another bottle of red and a double helping of *Schwarzwälder Kirschtorte* as Leon continued his performance with laudatory remarks on Britain's Brexit example for Germany once Merkel was out of the way, the wonderful way the president was transforming America, the debt we owed the Kremlin's bots for getting him elected, and how grateful his audience should be to the architect of the recent but wondrous results of populism, the fabled and fabulous Steve Bannon. *Now* was the time for the poor and overlooked to stand up and roar like lions to overthrow the heinous swamp created by the liberal intelligentsia who had ruled unchecked for their own benefit ever since 1945.

By the time the Black Forest cherry cake arrived, Farrago was up on his feet—well foot and a half—goose-stepping up and down the room shouting "*Sieg Heil*" and quoting Hermann Göring's famous line: "*Wenn ich Kultur höre...entsichere ich meinen Browning,*" which wrongly translates as "When I hear [the word] culture, I reach for my revolver."

Georg Büchner was impressed, very impressed, *so* impressed he ordered up a bottle of Ziegler schnapps to go with the coffees. By the time they were done, both men were very pissed but very happy as they toasted the upcoming Allianz Arena event.

"Gonna be a blast," said Büchner, teetering to the door to make his way home while Leon collapsed into his four-poster and slept the sleep of the just.

Ten

In *L'Ultima Cena*'s barroom, Mervyn was again pretty much sidelined as Taya Devine continued to consolidate her friendship with the woman whose albeit damaging relationship with her brother had serendipitously sparked so many new possibilities. Watching on, he was pleased to see how benevolently Lizzie responded.

"Mervyn's already told me his real name's Leon," she said, sipping at the spritzer she'd allowed herself.

"That's it. Devine like me," said Taya, giving her glass of *Montepulciano d'Abruzzo* the nose treatment and Mervyn the thumbs-up of a connoisseur.

Lizzie winked. "Not much divine about him, though, eh?"

"Never was I'm afraid. Always a bit of a naughty boy, our Leon," said Taya, before giving Lizzie the same outline of her brother's personality difficulties she had explained to Mervyn in Regent's Park, adding to it the fraught relationship he'd had with a domineering father and a loved, but powerless mother, and the vital one he'd retained with her.

Lizzie understood. "Families, eh? Can't live with 'em, can't live without 'em. Just as well *you* were around to help out, love."

Taya nodded. "I suppose so. For all the good it did. He still seems to have gone off the rails big time, but it's all an act, you know."

"A bloody good one, though. So all this Mister Macho image is just..."

"A bit of a façade, Lizzie. Okay, a very *big* façade. Leon was always one hell of an actor, at school and then at 'varsity. Footlights and all that."

Lizzie looked blank.

"A Cambridge drama group," Mervyn explained.

Lizzie sipped at her spritzer. "*Cam*bridge, eh? A brainy lad to boot then.

"On the IQ front yes," said Taya. "Straight As all his life. But when it came to emotional intelligence, there was always a screw or two loose. A dangerous mix."

"Still you've got wonder what he saw in me, don't you? Left school when I was sixteen with three O-Levels, I did. And one of them was in needlework."

"An Oxbridge education isn't all it's cracked up to be, Lizzie, let me tell you. For many of the golden youths who go there, it's no more than a useful ticket to high society and top jobs. Look at the current moron in Downing Street, for example. Might be able to speak ancient Greek but can't *think* beyond his next photo op. And anyway, hey, you're one hell of a bus driver, so Mervyn tells me. Great to see a woman breaking into a man's world, so don't run yourself down."

"I'll do but me best, love. It'd be a bit tricky anyway when I'm *driving* the bus, but I s'pose I could always jump out of the cab at the least minute and..." Lizzie steepled her fingers and performed a pretend dive.

Taya laughed, leaned over, and ruffled Lizzie's lustrous locks. "Atta girl."

"Yeah, yeah. Anyway, heard from your Leon lately, have you?"

"A couple of days ago. Said he was on his way to a job in Munich. Usual perky self."

Lizzie looked to Mervyn who, reading her hesitation, nodded.

"So you won't have heard the other news then," she said.

"Other news? *You've* heard from him since?"

"No, but there was this Mrs McGuire from California on the phone to me."

Lizzie paused and looked again to Mervyn, who again nodded.

"Shit, sorry. That must have been so embarrassing for you." Taya dunked a *grissino* breadstick into her wine then popped it into her mouth.

"Raaf, raaf," said Jürgen, so she gave him one too. And another to Suzie who'd taken an interest.

"Hope it doesn't get them pissed," she chuckled.

It was while she was still stroking both dogs that Mervyn took over from Lizzie and broke the news of Leon having had a bit of an accident over in California.

"Accident?" said Taya.

Lizzie took back the initiative. "'Fraid so, love. See, this other Mrs McGuire over there shot off two of his toes."

"*What?*"

"Must've got fed up with his shenanigans."

"Oh, God. Oh my *God*, poor, poor Leon." Taya paled and took a long swig at her wine. "*Christ*, I always feared it might come to this. And is Leon okay? Do we *know* he's okay? Apart from the toes, of course."

"I'm afraid we have no further information," said Mervyn. "One assumes there will have been hospital treatment and so on. It sounds as though this was just a warning shot across the bows, not a full-on murder attempt."

"Thank God for *that*."

"On the upside, though," said Lizzie, "Connie's now saying she'd like to set up a kind've women's defence group to stop gigolos getting their own way."

"Connie?"

"Horowitz. That's the California Missus McGuire's real name. She wasn't on the phone to just me. She also called all the other Missus McGuires around the world and they're, like, making a group for women's rights."

Swallowing back her fears for her brother, Taya nodded. "Sounds like a plan. At least Leon's done *some*thing useful in his life, even if more by accident than design."

Lizzie sucked in her cheeks. "On the downside, though, these Missus McGuires are out for his blood after what he done to them."

Taya bit her tongue, swallowed hard and paled. "Understandable I suppose. Which makes it imperative we find Leon ASAP and squirrel him away somewhere safe. Mervyn's told you about the Munich speech he's supposed to be giving the day after tomorrow."

"No, I didn't know about that."

Sensing this to be an opportune moment to delay further discussion of Leon's future and his and Taya's plans for it, Mervyn passed around the menu sheets on the bar and pointed out some tasty dishes he could recommend.

"The *Orecchiette alla Genovese*, pasta with pesto, is the speciality of the house I can recommend. Or else there's the *Linguine alla Pescatora*, ditto with seafood, and the *Risotto alla Boscaiola*, risotto with sausage and mushrooms, which are also good. Otherwise, you could always have a regular lasagna or Spag Bol or a pizza."

When the choosing was done, he signaled to Matteo they were ready to be shown to their table in the restaurant proper.

Matteo smiled. "*Prego*, my friends. Please to follow me."

~ * ~

After due consideration once they were seated, Taya and Lizzie followed Mervyn's *L'Ultima Cena* speciality advice, Taya going for the seafood, and Lizzie for the sausage and mushrooms while Mervyn himself stuck with his old favourite, the pasta with pesto.

"And for the wine?" asked Matteo.

"A Prosecco frizzante perhaps?" said Mervyn, reckoning it suitable for his and Taya's meal while at least a sip or two of semi-fizz would do no harm to Lizzie's bus driving as long as taken in moderation and mopped up with sufficient rice, sausages and mushrooms.

"*Perfetto*," said Matteo.

"Raaf, raaf," said Jürgen, hunkering down at Lizzie's feet.

"Farf, farf," echoed Suzie, who'd been affected by the *Montepulciano d'Abruzzo*-dunked *grissino* and was lying practically asleep at Mervyn's side.

After Matteo had stocked their table with the food and wine and the three of them were tucking in, Lizzie returned to the Munich speech Taya had mentioned.

"What's all that about then? Another one of his sales trips?"

"As I told you, Lizzie, Leon isn't a salesman, at least not in the normal meaning of that word," said Mervyn, "as I think we established at one of our Hand in Hand meetings. Remember how you were worried he was a criminal after what I told you and you got panicky?"

"Ah, right, *that*."

"Mind you, in a way I suppose the term still applies."

"What d'you mean?"

"It's just that it's not tangible goods like ladies' underwear he sells...it's dangerous ideas."

Lizzie forked a bit of sausage and frowned. "Dangerous ideas?"

"He never talked to you about politics?" said Taya.

"Never. Wouldn't have listened anyway. Reckon all politicians are knobheads, I do. Only in it for their own good."

Mervyn nodded. "Well, there's some truth in that, especially since twenty-sixteen."

"Which is so important why?"

"Because of the Brexit referendum and the American election," Taya reminded her.

"Ah, the knobhead of all knobheads *in* the White House and the Brits *out* of Europe. That what you're on about?"

Mervyn twizzled some pasta onto his fork. "Precisely. And that's what Leon's particularly interested in. You might remember what I told you after the meeting with my old MI6 boss, how he's become something of a loose cannon since he quit the secret services. The ideas he peddles wherever he can get an audience, as in Munich, are all directed at wiping out democracy as we once knew it, and replacing it with dictatorships."

"And he's very good at it," Taya added. "Proper little populist name he's made for himself."

Lizzie wanted to know what a populist was when he was at home. "Like Brian Epstein with the Beatles? He made them popular all right."

Mervyn smiled. "I wish it were as innocent, Lizzie. I wish the *times* were so, too."

It was Taya who took it upon herself, with a conciseness Mervyn admired, to explain the term as it applied to the changing political landscape worldwide, how power had shifted through carefully crafted slogans to bigots full of unreasoned hatred for others—people of colour, Muslims, Jews, women, intellectuals, foreigners in general, *any*one who didn't fit the new swinging-dick white male mould.

"Lies, all of it," she concluded. "But very potent ones."

Lizzie winced. "Christ, you don't reckon that's what John Beatle was on about with his power to the people song, do you? I loved our John. So sad he got shot."

"As Mervyn said, those were different times with *very* different meanings, Lizzie," Taya assured her.

"That's what I thought. But, shit, this brother of yours must be some twisted freak. Even more twisted than I thought. Sorry, don't mean to be rude, but..."

Taya sighed. "No need for apologies. As I said, he's always had his problems. Half the time I'm not sure he knows who he is or what he's saying or why he's saying it, or cares. To him, it may be just another performance in a play whose meaning he doesn't fully understand."

"Even though he was so bloody clever? Cambridge and all that."

"As I said, posh education isn't all it's cracked up to be, Lizzie. Also, there's that big gap between intellectual and emotional intelligence I spoke of. Plenty of so-called geniuses have the emotional IQ of pre-pubescents. Think of our new prime minister, for example, or the mental cripple in the White House. Spoilt little baby men with the sensitivity of playground bullies."

"*Any*way, Lizzie," said Mervyn, "We have a little proposal for you. Care to hear it?"

"Fire away."

So it was that Mervyn outlined the plan he and Taya had, with MI6 approval, to fly out to Munich, confront Leon with his demons at the end of his speech, bring him by hook or by crook back to the UK for treatment, and possibly even persuade him into a whole new anti-populist role in a drama with an entirely re-written script.

"That's a hell of a lot to expect," said Lizzie.

Taya nodded. "You're probably right. But at least we could get him home and off the circuit he's now on."

"True enough. And what is it you want me to do?"

"Good question, Lizzie. I wasn't entirely sure myself when Mervyn suggested it, but after I heard about the shot-off toes, I began to see an interesting angle to help persuade him."

"Which is?"

"That you come with us as a reminder of the monstrous regiment of women he needs to avoid."

"Say again."

"I can't imagine Leon would be all that pleased to hear of Connie Horowitz's plans to organize women in defiance of gigolos like him, especially not if he were to meet up with one of them again. Who knows what they might do? Shoot off even more of his toes, or worse."

"But how would *I* be of any use when I was one of them, too? I'm not shooting off anybody's toes, that's for sure."

"Which, paradoxically perhaps, is precisely the point," said Mervyn. "You would be there in the flesh to alert him to the danger, but also show if not sympathy at least a little unexpected understanding. Such a paradox might just stall him in the event of any naughtiness."

"You reckon you could handle that?" asked Taya. "Just a couple of smiles in the background would be all it would take. Mervyn and I would handle the rest."

Lizzie shrugged and blew out a long breath. "To confuse him?"

"As Mervyn said. Which might make it easier for us to persuade him to come home with us. It's a tough ask, I know, after what you've been through. You up for it, girl?"

"Yeah, I s'pose. I'm no actress, and I haven't been travelling for yonks, but if you think it would help, then okay. What about Jürgen though? I couldn't leave him behind all on his own, and there's nobody else around to look after him."

"Don't worry," said Mervyn. "Jürgen *and* Suzie will be coming along with us on special diplomatic immunity doggie passports. Oh, and by the way," he added, riffling through his pockets in search of the ten fifty-pound notes Sir Montmorency had given as payment for his son's debt to the Mrs McGuire of Wimbledon, then handing them over to Lizzie, "think of this as the resolution of the case for which I was first employed."

Lizzie stared at the money. "And this comes from?"

So Mervyn explained.

"And your cut is? Your fee?"

"Nothing. We've come this far, Lizzie Leah. Money is the last of my concerns."

Lizzie kissed him, which Mervyn liked. Then she kissed Taya too.

"Okay, I'm in," she said. "And, look, let me use some of this dosh to pay for the dinner, okay?"

Mervyn protested it was *his* treat, but Lizzie wasn't having any of that. "You and Suzie want a lift home in my bus or d'you wanna walk?" was her response.

She and Taya laughed when Mervyn raised his hitchhiker's thumb and waggled it about.

Eleven

Sergei Figov was on another super-mega-secure hotline to Hal Schornstein, this time from Munich.

"All good over there, Sergy?" said Hal.

"Kind of."

"Meaning?"

"Meaning I just met up with Büchner and the McGuire guy at his hotel over here, and he was kinda beat up."

"Farrago, the *Nor*man Farr*ago* guy," Hal corrected.

"Okay, the Farr*ago* guy was kinda beat up," said Figov, flipping Schornstein a finger he couldn't see because they weren't Skyping. The guy could be some pedant!

"Like he'd been in a fight?"

"Worse. He'd had some toes shot off."

"*Whut*? How many?"

"Two. By some dame in California."

"Holy shit. We know why?"

"First off, he said the toes were just busted after some skiing accident, but I wasn't buying that. Been on skis since I was a kid, so I know a skier when I see one and this guy didn't look the type. No way.

So I ask him some questions about types of snow and suchlike, and he can't answer any."

"Wanna cut a long story short here, Sergy?" Hal had little/no patience for long stories.

"Right, so I ask him to show me the busted toes, which is when he goes all gloomy, shows me hole where the blown-off ones were, fesses up."

"And?"

"He wouldn't go into the detail, only that the dame was pissed with him over other dames he'd been fooling around with."

"Just a domestic then. No harm done."

"Except for his toes."

"Yeah, yeah, *toes*. Minus a coupla toes he can still do the gig though, huh?"

"Sure, he's up for it. Only…"

"Only what?"

"I don't like the dames angle. We need our guys clean and with no bad news stories hanging around their necks. Could cause the organisation problems."

"*Fake* bad news, Sergy. Remember that. Never did the prez no harm anyhow, even if they're true. Nothing hillbillies and rednecks like better than a guy who can't keep his dick in his pants. Freakin' vote *winner* that is."

"Maybe, but later I did some checking around on the Horowitz dame's phone records."

"Horowitz?"

"The dame who shot his toes off."

"Right. And?"

"She's been talking with a whole bunch of the *other* Missus McGuires. That's what Farrago calls his whores—Missus McGuires—and there's, like, eighteen of them all over the world, one in the UK."

"So?"

"So the Horowitz has been whipping them into some kinda dame-self-help group with McGuire written all over it and they're after his balls big time."

"Fuck."

"Fuck is right. *One* dumb dame we could handle but eigh*teen*? You know how bitchy dames can get, Mister Schornstein."

Married and divorced six times, Hal surely did. "Spiteful," he said.

"On the money. And this we do not need. Okay, guys thinking with their dicks are good for business, guys who figure they're doing other guys a service. But a guy who could also be batting for both sides…"

"Excuse me?"

"You're not gonna like this, Hal, but I've got our Farrago/ McGuire/Devine figured for a maybe fag in disguise."

"Devine?"

"Is his birth name. You didn't know that?"

"No. And you know this how? The name and the fag deal?"

"One of those weird coincidences. I didn't put the pieces together till I met up with Farrago like I said. Something in the eyes brought it all back to me. I'd seen those eyes before."

"All what? *What* eyes?"

Which was when Figov recounted how, during his recent stay in Primrose Hill London, he'd liked to take walks in Regent's Park where he would stop at a café for a coffee and a cake, and how this one time he'd sat at a table next to an older guy and a younger girl who'd been talking a lot about her brother who was having problems with his sex life but hiding it behind a big macho image with dames all around the world. Sometimes she even wondered if he was gay. The guy was called Leon, the pair at the table Taya Devine and a dude called Mervyn Vincent who was ex-MI6 and interested in the plan the gal had to save her brother from himself by converting him to the other side.

"Which has what to do with the present situation?"

Figov shrugged. "Maybe nothing. Only the Leon Devine they were talking about was flying all around preaching populism. Can't be too many Brits on the circuit doing that. Not on Washington's dime anyhow. Washington's and maybe Moscow's."

"They *said* that?"

"The gal had it figured as a possibility."

"And you kept all this stored in your head until…?"

"Like I said, when I met up with the Farrago dude again. That's when something clicked. His eyes were the same blue as his sister's. And the same shape."

"Some memory you got there, Sergy."

"Why I did good with the old KGB. Once a spy always a spy. So, *any*how, I been doing a little research and it all fits: Russian mother called Svetlana, Brit diplomat-type father called Montmorency, both of them in and out of the States and the old USSR all the time."

Silence down the line as Hal thought this over.

"You still there, Mister Schornstein?"

"Sure I am."

"And?"

"The only things I can't live with are the crazy dames and the fag angle. The rest I can handle. MI6 ain't what it used to be, especially not now we got our guy in charge in Downing Street. Always assuming the story you tell me *is* more than only coincidence. But the fag and crazy dames' stories about our guy could be big time vote losers and *that* the organisation can't live with stateside or anyplace else while we spread our message."

"So damage limitation?" said Sergei.

"Possibly, but not yet."

"Still we keep a close eye."

"We keep a *very* close eye. And if your Mister Farrago/McGuire/Devine's troublesome sister or her MI6 friend should poke their noses too far into our business and find their cars suddenly driven off bridges into some river and they all drown, who do we point the finger at?"

Sergei Figov smiled. "We have options, Hal, that's for sure. Bad bitches top of the list, but then immigrants, liberals, Zionists, Muslims, the list goes on."

"Which will be *real* news, true news."

"Exactly. Meantime, let's see how the Munich gig plays out."

"Be in touch, Sergy."

"Bet on it," said Figov, yanking the super-mega-secure hotline wire from its socket.

~ * ~

Taya debated long and hard with herself whether or not to bring her mother up to speed on her son's current situation, particularly the missing toes aspect of it. Over the five years since Leon had left MI6 and taken to doing supposedly great business with an international company, Svetlana had been given only the censored snippets of hyped information Sir Montmorency had deemed appropriate. That was what Taya surmised from the secret weekly telephone conversations she had with her mother anyway. Whether or not the woman had any inkling of her boy's possible sexual preferences Taya had no idea, because her father had placed a strict albeit unspoken moratorium on such matters on the occasions he and Svetlana were in the UK and the family came together on school holidays. Mentioning sex in any of its aspects was pretty much the equivalent of doubting God's existence at the dinner table when Father was saying grace. For years during her early adolescence, Taya had often wondered how she and Leon had been conceived at all, although as she grew older rape seemed the most likely scenario. *Why* as an educated woman and concert-class cellist Svetlana had tolerated such a marriage, Taya had no idea. Her best guess was some spell cast by Sir Montmorency in his glory days, one now being consciously or otherwise echoed by his son, thereby still leaving Svetlana out of the equation.

"Poor son and poor mother," she said to Lizzie Leah after outlining this history. The friendship was an improbable one, but Taya knew no other woman who'd been intimate with her brother, who must have liked *something* about him, and to whom she might turn to offload her dilemma. It was the evening before their departure to Munich with Mervyn and the dogs, and the pair were sitting at a table outside the Wimbledon Station Starbucks over flat-white coffees and skinny blueberry muffins.

Lizzie shook her head in sympathy. "And poor you, love, in the middle of all this. Mind you, not that it's any consolation, but sex never raised its ugly head in our house either. And in school all we got were the mechanics. What a fanny was, what a dick was, where to put what and that was about the size of it. Oh, and condoms. Not that any of the lads ever bought them. Too scared or embarrassed or whatever, so if they ever worked up the guts to go to a chemists, all they ever came out with were bottles of Lucozade."

"Much the same at my school, but we didn't even have any lads to talk to, only other clueless girls with big imaginations. Same thing, from what he told me, in Leon's. Only for clueless girls, substitute rabid tossers. Yours was a comprehensive outfit, I assume."

"In Liverpool eight, not the world's best informed place. Me, I never even knew what homosexuals were till I came to London. Reckoned there weren't any in Liverpool. *Any*way, enough about me, it's you, your mum and my ex we're here to talk about, right?"

Taya nodded. "Sorry."

"Nothing to be sorry about, girl. Like I said, poor you, the go-between. And your poor mum. What d'you say her name was again?"

"Svetlana. British passport she has now, but she's still Russian underneath."

"Don't want to talk out of turn, like, but give me half a chance and I'd knee your dad in the nuts."

Taya laughed. "You're not the only one, Lizzie," she said, breaking bits off her skinny blueberry muffin and dunking them in her flat white. "It's what I do in one of my recurring dreams. Then I wake up crying."

Lizzie shook her head. "Guilt, eh? The thing that keep us from doing what we want but somehow know we mustn't."

"Ethics in the wider sense. A shame they're in such short supply these days, particularly amongst the political class. Mind you, Leon hasn't behaved much better, has he?"

"I s'pose not. It must have been hard for you watching that happen, but I guess it was his only way of fighting back, of *being* somebody when the ones who should have cared either wouldn't or couldn't. A little loving is what we all need as kids, a security blanket to hide under when times get hard."

"Wise words, Lizzie. Glad to see your lack of education hasn't hurt you none."

Lizzie smiled. "I know where those words come from, my old pal Paul Simon. That's some compliment. Thanks."

"My pleasure. I appreciate a person who can read the writing on the wall. They're rare these days."

"It's just the way I see things, that's all. Kind've black or white but nothing in between."

"Wood not trees, which is a gift. Anyway to get back on topic, here's my question. How much of Leon's current situation do you think I should divulge to Svetlana?"

Lizzie sucked in her cheeks, frowned, and followed Taya's example of blueberry muffin skinny-dipping. "None of it. Not *tonight*, if that's what you're thinking. For crissakes, Taya, there's no time. We're off to Germany in the morning."

Taya nodded. "True enough. But if not now, then when?"

"After the gig Leon's speaking at. After you and me and Mervyn have met up with him. That's going to be one helluva moment, Taya love."

"True enough."

"And depending on how it falls out, you will or won't feel like telling Svetlana those home truths. We need to give it at least that much time, right?"

"You're an angel, Lizzie. Anyone ever tell you that?"

"No. Mainly I was told I was lippy and out of my head. But who gives a fuck? Angels don't exist anyway. Ever seen pretty little things with wings that aren't birds flapping about in the sky?"

Taya laughed. "Nope. Anyway, look, thanks so much for the advice. I guess we should be making a move," she said checking her watch. "Busy day tomorrow."

"Ain't that the truth. Give you a lift home?" said Lizzie, nodding at the single-decker bus taking up nearly all the space in Wimbledon Station's tiny car park. Jürgen was sitting in the driver's seat wearing his special driver's cap.

"Raaf, raaf," he called through the window as Taya and Lizzie finished off their flat whites and headed in his direction.

Twelve

The Allianz Arena rally was a triumph for the alt-right. Not even Bayern München's home games attracted as many fans. Traffic around Munich was blocked for hours ahead of the kick-off as thousands of supporters, patrolled by almost as many police, marched through the streets shouting their slogans and waving banners mainly in German out of respect for the *Alternative für Deutschland* organizers, but with many in English and a range of other languages. A shame Steve Bannon was unable to attend; he'd have been proud. But then maybe it was precisely his role as *éminence grise* that determined his preference for skulking in the shadows. With or without his presence, however, Georg Büchner and Sergei Figov were delighted at the turnout.

As regards Mervyn Vincent, Taya Devine, Lizzie Leah, Jürgen, and Suzie, it was just as well Margery Middleton—under the alias of fervent pro-Brexiteer Sir Maurice Gubbins—had reserved seats for them ahead of the event or they might never have got in. From Lizzie's perspective, at least when it came to understanding proceedings, it was also an advantage that Büchner and Figov, under pressure from both the White House and the new incumbent at 10 Downing Street, had reluctantly agreed the lingua franca for all orators should be English.

Other languages, except German obviously, were to be permitted only as long as simultaneous on-screen translation could be provided.

Mervyn, however, was furious. "You have no idea how ashamed this makes me to *be* English," he told Taya and Lizzie as they took their seats in one of the special guests areas with the best view of the rock concert-type stage erected over the pitch's centre circle. "First the misery of Brexit, now the very foreigners we scorned being made to speak *our* language whether in British or American versions. A whole *new* and despicable version of the old colonialism."

Taya nodded agreement. "That's history for you."

"And a very nasty history it is," Mervyn was saying as Georg Büchner emerged from the wings onto the stage with a microphone and, to a stadium full of noise, national flags and fire crackers, welcomed the glorious coming together of so many brothers and sisters before announcing the order of events over the following two hours, each speaker being allocated fifteen minutes to state his case.

"Christ, we can't sit around listening to this fascist shit for an hour and three quarters until it's Leon's turn," said Taya when they learned Norman Farrago from the UK had been honoured with the valedictory speech.

Lizzie agreed. "Dead right. By the time we get to him, the noise'll be worse than the Anfield Kop when Liverpool are already thrashing some poor buggers eight nothing. Mind you, at least you get some laughs out of that. None of this sounds funny."

"Judging by this, it won't be," said Mervyn, watching on as a Milanese League Party official sporting a black shirt goose-stepped on stage, shook Büchner's hand and, ignoring any attempt at English, launched into a hundred-word a minute Italian diatribe against all forms of liberalism but especially those which had allowed and abetted the infiltration of his homeland by millions of blacks and Arabs from across the Mediterranean.

"Send...them...all...*HOME*...or...lock...them...all...*UP*," he proclaimed in conclusion as he conducted a band beneath the stage striking up *Giovinezza*, Mussolini's anthem.

Taya wiped her eyes. "And my brother is going to be a part of all *this*?"

"Look," said Mervyn, "why don't we use our time a little more sensibly while we wait for whatever Leon has to say?"

"By?" said Lizzie.

"Repairing to the VIP bar I see just behind us and blocking out the noise with a few beers. I know from experience the brewers of Munich to be almost as talented as Young's when it comes to beer and we have clearance with our tickets."

"Raaf, *raaf*," chorused Suzie and Jürgen.

And so it was, as the stadium behind them periodically erupted into thunderous noise, that the trio plus their dogs spent the following hour and a half speaking of many things, consuming a couple of *Steins* each of Löwenbräu, and, ignoring the *Rauchen Verboten* sign, puffing on their cigarettes of choice. The barroom's manager complained at this, claiming it was against all federal laws and he could face jail time for permitting it, but Mervyn shut him up with a fistful of euros and, in rapid German, the claim of diplomatic immunity to tobacco legislation guaranteed by the piece of paper he briefly wafted under his nose.

And what were the many things they spoke of? The final details of their current situation and how to resolve it when they met up with Leon clearly, but also, at Lizzie's request, a further outline of what populism actually meant for the guys outside shouting their heads off. She remembered well enough Taya's explanation of the term from their dinner at *L'Ultima Cena* but what, she wondered, did that mean if whole countries adopted it.

"Sorry to seem daft," she said, "but..."

Between them, Mervyn and Taya spent the following half hour or so giving examples of dictatorships of many kinds in many countries across many centuries.

Lizzie frowned. "It's not a new idea then?"

"Far from it," said Mervyn. "It's just been recently overhauled to make it sound relevant to the twenty-first century, that's all."

"But the bottom line remains the same," said Taya, "the rich tell the poor they're going to be looked after then continue to line their pockets at the poor folks' expense. Never mind what it was called—communism, fascism, royalism—the outcome was always the same.

Representative democracy was supposed to have sorted all that out and, for a time, it looked as though it might have succeeded, but the new populism looks like upsetting the apple cart all over again. Mainly by setting the people against their elected politicians by saying they are overeducated and over-liberal liars and cheats."

"Fuck, that's terrifying," Lizzie was saying as booming across the loudspeakers came the introduction of Norman Farrago to the stage.

Mervyn was the first to his feet. "Oops, time to get back to our seats, ladies."

And what they heard from Leon Devine was shocking indeed as he strutted up and down the stage like Mick Jagger on speed but with a leg problem. Jabbing angry fingers at the crowd, barking out the populist slogans he'd practised with Georg Büchner in a subtle mixture of Bavarian German and Roger Moore-type James Bond English as he implored his brothers and sisters in the stadium to take his message home with them from Munich and make sure it hit its mark.

And the message was? That they should all now follow the Brexit example of the UK and its wonderful new prime minister, a person even the glorious American president, The Chosen One, had called his kind of guy, and shake off the shackles of liberalism which had for so long chained them to neglect and poverty.

"If the UK's leader can bypass the mother of parliaments to get his way, so...can...*YOU.* What we are now looking at, *meine Damen und Herren,* is the brightest, the most *wunderbar* of new futures. Go away from this place and prepare for power. And be in no doubt...together we can! *Sieg Heil,*" he concluded with a Nazi salute before explaining his leg injury as having been caused by a post-ISIS madman and limp-stomping off stage to tumultuous applause all around the stadium.

It was the cynical linkage of Barak Obama's famous exhortation to Adolf Hitler's that caused Mervyn Vincent to ball his fists and bare his upper teeth.

"It is going to be *very* hard for me not to smack that brother of yours in the mouth when we meet him," he growled at Taya, who bowed her head. "Meanwhile, as I said, let's get out of here and back onto the terraces. Looks like he's headed this way with his cronies."

~ * ~

Mervyn didn't have long to wait to carry out his head-smacking threat, but by the time Georg Büchner and Sergei Figov had chaperoned a sweating Leon up many stairs past adoring fans to the bar behind him, he had managed with the help of Lizzie and Taya to take control of his temper.

It was Lizzie who tempered Mervyn's anger. "Cool it, love, smacking the bloke about wasn't the way we agreed to play this, right?"

Mervyn sucked in his cheeks and nodded. "He didn't see us on his way up, did he?"

"No," Taya confirmed. "Too busy lapping up the praise. And Lizzie's right, despite the shit he's just spouted, we've got to stay calm. It's the only way this will work."

"Fair enough," Mervyn agreed. "How long do we wait?"

"Long enough for him and his goons to get themselves sat down with their beers," said Lizzie.

"Then over we walk in cool as cucumbers and say hi," Taya added. "How he reacts will determine how *we* respond. Who knows, maybe your karate will come in handy after all, maybe it won't."

Mervyn raised a hopeful eyebrow. "With the goons, perhaps. Nasty pieces of work *they* look."

Lizzie, Taya, Mervyn, with Jürgen and Suzie on special leashes, waited another fifteen minutes before climbing from their seats and sauntering as blithely as they were able through the bar doors, ordering more *Steins* of Löwenbräu, then seating themselves at the table right next to that at which Büchner, Figov, and Leon were immersed in a bout of such voluble hubris they took no notice of anything in their surroundings. It wasn't until Leon rose with some difficulty from his chair saying he needed a leak and peered briefly at his neighbours that things kicked off.

Leon's recently proud puce face turned pallid. "Holy f-*fuck*, what the huh-*hell*'re *you* doing here?" he stuttered when Taya raised a hand, waggled her fingers, and said, "Hi there, big brother."

As he stared at Taya, Leon's mouth opened, but for once it was unable to articulate.

When Lizzie waggled her fingers too and said, "Hi there, Leo," his face moved from pallid to ashen and broke into dribbles of sweat.

It was as he was turning to run that Leon's good foot got muddled up with the white orthopaedic boot on his busted one, he pitched forward and, with a whimper, collapsed face first onto the floor, causing Büchner and Figov to leap from their seats.

"What the hell?" said Büchner, going to pick up the fallen populist, at which Mervyn raised a hand and said, "Leave him to us. We'll see to this."

"The '*we*' being, Doctor Vincent?" said Figov, recalling Schornstein's agreement to damage limitation. "Just family and friends, or perhaps MI6, too?"

It was Mervyn's turn to freeze. "How did you...?"

"You to wonder, me to know, Doctor Vincent. Little birdies tweeting, all manner of possibilities. Meantime, my advice would be for you and his sister to leave Mister Devine to *our* care."

"Or else?"

"Mister Büchner and me gonna need to look at a little persuasion. And trust me, that's the kind of persuasion you and the gals here ain't gonna appreciate. Hospitals and suchlike."

Behind his back, Mervyn prepared a karate chop, raised a doubtful eyebrow, and shrugged.

Joining the conversation while bending over to loosen Jürgen's leash, Lizzie said, "You and whose army, knobhead?"

"Grrrrr," said Jürgen, while Taya moved to her brother's side, cradled his head, and whispered that everything was going to be all right.

"Unnn?" said Leon.

"I...told...you...to...leave him a*lone*!" shrieked Figov, joined by Büchner doing his best to look fierce.

Needless to say, this altercation had begun to draw interest from other luminaries in the barroom. *And* the manager, who already had Mervyn, Lizzie, and Taya in his black book for their smoking laws contravention, and who was currently taking out his phone, doubtless to call the cops.

Time to act, Mervyn decided. Whoever these goons were, they would need to be dealt with...and fast.

It was Figov who accelerated his own and Büchner's downfall, however. To the uninitiated, the sight of a person reaching down to fiddle with his trouser cuff might have signaled no more than a person needing to scratch his ankle, but Mervyn knew better when it came to pistols in socks. Winking to Lizzie to unleash Jürgen therefore, he felled Figov with a carotid artery karate chop and watched on appreciatively as the Lurcher bit Büchner in the balls, causing him to sink to his knees, clutch his crotch, and vomit.

"Okay, folks we're out of here," he said as the wah-wah-wah of police cars neared.

"And Leon?" asked Taya,

"Make him an offer he can't refuse," Mervyn advised.

And, whatever the offer was, Leon didn't refuse. Just staggered to his feet and threw one arm around his sister's shoulder and the other around Lizzie's as the quartet plus dogs headed to the single stop elevator that would take them to the ground floor and the waiting Mercedes which would speed them to the airport where the specially chartered RAF VIP jet was waiting to carry them home. Once on board, Leon reckoned the plane wasn't as nice as a Gulfstream, but in the circs wisely decided to keep his mouth shut.

Thirteen

Hal Schornstein was understandably furious when, after paramedical treatment in the barroom, Sergei Figov regained sufficient strength in his vocal chords to call New York and inaccurately report what had happened in Munich. In Figov's version of events, Leon is still spirited away by the MI6 guy, the sister, and some other broad, but only after he and Büchner have put up a brave fight only to be cowardly ambushed by hidden spooks while their backs were turned, thus giving them no chance to fight back. No mention is made of testicle-biting dogs or doubts about Büchner's prospects for fatherhood, emphasis instead being firmly placed on Figov's sore neck, the overall enormous success of the rally, and the immense gratitude expressed to him personally for his part in it. How he had become something of an overnight alt-right hero, how medals were being minted in his name, how...

He wasn't best pleased, therefore, when Schornstein interrupted this self-eulogy with, "FUCK OFF, SERGY. 'HIDDEN SPOOKS,' MY ASS. YOU FUCKIN' *BLEW* IT."

Down the line, Figov tried swallowing the insult and coming up with a suitable rejoinder but what with the sudden return of laryngeal dysfunction plus a peculiarly associated sphincter problem, was only able to reply, "Uggghhh," which didn't impress Schornstein one bit.

"Fuckin Ruskies," he bellowed. "Give 'em one simple job to do and they FUCKIN' FUCK IT *UP*. Where the fuck *IS* the Devine/McGuire/Farrago fucker now anyways?"

To which question Figov had no answer, given he'd been blacked out at the time of Leon's departure with Mervyn & Co and aware only of Büchner on some distant planet wailing about his balls.

"The HELL shuh-should I nuh-know? I was outta it," he therefore gargled causing shooting pains in his throat and, again peculiarly, his anal canal.

Schornstein ground his molars "Jesus *H*. So put someone on the line who *does* fuckin' know. Must've been cops on the scene, right? You morons don't get beat up by some *women* without…"

"And an uh-MI6 guh-guy," Figov managed, forgetting the hidden spooks.

"With*out*…cops getting called," Schornstein ploughed on, ignoring the MI6 guy reference. "Any of *them* still around?"

As it happened, there were. Amongst them *Polizeihauptmeister* (Sergeant) Werner Weber, who had been a first responder and had stuck around until Figov recovered sufficiently to pass him the phone and give what had been a rather more accurate account of events than the one provided to Schornstein.

"Hold the luh-line."

"He spikka da English?"

"Yuh-yeah."

"'Cos I ain't got no Krautish."

With a name like Schornstein he *should* have, figured Figov. But this was no time for argument, not with his sphincter starting to play up big time. "Puh-passing yuh-you over," were the penultimate words he said before urgently signaling to a paramedic for a bedpan.

"His name?"

"Vuh-Werner Vuh-Weber," were the final two words Sergei Figov was able to utter before embarrassingly shitting himself.

It was from Weber, after he had noted and approved Schornstein's fake CIA ID in the name of Harry Fleet, that Hal learned the true story of the altercation in the Allianz Arena's barroom that Saturday afternoon, all of it gleaned from the manager and authenticated by a number of VIP rubberneckers.

"Pretty weird, huh?" Werner added.

"Weird is right. Any idea where the hostage got taken after the kidnapping?"

Which was how Schornstein learned from Weber, a police cruiser had been on the Merc's tail all the way to the airport and would certainly have stopped and arrested its occupants on the spot had it not been for a rear tyre blow-out only minutes from the destination.

"Piece of bad luck *that* was," said Weber, obviously enough unaware the tyre had been shot out by an outriding MI6 sharp shooter called Donald Picknett who had shadowed Mervyn & Co throughout the trip at a safe distance in case of just such an emergency. Figov hadn't been entirely mistaken about his "hidden spooks," although Picknett had been given no role inside the stadium.

"But these things happen, right? Nothing you can do about them," Werner added.

Through gritted teeth, Fleet/Schornstein agreed these things happened. As to what could be done about them, the dumb Kraut cops could at least have their car tyres checked more often was his unspoken response. Instead, he said, "You checked the fucking flight destination though?"

"Had to lean on the controllers a little 'cos it was military and private."

"And?"

"London, England."

"As I thought. Have a nice day."

Werner was halfway through wishing Hal the very same thing when he discovered himself to be speaking into a suddenly very dead line.

~ * ~

Ash blonde, svelte, five feet ten, and with a Berkeley Masters in Fine Arts, Connie Horowitz might have pursued any one of a number of careers, movie star pretty much top of the list. But though she'd played the Hollywood game for a while after college, ditsy blonde roles just weren't her bag. Plus there were too many assholes in the biz, all of them keen to take her clothes off. Ditto for the dance scene (too tall anyway), modeling (didn't like the clothes), TV soaps (too yuckie), LAPD (too many *Dirty Harry* wannabes), etcetera, et...cet...er...*a*. Apart from all of that, her type-A personality meant she liked to get a job done, and fast. No sitting on her hands for Connie Horowitz, which pissed off a lot of people. In a nutshell, being blonde and dumb was doubtless a career winner, but Connie soon discovered being blonde and super-bright sure as hell wasn't.

Once having learnt this lesson, she mooned around San Francisco for a while doing odd jobs, waitressing and suchlike, until one day she awoke knowing what she really wanted to do—make things. What point was there in having studied art if a person didn't *do* it? So it was she quit the city and moved off to the outer edge of Muir Woods where she could commune with the trees and animals and live in peace according to *her* tenets rather than someone else's. Play her guitar in the twilight, compose her own songs, practise with her guns, do what the fuck she liked, which was making things—*any*thing really, but mainly jewelry, pots, clothes, and, of course, paintings. These she sold wherever she could, car boot sales all around the Bay area, although mainly at the little shops in and around the Sausalito tourist trap. Guys came in and out of her life but she didn't pay them too much mind—until the McGuire asshole that was. So dumb even *she* had been to fall for him! Nice shooting to take out two toes though, and happy indeed she had been to inaugurate The Mrs McGuires Society which, given her type-A push-push-push personality, had blossomed once established on a number of Internet sites. Many hours per day Connie currently spent reviewing and answering the sorry stories emanating not only from Houston, New Orleans, Brooklyn, Belmont, Pensacola and Spokane in the States, but also women in France, Germany and Italy where self-help groups had sprouted and grown. In addition to *them*, there were also new contacts all over the world, the accent always on empathy and shared togetherness. The only person she hadn't heard from for a while was the Wimbledon UK Mrs McGuire who, she figured, must be either very busy or some kind of Internet Luddite. She would surely keep trying, though.

~ * ~

The offer he couldn't refuse Leon had been given by Taya back in the Allianz Arena barroom was: "On your feet and come with us, and I won't tell Father and Mother all I know about you and the bullshit you've recently been up to. Refuse and I will." This was said with some guilt but was the only angle she reckoned she could use, the hero-worshipped father and silently loved mother being the only arbiters she knew of whose judgement he would even consider. And at that moment of stress, she'd been correct. Beleaguered and shamed, he'd obeyed.

On the flight back to London however, during the early part of which he wore his DITA Mach-Five shades and remained obdurately silent through all queries about his wellbeing and offers of brandy and other sedatives, he must have reflected on this decision. It was as they were somewhere over Belgium he flung out a hand at Taya in the seat next to him, grabbed her auburn hair, tugged at it, and screamed "BITCH" in her ear.

Mervyn was the first out of his seat to grab the hair-tugging hand and deactivate it, but Lizzie came a close second in the rescue, taking Leon by both ears and twisting them backwards and forwards in opposite directions saying, "Leave go and shut the fuck up, knobhead, or next time it'll be your balls."

These ministrations had the desired effect as Leon collapsed back, albeit still spluttering imprecations.

"My advice, Mister Devine, like Lizzie's," Mervyn told him, "is to calm down double quick time, lay back and enjoy the flight. You may remember the MI6 method. Deep, deep breaths down through the solar plexus to reduce the blood pressure and give the brain the oxygen it needs to think rationally. Should you have conveniently forgotten this technique," he added, scything his karate hand before Leon's eyes, "I may be required to use this again. And you may remember the nasty effect it had on your Russian pal, whatever his name was."

"Grrrrr," said Jürgen, just in case Leon had also forgotten the fate that had befallen Georg Büchner's testicles.

It was all getting very noisy and fractious in the passenger compartment. So much so that RAF pilot Barry "Biggles" Sidebottom was obliged to call back from the cockpit, "Everything A-Okay back there, chaps?"

"All under control, Barry," Mervyn replied. "You just concentrate on your joystick."

Biggles laughed at that as *La Manche*—or The Channel as the English insisted on calling it especially since Brexit—appeared on the in-flight monitor.

"Fuck, fuck, *FUCK*," said Leon shortly before springing from his seat and limping to the passenger cabin door he evidently thought he could open in order to make his parachute-less bid for freedom.

"Oh, for...God's...*sake*," said Taya, stumbling to her feet and executing the decent rugby tackle around her brother's knees that caused him to scream "BITCH" again before banging his head on the jet's aluminium infrastructure and losing consciousness.

All in all it wasn't an easy flight and, on landing, Biggles Sidebottom was happy indeed to disgorge his passengers—one comatose—into the MI6 Land Rover waiting on the tarmac to take them any fucking where they wanted so long as it was out of his plane.

Fourteen

"Bit of a diplomatic hornets' nest you seem to have stirred up, old chap," Margery Middleton told Mervyn Vincent at her club the day after he returned home. "Ruskies cross with you for karate-chopping one of their agents, White House and Downing Street peeved about what they're calling 'interference in freedom of speech,' alt-right Germans wanting to know what justification Brits think they have to meddle in European affairs these days anyway. Bally media, social and normal, seem to have got hold of the story, too." she added, sliding over a copy of the *Daily Mail's* headline: BREXIT BRIT KIDNAPPED IN MUNICH MAYHEM.

Mervyn kneaded his knuckles. "Sorry, MM. It was a case of striking while irons were hot, I'm afraid."

"Couldn't you have lured the blighter away a little less publicly?"

"We would have preferred to, but given the minders we knew he'd have in Munich, it's difficult to see how or where we'd have found him alone."

"Ah well, *any*way, just so you know," said Double M, topping up their glasses of the more than decent Beaujolais. "No doubt some other bigger crisis will wipe away yesterday's news soon enough, but meanwhile there is the small problem of MI6 somehow having been implicated in the event, and Mister Narcissist at Number Ten is wanting to know how and why. I'm happy enough to tell him to go and stick his head up his bottom where it belongs but, from personal interest only, how could this have come to pass?"

Clearly, Mervyn had no immediate answer to that, although he remembered well enough Figov recognizing him as Secret Service. How, he'd had no idea then and no more of an idea now as he explained to Margery. Instead, he asked if the Ruskies had released the name of the agent in question.

"Of course not. And even if they had, it would have been false."

"So no other way of tracking him?"

Double M sipped at her wine. "You left The Circus a little before the Internet information revolution did you not, Mervyn?"

Mervyn shrugged. "I *am* something of a dinosaur in that regard, although, at least I can tell a computer from a television."

Margery smiled. "About *my* level of comprehension I have to admit, but at least if there are problems *I* can't fathom, I know a man who can. In this case, my top computer-whizz Arty Arthuro."

"A soubriquet, I assume."

"Of course. *Any*way just let us say a little poking around German alt-right sites by Arty turned up the names of Georg Büchner as prime organizer of the Munich bash and a certain Ruskie called Sergei Figov as general facilitator."

"Wow," said Mervyn prodding at one of the prawns in his prawn cocktail.

"Wow is right, Mervyn. And furthermore, trawling around some *very* arcane telephonic sites, Arty also unearthed a New Yorker called Halford Schornstein with whom this Figov had repeated exchanges on the subject of Leon Devine, the latest of which showed him to be inordinately displeased at the latter's failure to prevent the delivery of Devine into your hands."

Mervyn lowered his head and shook it. "The wonders of modern technology, eh?"

Margery raised her glass of more than decent Beaujolais in a toast. "Indeed, here's to Arty."

Mervyn followed suit. "To Arty. And do we know who this Schornstein *is?*"

"Not for certain. Arty found many blocks and fire walls around the name but, having broken through a few of them, was pretty sure it led one way or another to the White House."

Mervyn gasped. "*That* high up."

"So it seems. Which means, Mervyn, that from here on in we shall need to tread *very* carefully. You know how mentally unstable the current president is and, if *he* has anything to do with it, there's every reason to assume Schornstein and Figov will be briefed to come looking for Devine with potentially unpleasant consequences. And that must *not* happen on my watch, as I'm sure you will understand."

"Completely. I shall take all possible precautions."

"Good. If you need my help, just shout. Meanwhile, strictly *entre nous*, might I ask where you have secreted him?"

"With his sister at her flat in Putney. I offered my humble home in Wimbledon, but she insisted this was family business, and she would deal with it."

Margery nodded. "A brave girl. As I said, I should like to meet her one of these days, *and* the Lizzie Leah woman. The trip must have been something of an eye-opener for her too."

"It wasn't easy for either of them. But without them, *and* Lizzie's dog Jürgen, I alone could have achieved nothing. They deserve much credit. Sorry for the media fallout, MM, truly I am, but we are now where we are, so let us retrieve from the situation the best we can."

Margery smiled as they moved on to the post-prawn cocktail course of lamb cutlets *à point* with boiled spuds and *petits pois*, "Wise words, Mervyn. Especially in the context of this poor wrecked country being in the hands of yet another Eton/Oxford twerp, this one with the intelligence of an average sewer rat."

"There's always the chance of better to come," Mervyn replied, more in hope than expectation.

"Ever the optimist, Mervyn. One assumes you are referring to our little strategy of raising at least one small voice of protest in the face of rampant populism or what's left of it. Although from what you tell me of the journey home, Devine hardly seems ready for such a conversion any time soon. Are you *quite* sure it's safe for his sister to have him stay with her? He sounds to be at the very least unhinged."

Mervyn shrugged and shook his head. "She insisted the whole thing had been her idea and, in the circs, she had to take responsibility for his welfare."

"How?"

"From what little she told me, many hours and days of heart-to-heart conversation."

"Which will require patience."

"And love of a kind with which few of us are familiar."

Margery chopped off a slice of meat and chewed at it. "Indeed. With *that* sort of thing, The Circus is not best placed to help, but we could point a headshrinker or two in their direction if you see fit."

"Thanks. Give Lizzie and me a week or two to assess the situation? Obviously, we shall *both* be involved. As will our dogs. You may not be aware just how much an animal can contribute to a person's wellbeing. Even just stroking one."

Margery hiked an eyebrow. "Actually, Mervyn, believe it or believe it not, I *do*, although I am more of the feline persuasion. You are sworn to silence for fear of your life on this issue. Word gets around The Circus and I'm an ex-chief."

Mervyn crossed his heart and hoped to die.

"Okay then, for your delectation and yours only, the woman you're talking to sleeps with three cats, two of them Persians, Gloria and Mishkin, and the other a ragamuffin rescue called Mimi, all of whom are regularly stroked to within an inch of their lives."

Mervyn prodded a pea. "My lips are sealed."

"One would hope so. Now, back to serious matters. Whether Taya likes it or not, we are going to need twenty-four hour surveillance at the Putney flat. With so many folk so exercised at what happened in Munich, we can leave nothing to chance. Agreed?"

"Agreed. But nothing obvious."

Margery leaned back in her chair and steepled her fingers. "You really *have* become a little out of touch, Mervyn, haven't you? It will all be remote, cameras and so on. You don't really think we're going to post some goon at the door."

"And if something happens? If this Figov turns up, or Büchner or this Schornstein?"

"Then, on standby we shall have people who can be there in under five minutes. Nothing I'd like better than a little chat with any of those fellows, although they would be more likely to send underlings we've never seen. In expectation of which," said Margery, holding up a finger to prevent any further objection, "all unfamiliar phone numbers will be monitored, and Taya will always have a little red button around her wrist she can press in case of unexpected knocks on the door. You happy with that?"

Mervyn said he was. "Sorry to cause so much trouble," he added.

"No trouble at all, my friend. Let us just hope that somewhere down the line we can find a way to use Mister Devine's oratorial skills in a manner commensurate with the true interests of his country rather than in imitation of the gobbledygook currently emanating from the dork at number ten Downing Street and the clown in the White House."

"We'll do our best."

"I'm sure you will. Now, if you'll excuse me," said MM, checking her watch. "There are just a few hundred other cases I need to attend to."

~ * ~

Unaware that London was eight hours ahead of Muir Woods, Connie Horowitz tried Lizzie Leah's number at six in the evening local time, which wasn't the most convenient moment for Lizzie who was curled up in bed with Jürgen at her feet. Not that sleep was coming easily, which had been the pattern ever since her return from Munich. There was far too much circling around her head to allow the eyelids to shut as automatically as they once had, hence the endless squirming to find a tolerable position, the pummeling of the pillows, the re-positioning of the duvet, *and* the glass of red wine and packet of cigarettes on the bedside table that had replaced the supposedly infallible sleeping draughts from the chemist. All of which pissed Jürgen off big time, causing him to sigh and, when he could stand it no more, grumpily to decamp to his own bed on the floor, which at least stayed still enough for lying dogs to sleep. What made Connie's two a.m. call particularly unwelcome was that for *once* Lizzie had managed to doze off for half an hour.

"For chris*sake*," she therefore said, wrenching the phone from under a distressed pillow then, on the assumption the call was yet another scam about her phone being cut off unless she disclosed the details of all her credit and debit cards, told the caller to fuck off and die before hanging up.

Down the line thousands of miles away, Connie hummed, hawed, and scratched her head. Wrong number maybe, she thought, checking back through Leo McGuire's back-up phone favourites list. Weird though, when she found it, it was the right one.

It took Lizzie another couple of minutes of fighting with the duvet to think back on the call and reflect it had to be a pretty dumb scammer who would ring at two in the morning. Also, the American woman had known her name, which was unheard of. Normally, it was just "Hi there" before launching into threat mode, but this one had said, "Hi there, Lizzie" and that, as Mervyn Vincent knew so well, was the giveaway. Plus, her head clearing as she turned on the light and gave up all hope of sleep, she reckoned she'd heard that voice before. When, she had no idea, but...

It was as Lizzie was wrestling with this problem that the phone rang again and this time she answered it with a tentative, "Hello."

"Lizzie? Lizzie *Leah*?"

"Yes."

"Connie here. Connie Horowitz? One of the Missus McGuires?"

So *that* was why the voice was familiar.

"Oh *shit*, look I'm sorry. I thought you were a scammer. That's why I told you to fuck off and die."

Connie laughed. "Way to go with those assholes, girl. I get 'em all the time. Know what I say now?"

"You're going to shoot their toes off?"

Connie laughed some more. "Nice one, babe, but no. It's pricks if they're guys, tits if they are gals. That's after I say I know their address from my special phone gizmo and am gonna come looking for them with my Smith and Wesson."

"That a kind of gun?"

"Damn right it is. Anyhow, listen, can you spare me a little time? There's stuff you should know about The Mrs McGuires Society I set up. Like how we're all getting together to help other women suffering from freaks like the Leo you and I knew only too well. Going real good it is. We already got women friends all over the world. Plus, and this is the most fun, we have sworn statements from the eighteen original Missus McGuires if he *ever* turns up on their doorsteps again, he's looking at not just gettin' more toes blown off...that would be too easy...but years in the slammer with no hope of parole."

Lizzie froze when Connie asked if *she* had heard from the dipshit any time recently.

"Lizzie, *Lizzie*? You still there?"

"Yuh-yeah, I'm here. Only it's twenty past two in the morning here, and..."

"Oh *shit*, my bad. I didn't think of that."

"Yeah, well, I wouldn't know the time in California either. Look, could I maybe call you back at a better time?"

"Sure. Sure thing. Whenever you're ready. Just so you know whut's goin' down is all."

"Thanks, great to hear from you. I'll be in touch."

So it was that Connie Horowitz returned to her BBQ supper of burgers and fries while Lizzie Leah stayed in bed, although she didn't sleep a wink except for a fifteen-minute snooze around seven a.m. The only person in the Leah household to enjoy his rest that night was Jürgen, who dreamt that for the first time ever he'd *caught* the squirrel which had for years been eluding him by catapulting itself up the tree whose trunk he'd banged into and grinned down at him from an upper branch waggling its paws against its temples and going "yah boo sucks, motherfucker."

"Raaf, raaf, *raaf*," he mumbled while Lizzie continued to writhe and squirm, her mind a maelstrom of conflicting emotions, all of them sparked by a stupid relationship she dearly wished she'd never had. At the root of which was the question of where her loyalties lay: with Connie Horowitz or with the very cause of her troubles whom she now seemed committed to help reform? Life, she reckoned, was just one screw-up after another. Oh for those innocent days back in Liverpool, the now mythic city she wished she'd never left. But the past couldn't be revisited or changed, so...

Once the tears dried, she emailed Mervyn and Taya to tell them what The Mrs McGuires Society had in mind for Leon Devine should he ever resurface in their neighbourhood. That was information she couldn't just quietly file away until she decided on which side of the fence she stood.

Fifteen

Two weeks into their flatshare and, despite her best efforts, Taya wasn't feeling much less conflicted than Lizzie, albeit for a different reason, namely the guilt Leon was off-loading on her for having betrayed the trust he had put in the one person on earth in whom he'd thought he could safely confide. It was too late now to undo what she had already done and, indeed, what she had planned for the future, but nonetheless, Leon's accusations nagged at her. Not because they were any longer expressed openly or with violence, the very opposite. It was the protracted sulky silences that echoed night and day around the small apartment that got deepest under her skin.

"What's the matter, darling? Anything I can do to help?" she would ask, to which Leon would reply sometimes with tears and at others with the pathetic face of an adolescent who's been outed to the cops by his best friend for a covert heroin habit. Only ever dressed in the now wrong-sized pyjamas Taya had bought him before he'd lost weight because of refusing food, he would then crawl back to the rumpled bed he occupied night and day, pull the duvet over his head and noisily weep. What increased Taya's guilt for even allowing the idea into her head was the suspicion this could be just one more of her brother's famous theatrical skills. If so, she reflected ruefully, it was working a treat.

"Talk about rocks and hard places," she confessed to Mervyn Vincent on the phone when she could no longer pretend even to herself her guardianship was working let alone helping.

"So sorry to hear it, my dear. Truly I am. I'm sure you've done your very best."

"Which isn't good enough. I'm too close to the problem, so close I've *become* the problem."

"But still you think he could be playacting."

"I don't *know*, Mervyn. I can't *tell*. It's been years since we talked in the flesh. Everything was always by phone or email. Now, I barely know him. All I *do* know is he hates me."

"For shopping him."

"I was the only one who knew he was headed for Munich, so yes I suppose so."

"Taya, in the circumstances do you not think now might be the time to seek professional help? It's on offer from my old boss at The Circus, as you know."

"Shrinks?" said Taya, who had little faith in the textbook machinations of analysts whose idea the talking cure amounted to little more than an unearthing of the analysand's buried motivating passions and then the question, "And how did you *feel* about that?" as they batted the solution to the problem straight back into the sufferer's court.

"Yes."

"Leon could play them just like he might be playing me. Probably better in fact."

Understanding her reluctance, Mervyn nodded. "It's the best I can offer I'm afraid. But at least it would allow you get out of the house every now and again. Which would do *you* some good. Carers can become as extenuated as those they care for in these situations, you know."

"It would be a cop-out though, wouldn't it?"

"No, my dear. It would be a well-deserved relief. By the by, while I have you on the phone, you will be aware of Lizzie's email about the Mrs McGuires Society."

"Yes, I saw that. Only made things worse."

"Don't tell Leon, whatever you do."

"Of course not."

"There is, however, further problematic news, I'm afraid, which makes your own welfare even more of a priority."

"Which is?"

"That MI6 is insisting on hi-tech surveillance of your flat in the case of any angered populists coming over to seek revenge for what they're seeing as your brother's illegal abduction and trying take him back by force."

"Bloody hell. And how...?"

"Would they find you?"

"Yes."

"My dear, I have recently learnt more about the bally Internet than I could ever have imagined."

"Ah yes. No secrets safe."

"Indeed, and I'm sorry about it, although my old boss Margery Middleton will be taking steps to make them so. And it is she who is as concerned for your welfare as she is for Leon's, who also insisted on the surveillance. But look, if you would care to dodge the problem altogether, both you and Leon might consider decamping to my little house for a while. I have a spare room and a sofa bed in the lounge. You'd be more than welcome, and it would be one way of throwing the baddies off the trail."

"And what if they find *your* address? One of them seemed to know who you were."

"Yes, that was *very* peculiar. But don't worry, Margery's top computer whizz kid has also been instructed to throw more fire walls around it than even the Kremlin."

"Well, the invitation is much appreciated."

"So I can expect you?"

"*If* I can persuade Leon out of his bed."

"Leave that to me and Suzie."

"But I was trying to do this my*self*."

"Nobody can do anything *all* by themselves, Taya. How about Suzie and I coming over tomorrow morning, as early as you like?"

"You're a friend, Mervyn Vincent."

"I do my best. Would you like it if Lizzie and Jürgen came along too? I'm sure I could arrange that."

"The more the merrier. You want me to warn Leon?"

"Certainly not. Let this be a happening from the blue, news from nowhere. You never know how that might shake up whatever game he's playing."

~ * ~

Although Leon Devine *per se* was small fry in the worldwide rise of populist politics, the circumstances of his abduction from Munich continued to resonate in many quarters in case any fake bad news stories began to emanate from his captors, or indeed, if they had further, bigger, prey in mind. Even Mister Populist himself in The White House, already on the sharp end of criticism for his racism, misogyny, election-rigging and many other impeachment-worthy underhand dealings, was taking an interest, albeit covertly, through super-encrypted messages to Hal Schornstein, who assured him everything was under control even though it wasn't. Plus, the Russians were still peeved about Figov's treatment, as were the German *Alternative für Deutschland* crew about Büchner's. And similar fears for their own safety resonated around alt-right speakers all around Europe. The Brits, however, were no longer bothered, Double M had seen to that in a reassuring debrief to the Foreign Office, who had in turn slapped an updated D-notice on the affair so newspaper editors would leave it alone. They couldn't do that to the foreign press though, from whom articles concerning the whereabouts of "The Mysterious British Brexiter" continued to flow.

Most concerned of all these people, however, was Hal Schornstein, who had built a profitable career from populism plus his nefarious US/Russian relations and didn't want to see it flushed down the toilet by some Brit dork with personality and woman problems, particularly not with the president breathing down his neck.

"We gotta find this creep and shut his mouth," he told Sergei Figov, whom he'd had flown back to New York, neck and sphincter problems notwithstanding. "Plus, like we agreed, if bad things happen to his sister and her friends, amen to that."

"Right," said Sergei, less wholeheartedly than Hal would have liked.

"We know they're back in London, right?"

"We do?"

"Yeah. The Kraut cop I talked with told me that. Only London's a big place and I bin checking, but I can't find no addresses there for the sister or the ex-MI6 dude, Mervyn..."

"Vincent."

"Right, him, or the other dame. Don't know her name."

Figov shook his head. "Me either."

"Anyhow, needles in freakin' haystacks, right?"

"Looks like it."

Which was precisely what Margery Middleton had planned when she instructed Arty Arthuro to wipe Taya's, Mervyn's, and Lizzie's names and email or brick-built addresses from all sources of ID storage on the Internet or anywhere else. Once Arty had finished, nobody on the planet could have found them.

"Until I found *this*," said Hal triumphantly, giving Sergei the address in Henley-On-Thames of Sir Montmorency Devine and his wife Svetlana, about whom Margery had unfortunately forgotten. "Where else would a kid wanna hide but with his folks?"

Sergei could think of many places but didn't say so. Instead, with some reluctance, he said, "My job to go there and check it out, right?"

Hal drew a finger knife across his throat. "Your job, Sergy. And this time you do...not...fuck...up. Okay?"

With those jolly words echoing in his ears, Sergei took the red-eye back to London where the Primrose Hill airbnb flat was still in his name. During the flight, there was a surprise call from Georg Büchner wanting to know what was happening on the Leon Devine front, but Sergei wasn't disclosing such details in public, ex-KGB rule numero uno.

"Kinda top secret, Georg. But, listen, we could meet up in London you wanna. I got a rented apartment there," he said giving the address. "To talk would be good."

~ * ~

Georg Büchner flew into Heathrow the following morning and rang the bell of the Gloucester Avenue basement address at a little before two p.m.

Figov was looking thinner than before, with furrows across his brow and down his cheeks. "Good seeing you again, Georg. C'mon in. The place ain't big but then neither am I. Coffee? Tea?"

It was over machine-brewed espressos that the pair compared notes on the injuries they'd sustained in Munich, neither pretending heroics in the face of a still sore neck in one case and even sorer balls in the other.

"And all for *what*?" said Büchner ruefully.

Figov shrugged. "Fuck knows, only Schornstein is now even more pissed off than ever, lemme tell you."

"Schornstein?"

"Is one of the bosses of the populism outfit stateside. The reason I'm back here, you wanna know. To find out what happened to the Devine dude after the MI6 guy and his gals..."

"*And* their dog," said Büchner, rubbing his crotch for emphasis.

"And their dog...hijacked the guy and brought him back here."

"He's in London?"

"So Schornstein says. Found out from Weber. The cop at the scene?"

"Uh-huh," said Georg, who had been too worried about his testicles to bother about cops. "We know where in London?"

"Nope. Best, like *only*, guess is with his folks at a place called Henry on Thames, some name like that. I gotta check it out."

"And if you find him there?"

"I make sure he keeps his trap shut over the whole deal, better still fucks off and dies. Schtum is what Schornstein wants from him. Guaranteed omertà, like it was some Mafia sting."

"And if he won't agree?"

"There are other options."

"Like fucking off and dying?"

"I'll worry about that if, and when, I come to it."

Georg winced. "And you're up for that?"

"Do I *look* like I am?"

Büchner shook his head. "You look like shit on a stick. Sorry, but you asked."

"Apology accepted. Listen, you wanna take a walk? It's kinda pretty around here, and I could use some air. It ain't *great* air 'cos of climate change, and pollution, and pollen and all kindsa other crap, but it's still air…just about. Maybe we could also get us something to eat. Place is overloaded with eateries."

So it was that the Russian ex-spy and the German alt-rightist—continuing to use German as their lingua franca—headed up Fitzroy Road to Primrose Hill park, climbed the hill, and from the top stared out at the City of London landscape of towering tawdry temples dedicated to the worship of Mammon—temples which Brexit would empty of their banker occupants once they headed to safer climes than London to stow their money.

"You know, Georg," said Figov, "even *I* feel kinda sorry for the Brits. *Some* dumbass decision they made back in twenty sixteen. Leaving the EU and all that."

"Not in Downing Street's songbook. Not in the Devine guy's either. You remember the stuff he was saying at The Allianz?"

"Sure I do. But you gotta wonder if he's got his head on straight, dontcha?"

The *Alternative für Deutschland* man took a deep breath. "You figure the same could happen to Frankfurt if the bankers moved there, then Germany quit the EU?"

"I've been doing a lot of figuring since Munich, Georg, most all of it negative. You could say right now I'm kinda conflicted. Like what exactly is going down between the White House and the Kremlin? What secret plans they have for Europe between them? Russian money went into the Brexit vote, this much I know for sure. And you know how many people were locked up in Moscow this year, just for wanting free elections?"

Georg didn't.

"Three thousand. And wouldn't the American psycho in the White House like the *same* powers? Sure he would. So would his puppet in Downing Street. No more Congress or Parliament to get in their way. And if any joint Yank/Ruskie project were to flood Europe with populist wannabes, and they were elected, what future would democracy have there? None. Leaving who in power apart from the Chinese who couldn't give a rat's ass anyway?"

Figov shrugged at the obvious answer to this hypothetical question. "Okay, maybe you'll tell me I'm catastrophizing here but, hey, it's a possibility, right?"

Büchner winced but said nothing.

"Anyhow, *any*how," Figov continued. "You wanna eat?"

Sergei Figov and Georg Büchner strolled back down Primrose Hill to The Queens pub where they ordered themselves pints of lager and a lunch of burgers, French fries, and peas, which they took at an outside table on Regent's Park Road.

"Georg," said Sergei munching on his burger, "no pressure, but if you wanted to help me find Devine you'd be very welcome."

Georg forked a French fry and said nothing again.

Figov nodded. "Like I said, no pressure. You say no, you say no."

"And you're sure, sure, sure it's necessary. You couldn't just flip this Schornstein the finger and do a runner?"

Figov shook his head. "With the connections the guy has in Washington and Moscow, I'd be dead meat if I at least didn't try."

Büchner chewed his upper lip, not fancying becoming dead meat too.

"You don't *have* to come. It was only a..."

Büchner stopped chewing his upper lip, shrugged, and said, "Okay, why not? We've come this far together, you and me. I'm up for the extra mile if it helps."

"Much appreciated, my friend, believe me."

"And if we *do* find Devine?"

"We see what kind of shape he's in and act accordingly."

"I'm not in the business of offing anyone, Sergei, Devine or anyone else."

"Me either, Georg. You have to trust me on that. Between us we'll find another way."

"One guy with a sore neck and the other with sore balls from the last outing?"

Figov laughed. "Yeah, not a great combination. We'll just have to hope this time around it goes nice and easy. And look, you can stay at my place till it's sorted. That be okay with you?"

"Great."

"That's settled then. Meantime, how about another beer? It's not exactly Munich standards but it'll do."

Büchner passed over his glass and, while Figov was gone, took to facing his dog fears by patting a harmless-looking Dachshund called Rolf whom he reckoned might appreciate a little attention while his owners fed their faces at the adjacent table. What, he wondered, did "*Dachshund*" mean in English. *Hund* was 'hound' or 'dog' that much he knew, but the word for *Dachs*?

Mind you, Rolf didn't know he was a badger hound either, in German, English or any other language. Nor did he care. Just lay back and enjoyed having his ears tickled. Georg liked it too. Maybe not *all* dogs were ball biters.

Sixteen

The unfortunate events at the Henley-on-Thames residence of Sir Montmorency Devine and his wife Svetlana might have been avoided had Sergei Figov been able to locate a telephone number and make an appointment in advance of his and Georg Büchner's visit, but try though he would, he couldn't. The Devines were ex-directory in the ordinary telephone book, and they didn't appear on any of the Internet sites he hacked into either, so an unannounced visit was the only option.

It would also have been preferable for all concerned had Sergei and Georg understood Sir Montmorency's complex entry gate system, been a little more patient with his barked enquiries as to their identity, and not resorted to climbing the gates instead when he refused them passage on the grounds he suspected them of being hawkers, and foreign ones to boot. That way they wouldn't have triggered the alarms which immediately began screeching and flashing all around the grounds thereby causing Sir Montmorency to come marching out with his shotgun, shoot Sergei and Georg in their bottoms, turf both of them back out into the lane outside, and get himself arrested for his troubles when the pair understandably reported the incident to the local Thames Valley police. Okay, it was only pellets they had in their bottoms, but they stung. Also this wasn't America where anyone could shoot anybody else whenever they liked by claiming the Second Amendment, this was *Britain* where shooting people was meant to be illegal.

PC Gordon Roberts was both sympathetic and not, once he'd scribbled on his notepad the false names Sergei and Georg gave. "Trouble is, lads, the law's a bit funny on this one. Geezers like Devine *can* use guns on their own lands as long as it's only animals or rifle club-type targets they're shooting at. Plus, they'll say, like I'm sure friend Devine will, they're entitled to defend their property against intruders. It's all a bit murky."

"And what if he'd killed us?" said Sergei, spokesman because Georg's English wasn't up to complex argumentation.

Roberts had to admit that would be at least a felony, maybe a crime.

"And if he in*tended* to kill us but missed?"

"Well, we'd have to ask *him* about that, wouldn't we?"

"By arresting him?"

"I s'pose so. Only Sir Montmorency's a big wheel in these parts, and it might be a bit tricky, but..."

"Just do it," said Sergei, wafting a fake CIA ID under Gordon's nose, "Or what you gonna be looking at here is a shit storm that could reach all the way to Washington, DC. How does 'American Citizen Almost Shot to Death in England' in the newspapers and on TV sound to you?"

Defeated, Gordon nodded. The bloke's accent didn't *sound* American, even though he'd introduced himself as Clint Westwood, but then America was made up of foreigners, wasn't it? Plus he had the CIA ID, and Roberts didn't want the sort of shit he was talking about on *his* doorstep, so...

Which was how it came to pass the following morning that Sir Montmorency was awakened by the wah-wah-wahs of police cars outside his mansion and obliged to open the gates. Later, in his pyjamas, he was informed of his "misdemeanour," read his rights, cuffed, and taken kicking and screaming down the long driveway, all the way protesting his sovereign right to shoot anyone he liked on his own land, before being shoehorned into the back seat of a cruiser and driven away for further questioning.

Needless to say, he was held for only the stipulated twenty-four hours, during which he made it *very* clear to those questioning him they would lose their livelihoods, pensions, wives, husbands, bank accounts, etc should they have the audacity to bring *any* charges. Furthermore, the generous gifts he'd made to the Thames Valley police over the years would cease forthwith *and* on his return to his estate he would immediately be in contact with the "new chappie" at 10 Downing Street whom he knew personally from his days as Henley-on-Thames's MP and from whom he would expect full support.

When released the following day, it was a self-justifying and belligerent Sir Montmorency who strode back up his driveway and through his front door keen to tell his wife of his latest triumph in the face of "mindless moronicity," only to find his proud claims echoing through an empty mansion.

"Wife, *WIFE*?" his voice reverberated into the vacuum, but to no avail.

Why? Because the only person to have benefited from these happenings was Svetlana Lady Devine who, during her husband's merciful absence at the cop shop, had found the keys to his red Bentley Continental and hit the road to South West London.

~ * ~

From the get-go, Leon Devine behaved better at Mervyn's Wimbledon cottage than he had at his sister's Putney flat. No longer able to play the sibling guilt card, he had no choice but to co-operate with Mervyn's agenda, which did not include staying in bed moaning all day and night. Playing the hardball game he had used often enough during interrogations in his MI6 days, Mervyn was brooking no such wimpishness. Daily, Leon was roused at seven, fed, watered, and marched around Cannizaro Park, whence the pair and Suzie would return at around eight for what Mervyn termed "meaningful conversation." No visits to the Hand in Hand, no TV or radio, and certainly no surfing around on the computer. To all intents and purposes, Leon was in purdah.

On the first day of this routine—they were currently on their third—he had dared ask who the fuck Mervyn thought he was imposing such restrictions, so Mervyn told him who the fuck he thought he was and outlined in no uncertain terms the ground rules for his guest's sojourn.

"With me, laddie, you play no amateur dramatic games, okay? I've walked the boards myself, so I'll know if you try, and believe me, you won't like the outcome. Given your posh education you will have heard of nemesis, and I am perfectly happy to be yours. Play ball with me, on the other hand, and it's possible your hubris in recent times will be overlooked. Your choice."

"Meaning?" Leon dared ask, as they were leaving Cannizaro and heading back to the cottage.

"Meaning, it is within the powers currently extended to me by my, and your, ex-employer not only to publicize your recent murky history, but also to ensure you are never again at liberty to subjugate innocent women to your charms and extort money from them. And, of course, to ask serious questions about the wisdom of your continuing to trot the globe whipping up fascistic responses of the kind we saw and heard in Munich."

Leon couldn't deny the Allianz Arena speech, but fumed at the allegation he had ever abused a woman.

"How *dare* you? I have never in my life..."

Which was when Mervyn stopped dead in his tracks, placed a forefinger across his lips, outstared a puce-faced Leon, pointed him in the direction of the cottage, and said, "When we get back home I'll tell you the full story. And don't you *ever* raise your voice to me again, *capisce?*"

Reluctantly, Leon *capisced*, and they loped back to the cottage in a silence Suzie didn't appreciate. What or who *was* this new version of Master, she wondered. Never had she heard him so terse with anyone. Nonetheless, Leon interpreted her puzzled "raaf, raaf" as canine consolidation of her owner's stance. Never having lived with an animal, he wasn't best placed to think otherwise, and certainly didn't want to be bitten in the same place Büchner had been.

"Okay, laddie, so here's what I know of you so far," said Mervyn fifteen minutes later across the kitchen table, puffing at a fresh roll-up and sipping at a cup of Nescafé Gold Blend while Leon rotated the glass of orange juice he'd been allowed.

That was when Mervyn recounted the whole story from its inception. From how he'd been contracted by Lizzie Leah to discover her lost lover, through events leading up to the Munich trip, and concluding with the situation in which Leon now found himself. Nothing missed out, the whole nine yards. With special emphasis laid on the threats now posed to him by Connie Horowitz's Mrs McGuire Society, which Mervyn considered possibly even more of a danger than those from the likes of Schornstein, Figov, or Büchner.

"You know what hell can be like," he concluded. "How it hath no fury like a woman scorned."

Leon rotated his orange juice glass too fast, knocked it to the floor, and spilled all the juice but Mervyn paid no attention to that.

"Blokes can often be up for negotiation, but women..."

Bereft of a glass to rotate, Leon took to fiddling with his shin-high orthopaedic white boot.

Mervyn smiled. "How's it going in the toe department, by the way? Still a mite tender, is it? The way Lizzie heard it from Connie that's the very *least* you may expect if any one of the Mrs McGuires around the world ever finds out where you're hiding now."

~ * ~

All of that happened on the first day of Leon's sojourn with Mervyn. Day two was that bit more relaxed, and by the third he had become sufficiently compliant to be invited to the Hand in Hand to see if a glass or two of Young's Special might help loosen up his mind and tongue in the direction of honesty. Suzie was happy about that. What with Master having been so unusually bad-tempered and distracted all the time, she had barely slept a wink.

Once they were both seated and sipping at their pints outside in the continuing summer sunshine, Mervyn wasted no time getting to the point.

"Just answer me this simple question," he said, rolling a cigarette. "Do you actually be*lieve* the populist gospel you've been preaching, or is it just a mask for you to hide behind, another vehicle for your thespian talents?"

This was a far from simple question in Leon's book. Dumbfounded, he downed half his beer in one draught then stared off. Some kind of a nerve had been hit though. Mervyn saw that in the flexing and unflexing of the fingers of both hands.

"Don't go shy on me, Mister Devine. I ask purely out of interest and, like good old Voltaire, although I may not agree with your opinions, I respect your right to express them. To whom and where remains a moot point."

Leon remained silent except to ask if he, too, might have a roll-up. Mervyn made him one and handed it over with a lighter.

"Okay then, no response so I'll just outline a *reductio ad* possibly *absurdum* scenario to see if it rings any bells. Feel free to stop me whenever you wish. Some of it, I warn you, may be deemed *ad hominem* for which I make no apologies."

Leon blinked and puffed hard at his roll-up as Mervyn painted the picture of a socially privileged and highly educated young man who had hoped to impress his parents, especially the father, with his prowess in the big bad world beyond Cambridge, the MI6 James Bond lifestyle with fast cars and faster women, all that. Only some way along the road, the young man finds Bond was only ever a fiction blown into even more fabulous movies and much of the Secret Service work is disappointingly humdrum so he goes his own joyous way instead.

Leon twitched and stubbed out his cigarette with some violence.

"Which is why he begins selling guns and secrets to the highest bidders to make life a tad more exciting," Mervyn continued, "and gets the boot from the Secret Service for his troubles. But as a freelancer, the world suddenly becomes his longed-for oyster. Women in every port, jet-setting all over the globe, and how convenient for the times to provide him with the very philosophy that meets all his requirements—populism, which guarantees a macho image especially to those still locked into childhood disappointments by wiping

away history as 'fake,' and allowing its proponents the denial and/
or obfuscation of any missteps along the road to power, which is, of
course, the ultimate objective, never mind how many people's lives
are destroyed in the process. What one might term a dangerous but
as yet socially unrecognized psychopathy because it parades itself as
political acumen."

Leon knocked over his pint of Young's Special, got to his feet and
balled his fists at which Mervyn tutted and raised the karate hand that
had so damaged Figov's carotid artery.

"Don't even think about it, sonny," he said. "I would however be
interested in your response to this little story of mine."

If push came to shove, he still had the possible bisexuality card
to play but was hoping he wouldn't have to, mainly because it was
no more than Taya's suspicion and he also had no wish to breach her
confidences.

It was as Leon was still on his feet peering at the heavens as if
in search of some *deus ex machina* that Lizzie Leah appeared at the
gateway to The Hand in Hand at precisely the time she and Mervyn
had agreed.

She waved. "Hi there, Leo. What goes around comes around, eh?
How you doing?"

Leon froze. During the Munich fiasco and on the plane back to the
UK, he'd pretended Lizzie didn't exist, but now...

"And say hi to Jürgen. He's been looking forward to meeting you."

"Oh for *fuck*," Leon spluttered crossing his legs as the repressed
image of the hound from hell who'd bitten Büchner in the balls re-
materialised from somewhere in the mists of his mind.

"Raaf, raaf," said Jürgen.

"Don't worry, love, he won't bite," said Lizzie, but Leon wasn't
buying that.

"Kuh-keep huh-him away fuh-from me," he said, re-crossing his
legs the other way and clutching his crotch.

Lizzie obliged. "Okay. Sit, Jürgy, there's a good boy," she said,
restraining Jürgen who was all set to lope over to lick Leon's hand and
let bygones be bygones.

"I just thought it might be helpful for you to meet up with the Missus McGuire who hired me," Mervyn explained.

Leon clenched and unclenched his fists and stared wild-eyed back and forth between Mervyn and Lizzie. "Is thuh-this some suh-sort of a puh-punishment puh-*plot*?" he said, recalling only too clearly Mervyn's hell-hath-no-fury warning.

Lizzie pushed back her red hair. "No, love. Yeah, sure, I'm one of the Missus McGuires and I regret it, but the reason Mervyn asked me along wasn't to get my own back, was it, Merv?"

Mervyn shook his head. "Not at all, Lizzie means you no harm. She and I just thought there might be a more civilized way out of the mess you are currently in. A little chat, that's all we're asking for. You up for that?"

"Do I have a choice?" said Leon, still eyeing Jürgen and clutching his crotch.

"No. But I tell you what, why don't I go and get the beers in while you, Lizzie, and Jürgen re-establish contact."

Tentatively, Leon sat back down, frowned, and wafted a hand at Lizzie to join him.

"Raaf, raaf," chorused Jürgen and Suzie, both pleased to see each other again after the exciting Munich trip and, more importantly, to witness humans behaving properly.

Seventeen

When the ring came at the doorbell down in the street, Taya at first panicked, fearing the safety net around the house had been breached. It was only as the rings continued she remembered the surveillance had been transferred to Mervyn's cottage along with Leon, and felt safe enough to reply however tentatively.

"Yes?" she whispered into the intercom.

Which was when she recognized the voice she only ever normally heard on the phone, but this time sounding even less calm than usual.

"*Mama?*" Taya looked down through the curtains and saw the red Bentley Continental parked awkwardly with two wheels on the pavement. "What the...?"

"Just let me in. Just let me *in*," croaked Svetlana, nerves rattled by both the daring escape from Henley-on-Thames, and the terror of piloting a car for the first time in more years than she could remember. Never had Sir Montmorency allowed her to drive. It was either him or a chauffeur who did that while she sat in the back seat. Plus, there had been the terror of losing her way, particularly as she had no idea what a satnav was, let alone how to use one. But somehow—*somehow*—she'd found her way, partly in the old-fashioned manner of stopping and asking real live people for directions. And, after many hours, here she finally was, exhausted but at her destination.

Taya was downstairs to the front door so fast she twice tripped and practically ripped off the bannister while saving herself.

"*Mama.*" She took Svetlana in her arms from both love and the need to keep her upright. But her mother wasn't heavy. Tall, chestnut-haired, and just as beautiful as ever, but now bowed a little and weighing probably no more than six or seven stones.

"Tayara, my sweet darling," she gurgled into her daughter's neck. "I'm *here*," she added on a note of triumph.

"You are indeed, Mama." Taya disentangled herself from the embrace in order to sling an arm around Svetlana's waist and lead her back up the stairs to her flat, where the pair staggered through the open door and Svetlana collapsed onto the nearest sofa saying "*krovavvy ad* (bloody hell)." These were the only two Russian words she allowed herself. Although both women were bilingual, the agreement had been made on Sir Montmorency's insistence that English would always be the language in his house and like all his demands, the habit had become second nature.

"Can I get you something?" said Taya.

Svetlana raised a playful eyebrow. "Vodka. You have vodka?"

Taya smiled. "Would any self-respecting half-Russian daughter ever be without a decent drop of *votke* in her house. How d'you want it? With something or without."

"You know the answer to that, sweetheart. On the rocks, as the Americans say."

After two glasses of that and three chain-smoked Sobranie Black Russian cigarettes, Svetlana relaxed sufficiently to tell Taya the story of her escape.

"I am here to get away from that bastard father of yours for*ever*," she concluded. "Gonna wash that man right *outta* my hair," she added in a decent Ella Fitzgerald impression.

Taya nodded and laughed. "About time, Mama. You're welcome to stay here just as long as you like."

"*Merci beaucoup, ma chérie*," said Svetlana, who spoke fragments of many European languages, all gleaned from her work with orchestras before Sir Montmorency declared he had no intention of marrying a working woman, let alone a bally cellist. "Fiddle about on your own if you must," he'd told her on their wedding night. "But never in public. Not on my watch."

Taya frowned. "But won't Father come looking for you? It won't take him long to figure out where you've gone. *And* you've pinched his beloved car, which wouldn't be hard for the police to trace. It would just take a phone call, and he'll come knocking on the door."

"Let him, I don't care. For many years I have rehearsed the speech I will give him. Also, in the mirror, I have practised punching a person on the nose," said Svetlana with a determined but wobbly attempt at a right hook, which caused her to rotate sideways and fall off the sofa.

They both laughed as she picked herself up saying, "That's vodka for you. In any case, he's in trouble with the cops at the moment. I escaped when they took him away for questioning. What happens next depends on whether the intruders want to press charges or not."

"In*tru*ders?"

"Yes, two of them. Climbed over the gates they did, so Sir Monty Crockett shot them in their bottoms and chucked them into the lane."

Taya winced.

"It was only with the shotgun, though. Didn't blow their bottoms *off* or kill them or anything. Still, he got carted away to the cop shop for twenty-four hours, which was all the time I needed to pack a few things and vamoose. Anyway, let's just say he'll have other things on his mind, so no worries there. Probably won't even notice I've gone. *Any*how, my darling, how have *you* been? Haven't heard from you for so long. Everything going okay?"

"Yeah, I'm okay. Busy as usual," said Taya, fearing the question she was sure would come next. Which it did.

"And any news of that rascal brother of yours?" Svetlana continued, passing her glass over for another refill and firing up a fresh Sobranie.

Taya took a deep breath. There was always going to be a time when she would have tell her parents what had happened, but she had hoped it might not be yet. However, events in Henley-on-Thames had scuppered that plan. Okay, it was probably better to report the situation without Sir Montmorency present because he would have gone apeshit and started breaking things the way he always did in the face of news that didn't suit him. But given her continued belief in women's rights despite her bad marriage, was Svetlana really strong enough to take on board the events of not only recent weeks, but also news of the Mrs McGuire Society? Plus, her son's promotion of a political philosophy redolent of the post-Gorbachev era leading to the return of the vicious Moscow dictatorship she loathed. Leon, the misogynist *and agent provocateur* for the bad guys, would not go down at *all* well, Taya reckoned.

"A ruble for your thoughts, darling. Is the boy in trouble of some sort?"

Which was when Taya was left with no option but to give a stripped-to-the-bone but inevitably telling account of her brother's recent travails, including his brief sojourn with her and his current location not far away in Wimbledon.

Unsurprisingly, Svetlana broke down and wept, albeit for a shorter time than Taya might have expected. After maybe five or ten minutes of being hugged by her daughter, she righted herself and said, "Poor boy. Deep down I always knew he would come to a sad end. And there was nothing I could do to stop it, not with his father around. So gentle he was as a child, so loving, but..."

"Don't blame your*self*, Mama. You were caught in the same trap as him," said Taya, expressing for the first time the thought that had been on her mind for as long as she could remember.

Svetlana reached again for the vodka bottle and the Sobranie packet. "Do you think perhaps he might like to see me now I'm here?"

"I'm sure he would, Mama. But first, I will need to check with the guy who's looking after him."

"Who is?"

Taya explained who Mervyn Vincent was and why Leon was now staying at his house.

"Must be a very generous person."

"He is, Mama, but we will need a progress report before we muddy any waters, okay?"

"Strange to think of a mother muddying waters, Tayara dear. But, as you said about his short stay with you, maybe I too was part of the problem. I shall think on it. Meanwhile, I need to sleep. Do you have...?"

"Mama, you shall have my bed. I'm happy to sleep on the couch. I would like it, in fact."

So that was how mother and daughter passed the first night of their overdue reunion, although neither rested peacefully.

~ * ~

It was while Mervyn was still inside the Hand in Hand ordering up the beers and Lizzie and Leon were still sitting awkwardly on opposite sides of the table saying nothing that Jürgen decided to have another go at befriending the peculiar human who had rejected his previous advances, this time opting for the paws-on-shoulders manoeuvre normally forbidden by Mistress on the grounds it was poor doggy etiquette, especially for big dogs. But Jürgen sometimes forgot he was big, and anyway Mistress wasn't yanking at his lead or anything at the moment, so...

His embrace wasn't reciprocated the way he had hoped, however. Far from it as the strange human shrieked, collapsed to his knees, and took to headbutting the ground while producing weird gurgling noises from somewhere deep in his throat.

"Hrrmph," said Jürgen dismissively, but by then Mistress *was* tugging at the leash and saying he was a *very* naughty boy, so he just turned and took an urgent interest in his bottom.

Lizzie held up a reassuring palm. "Don't worry, Leo. Or should I call you Leo*n*? He was only playing. You can get up now."

"Some fucking game," Leon gurgled, his mind still awash with both Büchner's Munich testicular experience, and the fear of retribution from the Mrs McGuire Society to which Lizzie surely belonged. So much for the "little chat to re-establish contact." Some bollocks *that* was, particularly coming from Mervyn Vincent, whom he'd begun to respect, to trust even.

Surprised he was, therefore, when Lizzie passed Jürgen's leash to Mervyn, bent over, stroked Leon's hair. "Don't worry, love, like I said, I'm not here to hurt you if that's what you're still thinking. Yeah, you fucked me around but that's over now so we're looking at a new beginning."

Mervyn nodded approval as he set the glasses on the table. Some woman this Lizzie Leah, which was why he'd invited her to confront the cause of the whole story so far. No "hell hath no fury" for Lizzie Leah.

"Matter of fact, like Mervyn said, I'm here to help if I can," she continued. "And let's be clear, I know all about you now, the whole bag of tricks. From Mervyn here because he was my PI in the first place, but from Taya, too, because she's like a sister to me now, which makes us almost family, right? And your dad coughed up the dosh you owed me, so we're square on that front, too."

This was a lot of information for Leon to digest all at one go. To him the spiel still sounded like some trick, a set-up, but to what end? Plus, he was unused to understanding or sympathy or whatever you wanted to call it, never having received any in his whole life. To him, the thing had old dogs and new tricks written all over it, so he stayed where he was—quivering on the ground.

"Help you up, old chap?" said Mervyn, keeping Jürgen at a safe distance.

Like a child, Leon covered his ears with both hands. "Leave me *alone*."

Never had Lizzie seen him so craven. Always the guy in charge he had been. Always the Mister Big who could do anything he liked. Now *this*.

She knelt beside him. "Look, love, let's let bygones *be* bygones and draw the famous lines under stuff, shall we? Otherwise we're going nowhere fast. I can see why you might have trouble believing me. I got nothing to swear on, no Bible or any shit like that, I'm just what I am and, in the end, you can either take it or leave it."

"Leon, if I were you I'd take it," Mervyn advised. "It's your best hope, or if not best at least best worst. There may be others down the road, who can tell? Nothing much is straightforward in this life. 'Use your head, you're on Earth, there's no cure for that,' as Samuel Beckett noted."

Which rang a faint bell in Leon's befuddled head.

"*Endgame*?" he said, having once played Clov in a joint Oxford and Cambridge production of the play.

Mervyn wasn't sure of the exact reference. "Possibly, *very* possibly. But wherever it comes from there's a certain truth in the idea, is there not?"

It was as the result of whatever peculiar concatenation occurred in his brain that Leon Devine finally scrambled to his feet, Lizzie Leah climbed off her knees, and Leon bent to give her a helping hand up.

Eighteen

After spending the night at hospital in Henley-on-Thames getting their bottoms patched up and being drip-fed intravenous antibiotics, Sergei Figov and Georg Büchner returned the following afternoon to the police station from which Sir Montmorency Devine had been recently released, and told PC Gordon Roberts they'd thought things over and didn't want the hassle of pressing charges, which after all, Sir Montmorency's blustering and threats came as a relief to Gordon. Nonetheless, for the record, he needed a reason. The truth was the last thing Sergei and Georg needed was the sorts of publicity that might lead to their identification, but they weren't about to admit that to the police.

Sergei shrugged nonchalantly. "Can't be bothered. Whole thing was probably our fault anyway for climbing over the gates."

Gordon scribbled on his notepad. "There *is* that to it, lads. But why exactly might you have done that?"

"As you may have noticed, I am Russian," said Sergei.

"Foreign, I'd already worked out, laddie, even though you said you were American. But *Russian*, eh? Climbing over gates into other people's property the sort of thing Russians do often, is it?"

Sergei's eyes narrowed but he kept his cool. "No comment. I mention my nationality only because it's the same as Missus Devine's."

"Svetlana *Lady* Devine's," Roberts corrected.

"Whatever. *Any*way, all my friend and I wanted to do was convey to her, in person, best wishes from relatives back in St Petersburg, a perfectly innocent thing to do. But I can see how the husband could have misread the situation and gone batshit. Probably within his rights anyway."

Gordon concurred. "So he kept saying. And, like I told you, defence of property rights are all a bit of a murky business."

"Understood. So enough's enough. Let him go."

"I already have. His twenty-four hours were up, and we never charged him."

"Good, so no need to re-arrest him."

"Bit of a change of mind since you were last here and wanting to throw the book at him."

"Heat of ze moment," said Georg in a decent stab at English. "Now we have ze time over to sink."

Gordon scribbled some more. "Ah-hah. And you are, let me guess...Spanish."

"German."

"*Ger*man, eh?"

"*Ja.*"

"Okay then. Well, this is all very noble of you, gents," Gordon called after Sergei and Georg who were already heading through the door muttering to each other about British xenophobia. Within the hour, they were on the train that would take them to Paddington station whence they would hail the cab to take them back to Primrose Hill.

~ * ~

They spent the two days following the Henley-on-Thames debâcle wandering the area in the stormy post-heatwave weather. Apart from Primrose Hill, they strolled along the Regent's Canal and around Regent's Park speaking of many things. And when it rained, which was unseasonably often, they sat in the lounge of Sergei's rented

Gloucester Avenue flat smoking cigarettes, drinking wine, and tossing back and forth many of the same ideas they'd discussed on their peregrinations, top of the list being how they intended to proceed on the Leon Devine question.

It was on the morning of the third, mercifully cloud-and rain-free, day while sitting on a bench at the top of Primrose Hill peering out at the same London cityscape they'd seen on their last visit, that Büchner pretty much summed up the idea they'd both being veering towards.

"Maybe we should just let sleeping dogs lie," he said, cocking a raised eyebrow down at his shotgun-peppered bottom.

Sergei grinned and rubbed his bum, too. "That's one way of looking at it. And let Schornstein stew in his own juice. Tell him we did our best but the info he gave us wasn't sufficient. Not our fault."

Georg agreed. "Exactly. We just tell him the guy must've gone to ground somewhere we had no chance of finding him and he should get someone else on the case. Then we're free of the whole shebang, right?"

Sergei shrugged. "Maybe. At least we seem to be agreed neither of us wants any more to do with the populism roadshow."

This had been another subject much discussed as the pair walked and talked over the last couple of days. As Georg had worried previously from the same vantage point overlooking London, what if high finance moved to Germany which then itself imploded under the pressure of his very own *Alternative für Deutschland*? Also, what if other countries followed suit like dominos and, under populist pressure, the whole European Union collapsed? In Sergei's view, then the psychos in the White House and the Kremlin would be very happy because the map of Europe would look much the same as it had before the First and Second World Wars, lots of little nation states squabbling with each other with no common interest to hold them together and thus, easy meat for the big powers.

This was the conclusion he now repeated.

"A shame it took me so long to figure out. I guess I'd been brainwashed somehow. But, seeing things through new spectacles, I no longer want any part of it. You, Georg?"

Büchner shook his head.

As for letting sleeping Leons lie, however, Sergei had reservations.

"Yeah, I guess we *could* just walk away and bury our heads in some sand somewhere," he said. "But, you know what, Georg, I'd still kind've like to know how the guy's doing. Also, why he was of so much interest not only to Schornstein, but also to the MI6 guy and the woman with the dog."

Georg faux winced.

"The sister I can understand," Sergei continued. "I guess she loves him or something. Wants him out of harm's way or whatever. But what do the British Secret Services have to do with all this?"

"Good question. I see your point. But *how* do we find him? No joy from the parents, that's for sure. Not now. So..."

"Exactly, but before we were just following Schornstein's orders. Checking out the Henley deal, right? Now we're free agents."

Georg nodded.

"Also there may be another route to our Leon, one Schornstein couldn't have known of. You remember the time I told you about when I just happened to be drinking a cappuccino at the café table right next to the Vincent dude and the Taya dame in Regent's Park?"

Georg didn't.

"Well, anyway, I was. And I learned a lot from it, some of which I told Schornstein, which I shouldn't have, but I did. More fool me. *Any*way, something else just came back to me from that conversation."

"Which is?"

"Where the Taya woman works. At the University of Westminster... she's a Russian teacher there."

"So?"

"So she *must* know where her brother is. The university isn't going to give a total stranger her home address, that's for sure, but I've been checking online, and they have email addresses for all their staff so students can be in touch, which means we could contact her."

"But why should she want to get back to *us* of all people?"

"Because we're going to make her an interesting offer she, or more likely the MI6 guy, would find tempting. That be okay with you?"

"Offer? *What* offer?"

Sergei explained and Georg smiled.

"Right. Nice one. Why not? And you know what else, Sergei?"

"What's that?"

"I, too, would be happy enough to see the Devine guy again. Back in Munich at the hotel, there was something about him not quite right. Super-powerful, super-confident, all that shit. But underneath the mask, I dunno, there was this sad little kid trying to get out."

Sergei shook his head. "A shrink you are now, Georg?"

"Far from it, it's just..."

"So anyway, we're agreed to carry on the Devine search on our own account?"

"As I said."

"Okay then."

It was on this note that Georg Büchner and Sergei Figov walked back down the hill and again repaired to The Queens pub for what they reckoned to be fully deserved libations and something to eat. This time Rolf the Dachshund wasn't there, which Georg regretted. He'd rather liked Rolf.

Nineteen

It was on the morning of the fourth day of Leon's stay with Mervyn that his host received two phone calls, both requiring thought, tact, and diplomacy. The first was from Margery Middleton at MI6 asking for a further update on events since their arrival back from Munich. Mervyn had kept her in the loop where the facts were concerned, how the stay with his sister hadn't worked out too well so he'd come to stay at the little Wimbledon cottage and so on. But Margery was less interested in personal details than she was in the wider political picture.

"We did once speak of the possible indentation a reformed Devine might make into populist agendas were he to be refocused and took to contradicting what he'd claimed before, Mervyn," she said.

"Indeed we did, ma'am. Indeed we *did*."

"Which was why MI6 sponsored your snatching and possibly reforming him."

"Absolutely. Quite so."

"But not having heard from you since our last conversation, and now detecting a note of uncertainty in your voice, can I be assured that's still the plan, Mervyn?"

"It is early days, ma'am, *very* early days. Many balls in the air, so to speak."

"Not Devine's, one hopes."

Mervyn chuckled. "No, he seems to be calming down a little, but it's very much a case of one step at a time," he said. "Right now, I've no idea in which direction those steps might lead. The man's mind is somewhat scrambled, shall we say."

"Perhaps a visit from me along with one of my super-headshrinkers?"

This was the time for tact and diplomacy on Mervyn's part. "I'm sure that would be *most* welcome...in...due...course. When the dust has settled."

"Strong on the tropes today, Doctor Vincent. First the balls, now the dust."

Mervyn chuckled again but only to win himself a little time for thought, specifically about how he could best keep Margery on board while at the same time protecting Leon from premature messing with a head still barely able to sit comfortably on its own shoulders.

"Margery, the rest of the team and I remain deeply grateful to you and your MI6 colleagues for all your support, and will contact you for more as and when. But at this stage, our feeling is we don't need a hammer to crack a nut."

"*More* tropes, Mervyn," said Margery, but at least she too was now laughing. "Just always remember we're on the same side, okay? I would, for example, be perfectly happy to visit with*out* any headshrinkers if you deemed it appropriate."

"I shall bear it in mind, Margery, and many thanks. Whoops, there's someone on the other line. I'm going to have to love you and leave you."

~ * ~

Mervyn didn't have another line but as chance would have it his antiquated landline phone trilled again only moments after he'd settled it back on its rest.

"Taya. Great to hear from you, how's tricks?"

Which was when Taya explained Svetlana was in town having done a runner from Sir Montmorency and was longing to see her son again.

Mervyn's eyes widened. "Done a *runner?*"

"Yes. Stole his Bentley while he was in jail and..."

"*Jail?*"

"The old bastard shot some intruders in their arses and got arrested for his troubles."

"Serves him right. I hope they bang him up for the foreseeable," said Mervyn, remembering the sad wave Svetlana had given him from the balcony of her mansion/prison.

"Me too, but I doubt it. He has clout in Henley, and you can be sure he'll use it."

"And once free, he'll come looking for her. That's what you're worried about."

"I am and it won't be pleasant."

"Is the car still there?"

"Yes."

"Ditch it somewhere improbable. It might at least slow him down."

Taya sighed. "Sure. But car or no car he knows where *I* live and he's sure to think that's where Mama is. Where else would she go?"

"True enough. Call me night or day if you need help."

"Thanks, you're an angel, Mervyn."

"I wouldn't go that far. *Any*way she wants to see Leon, you say."

"Yes. What d'you reckon? She's longing to see him obviously but, being the woman she is, she's also aware of having possibly been part of Leon's problem and has no wish to dig up old wounds. She and I have talked the thing over again and again and come to no conclusion. You will remember how he behaved at my place."

"Playing the guilt card," said Mervyn who, never having been married or sired children, was beginning the feel a tad out of his depth, neither of his careers as MI6 agent and private eye having prepared him for family counselling. To Mervyn, the human mind, particularly the female version, remained as much of a mystery as it always had.

Still, there was always a first time for everything and learning never ended, so....

"Exactly. Which is the *last* thing Mama needs right now. As you can imagine she's not at her strongest. But still..."

"Cleft stick time, eh? Damned if she does, damned if she doesn't."

"Exactly. Just tell me how Leon's getting along with you. He's only been there a few days, I know, but is there any improvement? Man to man stuff and so on?"

Mervyn couldn't deny it. "Not the third-degree, but let us just say I've given him the facts of the matter as I understand them."

Taya smiled. "Knowing you, with at least a smidgeon of sympathy."

"One does one's best."

"And?"

"Well, he gets up in the morning now."

"A triumph then."

"Of sorts," said Mervyn, going on to tell Taya how Leon had also met up with Lizzie, which had gone better than expected. How she had offered to stay over with him at Mervyn's place, but he had reckoned that might be a little premature so she and Jürgen had gone back home again.

"And he knows about the Mrs McGuires Society?"

"Yes, I told him. But Lizzie said she'd call the Muir Woods woman to see if the heat can be taken off, for the moment at least. She was going to explain why."

"Mervyn, that's *some* progress."

"I guess you could call it that," said Mervyn before going on to recount the recent conversation with Margery Middleton, how she'd offered MI6 psychoanalysts to help with Leon's case to get him ready for a return to the field with a whole different script.

"Hope you told her *no* to both."

"I did. But I need to keep her on board. After all, she has her reputation to think of, and it was she who funded and arranged our Munich operation."

"True enough. Strange times, Mervyn."

"Strange indeed, Taya. We are living through many changes on many horizons, both personal and political, but back to Svetlana. What is *your* view of her and Leon getting together? Is she listening in to this call by the way?"

"No, she's sleeping. I gave her one of my little potions."

"Of?"

"Warm vodka with just a drop or two of Valium."

"A knockout brew."

"But she knows I was going to call you. And when she wakes up..."

"She'll want an answer on the Leon front."

Taya laughed. "Knowing Mama, *da*."

"So," Mervyn said, crossing fingers and casting trepidation to the four winds. "How about we set up a meeting tomorrow at the Hand in Hand? Early afternoon around two?"

"The Hand in Hand?"

"It's a pub just along from Cannizaro Park that has served us well so far in this case. Come to my place first and we'll go together. Sir Monty's Bentley's bound to have a GPS monitor and, while we're about it we can ditch the beast in Wimbledon Common car park with the windows rolled down and the keys in the ignition. Which will be tantamount to sticking a note on the windscreen saying STEAL ME, I'M YOURS. Fat chance of Sir Monty finding it ever again."

"Cunning thinking, Sherlock. And meanwhile, you'll alert Leon to our visit."

"Leave it to me," said Mervyn, replacing the overheated phone on its rest and crossing even more fingers.

~ * ~

Given the university was on summer vacation, Taya wasn't bothering to trek all the way up to town to collect any paper snail mail, and emails she could pick up at home—which she did once she got off the phone from Mervyn. Not that she much felt like it, cursing the day Higher Education succumbed to the computer age. What with lectures being on the Web and essays marked according to set pro-formas and returned by email, teachers barely ever saw students face-to-face at all. But that didn't mean they were never in contact. They were, all the time, spectrally via hi-tech. Most of the time complaining they hadn't received a justified assessment of their last piece of work and threatening litigation if it were not raised to what it deserved i.e. at least the seventy percent first-class mark they were paying through the nose for. Even in the holidays, from some louche resort in the sun or more likely in a break from their mac job, they would tap away at their phones making sure they weren't forgotten. Such was the crammed mailbox today as Taya scrolled through the hundred or so complaints and urgent queries about this, that, and the other.

"Bugger," she sighed, knowing she would face a Vice Chancellor's enquiry were she to fail to reply.

But then, sent yesterday, one stood out from the rest and, shaking, Taya was obliged to sit down and re-read it three times before it made the least sense.

The text was:

"Hi Miss Devine,

This message comes from me, Sergei Figov, and my friend Georg Büchner. You will not know these names but, if you think back to the Allianz Arena in Munich, you would recognize our faces. We were the guys looking after your brother until you and your comrades took him away. And let me be clear at the start, we mean neither you nor Leon *any* harm!!! This you must understand. All I ask is that you grant us the chance for a meet-up. Many things have changed in our lives since Munich, things we may be able to discuss. We are in London and always available. Although we would wish to, we do not need to meet with Leon, or you, or your other lady friend if you do not want. But we would like to talk with the guy who was with you, Dr Mervyn Vincent, because there is an offer we would like to make him.

Hope to hear from you soon.

Sergei."

Taya was straight back on the phone to Mervyn, who picked up his black bakelite only moments before it went to message.

"So sorry to bother you again," she said. "Only I've had this email from the Munich guys."

Mervyn had been sprawled on a couch staring at a wall while Leon fed Suzie her lunch. "What Munich guys?"

"The ones we took Leon from. The one you karate chopped, he's the one who sent the message, is called Sergei Figov and his friend is Georg Büchner."

"The one Jürgen bit in the personals?"

"I assume so. Anyway, can I read it to you?"

"Sure."

Mervyn sat bolt upright when he'd heard the whole text. "Well, I'll be blowed."

"What the hell can it mean?"

"I don't know."

"D'you want me to reply to it?"

"No, no. If anybody does, I will, but not just yet. Give me the address, please. How the hell did they find yours, by the way?"

"It was in my university profile. I have no idea how they found out I worked there."

"Mmm, curiouser and curiouser. Anyway, leave it with me, Taya. If there's any news, you'll be the first to know."

Twenty

Mervyn was starting to have second thoughts about the Hand in Hand meet-up between Svetlana and Leon. After all, it was not his position to act as arbiter or go-between in a mother-son relationship, not at least without first consulting Leon, and if he threw a wobbly and refused, then the whole thing would have to be called off, or postponed or whatever. The difficulty was judging or predicting the man's moods after so short a time ,although, while Leon was still nothing like a fully rational human being, he had at least made some progress in that direction as evinced by the meeting with Lizzie. Who would have for a second suspected the pair might get along together like civilized divorcees? Not Mervyn, that was for sure. Okay, he knew Lizzie well enough by now to trust her to put any past resentment to one side and behave with reason rather than emotion, but that Leon had managed almost the same civility had been a welcome marker of progress. Gone, or at least well hidden, had been the old brash macho Leo McGuire, to be replaced by something almost gentlemanly as they sat together in Mervyn's lounge while he excused himself and fiddled about in the kitchen ostensibly cleaning things. Afterwards at the garden gate, before she and Jürgen took their leave, Lizzie expressed astonishment at the change.

"That's a new bloke," she told Mervyn. "Some miracle you've achieved. Should've been a shrink, you."

"One does one's best," said Mervyn in what had become a familiar response. "Unless it was all just another piece of theatre."

"I don't think so, love. I'm old enough to know when a bloke's fooling and when he's not. Call it a woman's intuition."

Mervyn didn't remind her of the misrecognition that had led to this whole story but he didn't need to because Lizzie did it for him.

"Yeah, yeah, I know. I was daft as a brush with him before, but I'd have been even dafter not to have learnt a lesson, right?"

"Older and wiser, eh?"

"Older, wiser and maybe also sadder, but that's life. Anyhow, there's always got to be a reason to pick yourself up, dust yourself down, and start all over again, hasn't there?"

"Too true." Mervyn took her in his arms and kissed her on the forehead, paternally. "I shall mark your words. Meanwhile go well," he was saying as Lizzie returned the compliment with a smackeroo right on the lips.

"You are a good man, Mervyn Vincent. We shall see each other again, soon," said Lizzie, waving back as Jürgen yanked at his lead and tugged her away.

Watching her sashay off onto the path whistling, Mervyn was an emotionally confused man as he returned to the cottage to find Leon sitting on the old American rocker staring at a print of Picasso's *La Joie de Vivre* on the wall opposite.

"Like it?" Mervyn asked.

Leon nodded. "Just let's say it speaks to me. Which is what art should do if it's any good. Not a question of meaning, more one of implication, a puzzle with any number of interpretations. Thanks for asking Lizzie around, by the way. She was kind to me, which I didn't deserve."

"She's a good woman, Leon. And who's to say what a man deserves and what he doesn't? The opportunity to change is always available. Or, better perhaps, finally to understand who he *really* is and, if he finds goodness there, have the bottle to act on it."

"So as not to go to hell?"

"This has nothing to do with religious narratives, Leon. Simply a matter of who we *want* to be in the short time we're on Earth. Unlike other animals we supposedly have the ability and right to make such a choice, and there's nothing transcendental about it."

"I wanted to be James fucking Bond."

"And do you still?"

Slowly and deliberately, still gazing at *La Joie de Vivre*, Leon shook his head.

It was this exchange that had formed the basis of Mervyn's belief it might be possible after all to shuck off the arbiter role with sufficient confidence to trust in Leon's decision when it came to seeing his mother again after so many years.

"She's *here*?" said a suddenly agitated Leon when Mervyn went on to describe Svetlana's escape from Henley-on-Thames.

"Staying with Taya in Putney."

"Holy Christ. How did she...? Father'll be going *ape*shit."

Mervyn outlined Sir Montmorency's current difficulties with the law, at which Leon stopped staring at the Picasso and took to smacking his temples.

"Sorry for the cliché but what goes around sometimes comes around," said Mervyn, fearing the worst as Leon continued to smack himself around the head. "An intelligent person cannot live her *whole* life in chains."

Leon took several long, deep, yoga-type breaths.

"She'd love to see you, so Taya says. And who knows, maybe *you* could help *her* out in these strange times."

"You think?"

"This is your decision, Leon, but if my opinion counts for anything then yes, why not? It can do you no harm and will surely help her."

It was while leaning down to stroke Suzie that Leon whispered, "Call her. Call Taya and say okay. Only she must come too."

"Of course. Your mother would never find the way without her."

~ * ~

Hal Schornstein and Sir Montmorency Devine were dissimilar in so far as they lived on opposite sides of the Atlantic and were of different generations, but that's where the distinction ended. Otherwise, they had three defining features in common: inordinate wealth, the belief that women were a lower form of life and, stemming from these two factors, the automatic assumption they were innately superior to other people who would therefore always be expected unquestioningly do their bidding. In these ways, they marched through life in the much same manner as the misogynist billionaire in the White House and his equivalents in both the Kremlin and 10 Downing Street. Cross any of these psychos and you'd be, at best, publically mocked or fired or both and, at worst, stiffed or jailed. Schornstein and Devine didn't have these latter powers available to them in reality, but in their dreams they were made of the same stuff, which was why neither respected any authority other than their own.

In recent days, however, they had come to share a further affinity, which was driving each of them crazy—namely the arrant disregard for their tyranny by in Schornstein's case Sergei Figov, and in Sir Monty's by his wife, Svetlana. How *dare* these infidels flout the wishes of their masters with such evident disdain? Figov had called just the once to explain to Hal he and Büchner had given up the Leon Devine hunt and, thereafter never once answered his phone. And Svetlana hadn't even had the courtesy to leave Monty a message before vanishing into thin air from the house it was her responsibility to keep in tiptop order.

"Fuckin' *ass*hole, where the fuck *are* you?" shrieked Hal on a daily basis as he stumped up and down his NYC office dialing and re-dialing Sergei's number and only ever getting white noise as an answer. But how could he have known both Sergei and Georg Büchner had had the good sense to toss their old phones into The Regent's Canal attached to chunks of lead and bought themselves a couple of throwdown replacements programmed only to receive calls or emails they would answer? *No* way, that was how. The thought never even crossed his mind, believing instead something must have gone seriously wrong with Figov's brain, something Hal intended to check out with Moscow

ASAP. The White House was on the blower every fucking day for crissakes, *still* wanting a progress report on the Munich hijack of the Devine creep in case he spilled confidences that could ruin the next election bid.

Having lost his car *and* his wife, Sir Monty faced a similar dilemma as he paced around the manor house and the estate looking for clues to his wife's disappearance and, finding none, eventually concluding the only place she would have gone would be to her daughter's, and on that assumption, trying her phone, only to be faced every time with static just like Hal's. Why? Because fearing such an eventuality, on Margery Middleton's advice Arty Arthuro had provided Taya with a special phone like Sergei's and Georg's equipped with a device that blocked and binned unwanted calls from specified numbers.

"Jesus H on a sodding *bike*," he howled, his pointless shotgun swinging down by his side. "Bet your life that no-good Mama's boy son of mine is somewhere at the root of this, and I can't bloody well find *him* either."

In New York City and Henley-on-Thames, therefore, there dwelt two very pissed off egomaniacs both in one way or another in search of the catalyst of all their angst, Leon Devine, who remained blithely unaware of *this* aspect of the trouble he'd caused. Which was just as well because contact with either, especially his father, would have slowed his progress to relative sanity exponentially.

~ * ~

"Sorry I'm busy right now, but I'll get back to you soon as I can," was the message Lizzie got when she phoned Connie Horowitz. And this wasn't an excuse. Having heard rifle shots close to her trailer, Connie *was* busy doing her self-appointed ranger duties, given the real Ranger Station was so far away. This entailed patrolling her fringe of Muir Woods with her Winchester for any asshole dumb enough to try shooting any of her precious animals, especially the deer that were so prized for their meat, or worse still, the Northern Spotted Owls which were listed as an endangered species. Plus, there were all kinds of smaller fry, raccoons and suchlike. Life was life, and Connie didn't give a rat's ass *what* the hunters' target was as long as she preserved animal wellbeing in her patch of the woods. And sure enough, after only a few steps into the trees there he was, some wannabe macho dickbrain loosing off at anything that moved. Kitted out in all the hunter's gear like he was Davy Crockett or someone. He was also wobbly on his legs and chuckling, which Connie attributed to the bottle of Jack Daniels poking out of the back pocket of his baggy khaki green pants.

"Pow, pow, kerrrrr-*pow*," he yelled as he pointed his gun in any direction that took his fancy, upward to the tops of the giant sequoia, downward to their trunks and roots, sideways into the bushes, randomly *any*where.

Which wasn't wise of him with Connie Horowitz around. Her priority was animal life, but trees came a close second, especially when chunks of them were being splintered and shot off by this soused dork. Connie believed in the wisdom of trees.

Without a second thought, she shouldered her Winchester. "Hold it right there, bozo. Put your gun down and walk away or you're gonna regret it."

The bozo, named Hank Reilly, was either too oiled or too stupid or a combination of both to obey this order. Instead, he turned bleary eyes on Connie, called her the kind of dumb bitch who couldn't tell shit from Shinola and, through a lot of spittle, asked her who the fuck she thought she was, Annie Oakley? She wasn't no ranger, that was for sure. Which was enough to raise Connie's hackles to their full height. But Hank's worst mistake was then to raise his rifle and point it at her because that's when Connie shot off his Boonie hat and told him the next bullet would take off the head beneath it.

At which Hank scarpered as fast as he was able, which wasn't very fast what with the Jack Daniels inside him and everything. Stumbling over undergrowth on his rickety legs he went with Connie right behind him asking how he would feel to get his ass shot off too.

"Move it, fatso," she brayed, poking the barrel of her Winchester in said ass. "And dontcha come around these parts no more."

By this time Hank was whimpering a lot and, which pleased Connie, appeared to have soiled his trousers.

"Promise me," she commanded.

And Hank did. "Kuh-cross mah huh-heart an' huh-hope to duh-die," he mumbled as he staggered back to the hilly and curvy road where his American Iron Horse motorcycle was parked. To encourage him still further as he mounted the beast and it coughed into life, Connie loosed off a round over his head. No wonder she was a little breathless when she picked up Lizzie's call and returned it.

"That you, hon?"

"Yeah, it's me, Lizzie the Wimbledon Missus McGuire. You all right, Connie? You're sounding kind've wheezy."

"Yeah, I'm okay, babe, never better in fact. That's how I always get to feel when I shoot a klutz's hat off," said Connie going on to give Lizzie a brief account of her recent escapade in the woods.

Lizzie laughed. "No toes this time?"

"Nah. He had these big biker's boots on. Bullet would likely have bounced right off."

Then Lizzie's reference clicked and she laughed too. "On that subject, I never did find out what happened to the Leo guy. Me'n the other Missus McGuires still looking for him, ya know. All we got to go on so far is a TV news story picture of some dude called Farrago getting himself hi-jacked after some big politico speech over in Germany. Looked one helluva lot *like* Leo. Plus he was wearing this white boot thing on one foot and limping. Missing toes could've explained it. Other than that nothing, like a big fat zilch. You see that story, too?"

"See it, love? I was *in* it."

"Ex*cuse* me?"

By the time Lizzie had ensured she was on a safe phone connection and given a potted version of events starting with the appointment of Mervyn Vincent, Connie was even more breathless than after shooting Hank Reilly's Boonie off.

"Huh-holy *fuck*. You couldn't *make* it up."

"I'm not, love."

"And you've *seen* him?"

"Yeah. He's staying with the PI bloke I told you about."

"Wow, I gotta tell all the other Missus McGuires in the Society about this. You get in a punch in their behalf already? Plus mine?"

"Actually no, Connie. That's why I was calling. And this may not be the best time to tell all the other ladies in the Society."

"You didn't smack him around at *all*? What's the matter with you, girl? An eye for and eye and a..."

"Toe for a toe?"

"Don't make fun of me, hon."

"I'm not. All I'm saying is this doesn't look like the right time for revenge."

"Why the hell not?"

Lizzie used quite a lot of her remaining battery time explaining not only the gentlemanly manner in which Leon had recently treated her but also the complexities of his family background as far as she understood them.

"So he's a poor screwed-up kid, so what? We have a lot of guys like that stateside all the way up to the freaking baby-man president. Man would I ever like to shoot *his* weenie off. And trust me it...is... weenie."

"I can see where you're coming from, Con. *That* bloke deserves all he gets. It's just, I don't know, sometimes it seems to me, and his sister, and the PI bloke, that forgetting and forgiving might be another way of dealing with stuff. At least until we see if it works."

"And if it don't?"

"Then we might need to think again. All I'm asking is you keep schtum for the meantime before you say anything to the other Missus McGuires. He knows you're all on his tail and he's pretty scared, let me tell you."

"So he fuckin' should be."

"I'm just asking you a favour, Connie, woman to woman. Maybe if *you* were to meet him you'd see what I'm saying."

"And leave Muir Woods to fly all the way to Britland? You gotta be kidding."

"We could always arrange a phone call. It might help you see what I mean."

A long silence while Connie thought this through.

"Okay, mebbe, I guess," she eventually said. "How're the guy's toes by the way. He grown any new ones?"

"Prosthetics."

"Okay," said Connie non-committally.

"And until the phone call, you'll tell nobody?"

"Maybe a raccoon or two, but elsewise…"

Just as she was about to thank Connie, Lizzie's battery finally went flat. Nonetheless, she was pleased with the email that pinged into her box once it was charged again.

"With you on this one, hon. I'll hold my horses," it said.

Twenty-one

Mervyn puzzled long and hard over whether or not to reply to the Figov email. That the bloke should even have known Taya's name, and indeed his, was the initial problem but that he resolved quickly enough by casting his eidetic memory back to the Allianz Arena episode as Figov suggested. Looking at the picture frame by frame Mervyn remembered Taya had indeed referred to Leon as her big brother, and one of Leon's minders, presumably the Figov person, had known Mervyn's name too. How, Mervyn still had no idea, but he *had*.

"Mmm, and the email address for Taya?" he muttered lying back on his bed and closing his eyes.

But in this miracle of miracles Internet age from which nobody could hide, he supposed that problem wouldn't have been too hard for Figov to crack. There couldn't be many women in London named Taya Devine, and that one should pop up at the University of Westminster teaching Russian when her brother also shared Russian ancestry would have been worth a try anyway. All pretty circumstantial, and still not explaining Figov's familiarity with *him*, but it was the best Mervyn could conclude.

And now this pair of what he could only guess to be agents in the populist putsch across Europe, one also Russian he assumed and the other German, were in London claiming second thoughts of some sort and with a deal they wanted to offer him. Not since his spy days of dubiously self-professed double agents had Mervyn come across anything so spooky.

"Tread carefully, Mervyn Vincent. Tread *very* carefully," he said to the ceiling. "This is not a decision you should be making without consultation."

And so it was that he picked up the phone and punched in Margery Middleton's super-encrypted number. She picked up on the second ring.

"Mervyn, hello. How're tricks? Still working away on our Mister Devine?"

"Indeed I am, ma'am."

"With any success?"

"Some. Quite a lot, in my humble opinion."

"Pleased to hear it."

"Another matter has cropped up, however. On which I would value your advice."

"Fire away, old chap, but keep it short. I'm expecting a call from the Nazi in Number Ten with some nefarious job he wants done in Washington."

Mervyn laughed. "Which you'll refuse on principle."

"That and along with it the offer to help him shove his head up his bottom where it belongs. Meantime, how may I be of assistance?"

Which was when Mervyn told Margery of the Figov email and reminded her of the work her hacker Arty Arthuro had done when unearthing the names of Figov, Büchner, and Schornstein.

"The very people we do *not* need on Devine's trail," said Margery.

"Quite."

"And this offer Figov and Büchner want to make us?"

"No details. You reckon it could be a ploy to help them find him?"

"Very possibly."

"In which case I should either *not* reply or tell him where he can go and shove *his* head."

"That would be my first response."

"And your second?"

Margery Middleton always had second, third, and even fourth responses to any conundrum, not that she ever dithered over selecting her preferred option.

"We play his game. No good sitting on the subs' bench sucking one's thumb when one could be on the pitch and playing," said the one-time captain of Lady Margaret Hall Oxford's cup-winning inter-varsity women's hockey team.

Mervyn nodded. It was the sort of response he had expected.

"But not without back-up," he said.

"Indeed not. Far too tricky. No, no, should the meet-up go ahead, you would require a team of my chaps and chapesses skulking and lurking in the background with listening-in recording equipment. Armed too, just in case of any overt nastiness. Not a good idea meeting at some regular restaurant, therefore, in case of any collateral damage to the innocent. Equally outside on the street would be no good, too much foot traffic, *and* real traffic that would blur the mikes. An open-air venue with shelter and bushes and trees and things would be best. Know of any such place, do you?"

Mervyn thought of The Hand in Hand or The Windmill Tearoom on the Common as possible Wimbledon venues but, on reflection, considered their outdoor spaces too constricted. Then he remembered where he'd first met Taya, The Broad Walk Café in Regent's Park, which matched most of MM's requirements.

"Sounds good," said Margery. "Go for it. Let me know when it's arranged and I'll get my guys prepped. Whoops, there's the other phone. Probably with the Nazi on the other end."

"Tell him I'd be only too happy to help with the head-up-the-bottom scenario."

"Thanks, I'll be sure to," said Margery, cutting the call.

~ * ~

It was with some trepidation that Svetlana parked the Bentley in the lane outside Mervyn's cottage from where Leon would take the party to the Hand in Hand.

"You're quite, *quite* sure Leon said it would be okay?" she asked Taya, sitting alongside her.

"Doctor Vincent said so, Mama."

"He won't hate me for running away from his father?"

"Mama, how can I *know* that? There's only one way to find out. And remember, when Doctor Vincent called a second time, he said Leon was looking forward to seeing you."

"Maybe the boy was lying. He seems to have lied a lot since I last saw him."

"About him*self*, Mama. To conceal the real person who hid behind the smoke screen he set up."

"And that's all gone now, the smoke screen? Been blown away?"

Taya shrugged and splayed her palms. "Mama, I don't *know*. Doctor Vincent—Mervyn—said Leon was a lot better, but you can't expect a person with a severe personality disorder to be cured overnight, can you?"

"I suppose not."

"So let's look at it this way, we're here to help him a little further along a hard road. What else is family for?"

"True enough. It's him I should be thinking of, not myself."

"Exactly."

"Okay then, here goes," said Svetlana, wiping a tear from her eye, switching off the engine, leaving the key in the ignition as Mervyn had requested, then opening the door to step onto the pathway, where she smoothed down her calf-length blue skirt, patted her still lustrous hair, and straightened her shoulders.

"Atta girl," said Taya, following her around the Bentley's bonnet and taking her in a Russian-type bear hug.

"You go first," said Svetlana, breaking free. "I'll be right behind you."

~ * ~

Inside the little house, as the clock ticked on towards the appointed time, Leon and Mervyn had a similar conversation, Mervyn playing the Taya role and Leon that of Svetlana.

"You said she'd know all about me, what I've done, what I've *been*," said Leon, fiddling with a roll-up and spilling tobacco all over himself.

"We thought that best," said Mervyn.

Leon swatted at his trousers. "So she'll think I'm bad, or crazy, or both. Maybe this wasn't such a good idea after all. Maybe we should…"

"It's too late to call it off, Leon. They'll be on their way already."

"And Taya's coming too? You said Taya would come…"

"She promised she would. Does that make a difference?"

Leon stopped swatting at his trousers and held his head in his hands. "Taya and me, we always talked. But Mama was in the dark. She'll have believed my lies. And now…"

"Now, she's coming here especially to see you, Leon. Why would she, your mother, do that if she didn't think there was hope for the future? The past is the past, let it be."

"And Father? What will *he* think?"

"Your father doesn't know where your mother is and, if I have anything to do with it, isn't about to find out."

"You're sure?"

"Positive," said Mervyn, going on to explain his plan for the Bentley Svetlana had used to make her escape.

Leon laughed at that. "Serve the old bugger right. Some role model *he* was."

Mervyn nodded at the recognition. "As your mother would surely agree."

"I was never allowed to see too much of her. *He* kept her away on one excuse after another."

"So here's your chance of a catch-up. And if I were you, I'd take it with open arms," Mervyn was saying as there came a tap on the front door.

~ * ~

Frustrated to the point of frenzy at being unable to contact his daughter telephonically, and having for two days imbibed more whisky than advisable on a stomach empty except for a couple of sloppily made egg sandwiches, Sir Montmorency Devine took from one of his garages an elderly Harley-Davidson Road King, donned leathers and a dented crash-hat, and lit out for London. Even if Taya's phone didn't work, he had her address in Putney and intended to shake the girl till her teeth rattled until she admitted sheltering her rebellious mother to whom he would demand immediate access.

To begin with, the trip went well enough as Sir Monty raced along the M4 motorway weaving through traffic and zigzagging across lanes at around ninety miles per hour just like a proper Easy Rider. Thumbing his nose at honking motorists in all three lanes as he threatened their lives, and avoiding jams by zooming along the hard shoulder cackling at the idiots who didn't follow his lead. In short, Sir Monty truly was a king of the road. Until the outskirts of London that was, which was when he heard the wah-wah-wah of the cop car behind him and turned to see the flashing blue lights.

"Fuck," said Sir Monty, but not in resignation. No siree. Instead, he simply wound the throttle to its full extent with one hand, flipped the cops the finger over his shoulder with the other, and added a screamed "you" to the "fuck." What with one thing and another, Sir Monty was pretty pissed off with coppers. First the nonsense about his right to shoot people on his own property, now the audacity of the bastards to try stopping him from reaching the daughter who was almost certainly harbouring the wife who'd had the audacity to escape in...his...prized...Bentley. To the screamed "fuck you" and, to make matters *quite* clear, while still riding with only one hand on the bars and swiveling around on his seat to outstare his pursuers, he therefore added several V-signs.

"Some weirdo," said driver PC Angus O'Connell to PC Jim "The Taser" Tomlinson in the cop car's passenger seat.

"We'll get him. Put your foot down, Ang," said Jim.

So Ang did, thereby narrowly the gap between the suped-up Ford Focus and the wildly swerving Harley to a mere twenty metres.

"Bastards! Swine! Turds!" Sir Monty howled as he began to appreciate the proximity of the coppers, which would surely soon lead to him being pulled over, grilled to within an inch of his life, fined, and possibly even arrested again.

He was still bellowing foul imprecations when the Harley's front wheel hit the fallen branch of a roadside oak and sent him flying across the handlebars into a soggy ditch, his dented crash-hat getting yet further dented and doing little to protect him from the impact.

"Aaaaaaggghhh," he said while still in the air. But once he landed he said nothing.

"Oops," said Jim "The Taser," leaping from the Ford Focus which had narrowly missed crashing into the fallen Harley and slithering down the ditch to investigate.

"Nasty," he called back to Angus. "A white coats job by the looks of it."

A fan of American cop shows, Angus shouted back "ten four," and got on the blower.

Until the ambulance arrived half an hour later, PCs O'Connell and Tomlinson spent their time administering CPR, which worked sufficiently for Sir Monty to open his eyes and tell them to fuck off again.

For one awful moment, Jim toyed with pulling out his Taser but thought better of it. What, after all, was the point of again knocking out a bloke who'd only just regained consciousness? There would be time enough during the hospital interview to remind the old bastard that whatever the case was he presented for his lunatic biker display it was sure to be exacerbated by having told the two officers who'd saved his life to eff off. Grim penalties there were for such behaviour.

Twenty-two

Sergei Figov and Georg Büchner were pleased by Mervyn's positive response to the meet-up, but also wary of his unconditional acceptance of the idea. Especially Figov, whose experiences in the spy trade had taught him the same lessons learnt by Mervyn, namely always to beware gift horses. Had the message come from Taya, it might have been different. The pair shared the same language, for one thing, so there was less of a chance for misinterpretation. Plus, she was an amateur, which Sergei reckoned would have given him a natural advantage. But although she would be attending the proposed meeting, it would be the one-time MI6 guy who would be in charge of it and what kind of a game was he playing? Would he, as he appeared to be suggesting, understand the reasons for which he and Büchner were making the offer of information, and use it the way they intended and hoped? Or would he just take it, say thank you very much, and nonetheless, still hang them out to dry? He couldn't completely have lost touch with his old masters, after all.

Sergei also found it eerily coincidental the proposed venue for the meet-up should be the very same café in Regent's Park at which he'd overheard Vincent's conversation with the Taya woman all those weeks ago. What if the truth of the matter were the hinted whisper of prior knowledge? Yet how *could* the guy have known? What with one thing and another, Sergei was beginning to wonder if some double game were being played here and the contact he'd made with Taya Devine had been wise after all.

"What d'you reckon?" he asked Büchner as the pair sat drinking beers and smoking cigarettes at a picnic bench outside The Lansdowne pub opposite the Gloucester Avenue apartment.

Georg shrugged. "See where you're coming from, pal. A bit late in the day for second thoughts though, eh? They know we're here. They have the email address. I guess there could be ways of finding us if they wanted. Unless we call the whole thing off and get the hell out of here fast."

"Still a possibility."

"But apart from your trap idea, there are three other aspects to this."

Sergei raised his glass. "Good to have you on board, brainbox. So shoot."

"One is *we* made the move, so we see it through whatever the circumstances and take our chances. After all, this was our way of trying to climb off the populist bandwagon and even reverse some of the damage we may have done."

Sergei nodded. "True enough. And two and three?"

"Whatever the Vincent guy might think of us, he will know from Leon we never hurt him. Just helpers along the road he'd chosen, that's all. It's also within the bounds of possibility Vincent *believed* what we said in the message about the many things that had changed in *our* lives, reckoned we weren't enemies, and was open to our story with no strings attached. There must be *some* human beings left on the planet who don't believe everything's a trick."

"And three?"

"Although we didn't specify the offer we're gonna make, Vincent is bound to be curious. You will remember from your time with the old KGB. Sure you might sniff a rat, but what if the info turned out to be useful and you let it slip through your fingers?"

"Also true. So we go for it and let the devil take the hindmost?"

"Would be my advice. And look, Sergei, how hard can it be to persuade the guy and the Devine girl we mean what we say? Flimflam is one thing, but truths are hard to mistake, even by the most suspicious."

"All cards on the table then?"

"*All* of them."

"You're a persuasive guy, Georg."

"One thing I'm still not clear about, though. What exactly *is* the gen we're gonna hand over?" asked Georg.

"In a nutshell?"

"Please."

"The names and addresses, including Schornstein's, of many of the agents currently involved in the planning of the populist domino effect in Europe, *and* who I suspect in Washington and Moscow of masterminding the whole death of liberalism anti- democracy can of worms and why. If our friend Doctor Vincent still has open ears at MI6, I would hope he would be able to pass along such information to somebody who might be able to use it to some purpose. We're not going to change the world with this, Georg, but at least we can feel we've given it our best shot."

"And cleared our own consciences."

"There is also that to it."

"Okay then. So you'll get back to Vincent for a date and time?"

"Just as soon as I get back to the apartment. But before that, how'd you fancy another pint of the local brew? A bit like gnat's piss after your German beer, but..."

Georg grinned. "Better that than a smack in the face with a dead haddock. You stay where you are. This one's on me."

~ * ~

Thinking back on her conversation with Leon at Mervyn's place and her subsequent chat with Connie Horowitz, Lizzie Leah was beginning to experience strange and confused emotions about the man who not so long ago she'd appointed Mervyn to hunt down, and all for the sake of five hundred quid. Okay, she'd also felt humiliated and angry, like all the other Mrs McGuires no doubt, by the experience of being taken for a ride by a serial philanderer, but what was really weird was she now found herself quite liking him. And after all, even back in the bad old days, he'd never knocked her around or anything.

"More sinned against than sinning, I'm starting to think," she told Jürgen who was lying alongside her on the couch of her tiny South Wimbledon lounge.

"Raaf," Jürgen grunted half-heartedly. Woman had been muttering at him for days on this subject and dogs needed their sleep, perchance to dream of one day finally *catching* that elusive squirrel.

"When you think of what he went through at home, it's no wonder he went a bit doolally."

"Rurff."

"Mister Big Balls for a dad, and a loving mother who wasn't allowed to show her love. P'raps he was just a bit more sensitive to those things and more extreme in his answer than most blokes in a similar situation, but that's not a bad thing, is it Jürg? Understandable even."

"Prrrr."

"You *listen*ing, Jürg?"

"Raaf."

"That's better. Anyway, let's just say I'm starting to see him in a different light," Lizzie was ruminating when Jürgen rolled off the couch, stretched, and wandered off for a pee in the patch of garden.

"*Hu*mans!" he muttered, lifting his leg against the honeysuckle that kept failing to grow.

Lizzie sighed, stretched herself into the couch space Jürgen had vacated, and tuned her IPod to Paul Simon's "Slip Slidin' Away" about folk who get close to their destinations then, for one reason or another, miss them. Lizzie reckoned that pretty much summed up her experience of the people in *her* life so far. Which, of course, they found hard to admit either to themselves or anybody else and so continued to promote the idea they'd achieved the most remarkable things even though that was a patent lie. And this, Lizzie reflected as she sang along with Paul about a woman who'd become a wife then regretted it and wondered about how things might have been, seemed to be a feature common to the human condition. Although, she further reflected, she could hardly include Mervyn Vincent in such a category. He seemed more or less oblivious to who he was or what image he projected. He just *was*.

"Mmm," she said to herself, as Paul went on to tell of a man who travelled a long way to tell his son the reasons for the things he'd done but chickened out at the last minute, kissed his sleeping son, and headed home again.

"Reminds me of *my* dad," she told Jürgen, who'd returned from watering the honeysuckle and wanted back his place on the couch. "Nice enough bloke, but got all twitchy if you ever asked him anything about his past. Mind you, he wasn't the only one. Lots of the fellas I hung out with were the same. Reckoned they were super-heroes but never told you how or why. Like Ma said, I have a history of going out with headcases. She could talk though. I never *did* know why she married Dad."

Jürgen yawned. *That* old story again.

"And that's what I thought Leon was, just another lying bastard. But, like I was telling you before you went for a pee, there are at least *reasons* for it. Underneath all the garbage, I reckon there's a bloke who's *not* a total bastard but had just kept it well hidden. Think that's right, Jürg?"

"Raaf," said Jürgen, which could have meant anything but Lizzie took it as confirmation.

"The way he helped me up at the Hand in Hand. The chat we had at Mervyn's when he said he was sorry for what he'd done and wanted to make up for it. Looking me straight in the *eye*, Jürg. I know he's a good actor, but eyeball-to-eyeball lying is a hard trick to pull even if you're Sir Laurence fuckin' Olivier. *Any*way, doggo, you know what?"

Which was greeted by another meaningless "raaf" from Jürgen.

"I'm going to put my new ideas about Mister Leon Devine to the test. An interesting little plan I've got for him. And, if he buys it, I might even love him," she told Jürgen, albeit with no response because Jürgen was already asleep and snoring.

~ * ~

It was Leon who, at his own insistence, opened Mervyn's door to Taya and Svetlana. Mervyn had been all set to do it, but Leon had gently pulled him back.

"No, no, my friend, this is *my* job," he said, which Mervyn took as a good sign. He gladly hung back and watched on as Leon walked through the door into Svetlana's open arms.

Behind them, Taya raised a welcoming palm at Mervyn before herself being tugged into the family hugfest, Leon showing no sign of the resentment he might have felt in the knowledge of what she'd told Mervyn about him. With Taya's agreement, Mervyn had come clean about that and Leon had accepted it with little more than a nod.

"What she did was probably for the best. Sis only ever looked out for me, and I guess that was what she was still doing when she offloaded on you."

"Good of you to see it that way."

"I'm starting to see a number of things in new lights, Mervyn. Thanks mainly to you."

Mervyn had shrugged as normal when complimented, yet he now was witnessing tangible evidence of at least one of those new lights as the Devine family hugfest continued with some tears but no words. Mercifully, from Mervyn's point of view, there was no wailing or gnashing of teeth or anything overly emotional either, nothing of the kind one might have expected from two long estranged and guilt-ridden semi-Russian siblings and their full Russian mother. All in all, the whole thing was rather British.

It was Svetlana who eventually broke the hugfest and, over the heads of her children, treated Mervyn to the same smile she'd given him from the balcony of the Devine mansion back in some other lifetime.

"How kind of you to welcome us all," she told him. "And what a lovely home you have."

"Humble but mine."

"May we step inside?"

Mervyn fully opened the door, bowed slightly, and wafted an inviting palm behind him. "With the greatest of pleasure."

"So, Leonka and Tayara, shall we accept Mister Mervyn's invitation?" asked their mother of the brother and sister still locked in a seemingly unbreakable embrace.

"Raaf, *raaf*," said Suzie, who'd come out to see what all the fuss was about and decided all three visitors needed a good licking. Which, along with reciprocated strokes and pats of the kind Suzie appreciated, was what finally brought everybody together in Mervyn's lounge, on one of whose walls still hung the Picasso *La Joie de Vivre* print Leon had so liked.

Svetlana laughed the moment she saw it. "Our funny, sad, and puny little lives, eh?" she said. "Good old Pablo."

Twenty-three

Still having failed to contact Sergei Figov, still under pressure from the White House, *and* having met with a brick wall when he tried contacting the Kremlin to see if its agents knew what might have become of Sergei Figov, Hal Schornstein opted for the faux mental collapse he hoped would get him off all these hooks for the foreseeable future. Before calling in the shrinks in order to be certified, sectioned, or whatever it was shrinks did with dangerous crazies, however, he practised what he tried to imagine would be the sorts of symptoms that would ensure he was whisked away from his Fifth Avenue NYC apartment ASAP and placed in a secure facility well away from any more hassle.

There was a problem with these rehearsal sessions before the floor-to-ceiling mirror in his dressing room though, which was that never having met a full-blown and obviously certifiable crazy and not being a very imaginative person Hal was uncertain quite what the most recognizable and foolproof madness symptoms *were*. He tried girning and jabbering gobbledygook while slouching and pulling at his hair. He tried going cross-eyed, standing on one leg and howling lupinely while chewing on a banana—like he *was* bananas. He even tried lying flat on his back dressed only in his stars-and-stripes boxers while juggling three plastic goldfish. All of which seemed okay but *still* left something to be desired, a certain *je ne sais quoi*, which by its very nature escaped definition.

In search of the expert sure-fire knowledge he sought, Hal Googled the American Psychiatric Association but, after only a couple of dense pages of one of its most recent reports, came to the conclusion that shrinks were themselves nut jobs who argued with each other about affective treatments for even such commonplace maladies as arachnophobia, which Hal had to look up in a dictionary anyway. Freudians and Kleinians there were...Jungians, Lacanians, Lßaingians, so many -ians they were driving him crazy. Hal grimaced at the irony.

"Hi there, Mister Shrink," he imagined himself saying, "I've been driven crazy by reading about you."

"Harrrumph," he added, the problem still not solved.

When the harrumphing was over, however, it struck Hal that some of the worst crazies, the ones who had committed the most terrible crimes, didn't even *look* like crazies, indeed looked saner than the average shrink featured in the APA. John Wayne Gacy, Ted Bundy, Mark Chapman, the guy who'd shot John Lennon, Lee Harvey Oswald...the list went on. Regular guys just like the kids going on mass murder sprees in schools all over the States right now, which was how they were able to do their killing without anybody suspecting anything beforehand.

"Mmm," he mused.

As a result of this musing, Hal decided on what he considered a slam-dunk win-win strategy to ensure he was kept off the political map and out of harm's way in some nice cosy jail, namely to call the cops, tell *them* he was disturbed by murderous phantasies, and hand himself in. That way, he could stay looking and speaking normally like the arch villains but, nonetheless, outline a crime so heinous the cops would have no choice but to take him out of circulation. Helluva plan, Hal reckoned. Every chance the cops would even be grateful to him for saving them precious resources by preempting the need for solving a crime that hadn't even been committed yet.

"Hi, there," he said in a gloomy voice to desk sergeant Tom Bosch at NYPD. "Something you gotta know, buster."

"Yeah? And your name is, sir?" replied Bosch, who was only minutes away from his lunch break.

"Hal. Hal Schornstein. See, I had this vision last night where I was killing the president and eating him."

Bosch yawned. "And your address, Hal?"

Schornstein liked this. It was going good. He gave Tom the address, plus two cell phone numbers.

"Killing the president, huh?" said Bosch.

"Yup stone dead with an AK47, *and* eating him. Next time he's in town. I just don't think I'm gonna be able to help myself. It's driving me crazy. I see his fat face everyplace I go and I...I...I'm gonna wipe that stinking grin off of it forever and eat his fingers deep fried on toast. You need to get me sectioned somewhere safe or else..."

"Hal, *Hal*, take it easy, huh? Calm down."

"Calm down. Calm *down*?"

"Hal, sorry to disappoint you, pal, but you're the fifth caller this morning wanting to kill the president. Most days there are at least a dozen, all of 'em hoaxes, we figure. Same story every time."

"All of them wanting to *eat* him?" said Hal, ramping up *his* crime in the hope of special attention.

"Some of 'em. Why you guys call to tell me, I don't know. You think we have the manpower to check 'em all out? Anyhow, just so you know, I'm right with all of you wannabe killers. The guy is an asshole and deserves what he gets. Good luck," said Bosch, hanging up and checking out of the office for the burger and fries he'd been longing for the whole of his shift.

"Oh...for...*FUCK*," screamed Schornstein, hurling the phone at a wall, yanking at his hair and gibbering gobbledygook just like in one of his practice crazy scenarios.

When the White House called on the other phone only minutes later demanding an immediate update on the Devine situation or else he could expect the worst, Hal threw that at a wall too, burst into tears, crawled into his bed with a pack of anxiolytics, and turned out the light. Now he finally knew what crazy meant.

~ * ~

Leaving Leon, Taya, and Svetlana in the lounge to work through their family issues, Mervyn repaired to his little study upstairs to fiddle with his computer, catch up with the latest developments on the wannabe alpha male oligarch in 10 Downing Street, and check his emails. To his horror, as he scrolled through the news, the PM, doubtless abetted by his Rasputin-esque adviser, had yet again disregarded legal approbation and prorogued parliament for the foreseeable future in order further to build his power base. *The Guardian's* editorial opined his ultimate objective, like his heroes Winston Churchill in 1945 or Oliver Cromwell in 1653, was to rid himself of parliament altogether so he could get his own way unhindered by "pointless twaddle."

"Bastard!" Mervyn whispered for fear of disturbing the Devines who, to judge from the lack of weeping or shouting downstairs, he could only conclude to be reaching agreements at least...at best, harmony.

"Like some godforsaken feudal monarch. Like an autocratic bloody dic*tat*or," he hissed. "So there's democracy as we knew it down the toilet. Poisoned from within. And in Britain of all places," he added, biting his lip as he thought back to the Munich speeches, the populism now rampant in the US and Europe, the numbers of effectively disenfranchised electors like him who could only stand by and watch on helplessly as the liberal governance they had taken for granted for so long was wiped away at the flick of a finger by an out of control executive branch. And all in the name of what? White male sovereignty, nationalism, chauvinism, hubris, xenophobia, racism, sexism, narcissism...the list went on.

"C'*mon* nemesis, do your worst. And do it now," he spluttered.

Mervyn ruminated on these matters for a further ten minutes or so, then as usual when faced with the sickening maelstrom of current domestic and international politics, switched off. It was his only way staying sane. R.D. Laing's idea about insanity being a perfectly rational adjustment to an insane world was all very well and might even have explained some of Leon's problems, but it wasn't for Mervyn Iain Vincent, thank you very much. Any more than was "If you can't beat 'em, join 'em."

For focus he turned to his emails. The two in Sent were the ones he'd had written to Sergei Figov and Margery Middleton setting a date for the meet-up. The third, in the Inbox, was an interesting idea from Lizzie Leah that had just pinged in. It was as he was still smiling at Lizzie's proposal should Leon's situation continue to improve that Taya tapped on the open door.

"May I?" she said.

A puce-faced Mervyn closed down the computer. "Of course, my dear. Do take a seat while I switch this off."

"You all right? You look a bit..."

"Sorry, my dear. Just read the bally news, that's all. It can have that effect on a person. *Now*, back to planet Earth. How are things going downstairs? No wish to pry, of course, but I am obviously curious."

Taya took a chair on the other side of Mervyn's desk and gave him the thumbs up. "They're going well, you could almost say miraculously. Leon's smiling and seems relaxed. And I would know if he were just playacting. In such a short time, I don't believe any number of psychiatrists could have achieved what you and now Mama have."

"And *you* too, Taya. You must have played a part."

Taya blushed and nodded. "I suppose."

"And to what do you attribute this progress?"

Taya took her time and thought. "In a nutshell?"

"Please. I'm not great with periphrasis."

"Empathy is, I believe, the fashionable word but I would prefer rapport, or fellow feeling, the sense that people are on your side. When Leon was young, Father was forever hectoring him for not doing or being what he was expected to be. And whenever he tried to satisfy the expectation, the goalposts would move until he no longer knew *what* he was supposed to do or be. Which, I guess, is why he finally escaped into his own invention."

"And you and Svetlana have...?"

"Told him we were always on his side and apologized for being either too feeble or too blind to give him the help he needed when it was *most* needed."

"And all this in the short time I've been up here fiddling with my computer?"

"We cried together for a bit, but essentially yes. Mind you, without the groundwork you put in, I doubt it would have been as straightforward. He was already *ready* to talk. And to listen."

"Well, young lady, all I can say is I'm glad. And well done you. Might now be an appropriate moment for me to join the party?"

Taya rose from her chair and went round to Mervyn, whom she hugged and then kissed.

"Now would be a great time. We were rather hoping for a little celebratory visit to that pub of yours. What was it called again? The Hand in…"

"Hand. And all the food and drinks are on me. Not so, Suzie?" Mervyn asked the little London Terrier who'd been sitting at his feet while the humans got on with their arcane business.

"Raaf, *raaf*," said Suzie, tail wagging while she shook herself in readiness for walkies.

Twenty-four

Once he'd been checked over by the paramedics, Sir Montmorency Devine was handed back to PCs Jim Tomlinson and Angus "The Taser" O'Connell to do whatever they wanted with him.

"Doesn't he need to go to hospital?" Angus asked lead paramedic Doctor Julie Tulip.

"Nah, no good overloading the poor old A and E, they're on their knees already. And the old bugger's all right as far as we can tell. No broken bones, cardiac function back to normal, bit of a lump on his bonce but no cerebral damage. He'll have a headache for a week or two, but that's about the size of it. If he *does* develop any funny symptoms *then* you can parcel him off to hospital. Meanwhile he's all yours... have a nice day. Oops," she said whipping the flashing pager from her belt, "there's another call, some dead or dying bloke hanging from a tree. Gotta love you and leave you, guys."

And with that off she and her team sped in their emergency ambulance, blue lights flashing and wah-wah-wahs at top volume.

"Right then, chum," PC Jim told Sir Monty who was still lying in the ditch, "looks like you're fit as a flea, so up you get."

Sir Monty really *shouldn't* have told Tomlinson to fuck off *again*, let alone clamber to his feet and try to headbutt him, but that's what he did and why he came to be faced with one of the grim punishments available to policepersons for such behaviour, namely being tasered by PC Angus O'Connell before being dumped inert into the back seat of the suped-up Ford Focus and driven off to Paddington Green police station in handcuffs.

Tottering and still whoozy but in no better temper when they arrived, Sir Monty wanted to know where his beloved Harley was.

"Stolen it, you bastards, have you?" he growled at Tomlinson and O'Connell from the back seat as they pulled up outside the cop shop. "Going to sell it on the sly?"

"It's still in the ditch back on the road. One of our trucks will pick it up and bring it here," said Jim Tomlinson as politely as he was able through gritted teeth, which wasn't very politely at all.

"Cretin, moron. I'll have you know I'm a peer of the realm," spat Sir Monty, whose cerebral cortex appeared as undamaged as Julie Tulip had diagnosed even *after* being tasered. "And I'll have your balls for breakfast, you'll see if I don't. I'm a man of influence in these parts."

Which, sadly for Sir Monty, wasn't *quite* accurate, seeing as he was no longer in the parts where he had influence, namely Henley-o-Thames. He was in West London where folk didn't know him from a hole in the road. Perhaps the slightest of glitches in the mental functions after all, therefore. He was still blethering insults and accusations as he was read what little there was left of his rights and led away to a holding cell before further questioning in the morning.

"Swine, perverts, just wait till my pal in Downing Street hears about this," he was still ululating as the steel door hissed shut on him.

"The Nazi in Downing Street, eh?" said Tomlinson to O'Connell, neither of whom had much time for the new prime minister. Not since they had read about many of their colleagues having been drafted in to protect peaceable democracy protesters in Trafalgar Square only to be spat on by the newly liberated hordes of far-right hooligans glorying in the further proroguing of parliament and the novel freedom of insult to which they felt that entitled them. To the Cable Streets riots of 1936 some journalists were comparing the event.

"Chaos monger he is, you ask me." Angus agreed. "Bleedin' Eton toff talking through his arse about the people against the politicians. Settin up a phony civil war for his good and his good only."

Unusually for a policeman, PC Angus "The Taser" O'Connell was also something of a political philosopher.

"And a fat lot of good it's going to do our boy Devine being a pal of his if I've got anything to do with it" said Jim Tomlinson.

"Bet on it, mate."

~ * ~

In order to allow a little more time for Leon's reunion with Svetlana and Taya to cement and, he hoped, flourish, the date Mervyn had set for the meet-up with Sergei Figov and Georg Büchner in Regent's Park was a week after the happy occasion at his house and then The Hand in Hand. After all, Taya would need to be present and at her sharpest. Plus, he would himself need to get his head straight over the kind of script he would wish to follow, and, of course, Margery Middleton would need time to brief her boys and girls and requisition equipment for the task. If this were a set-up and there were any unforeseen trouble, Mervyn would need professional backup, no question about that. And then, of course, there was Leon's reaction to take into account. Mervyn had no idea what *he* would think of such a meeting, although he had every right to be informed of it.

So a week had been decided upon as a sensible interval during which, to his great pleasure, the Devine trio became pretty much inseparable. Never did they gather at Taya's flat in case a furious Sir Montmorency were to turn up demanding both his wife and his car back. Not that he was in any position to do so, given his ongoing problems with the police, but nobody knew about those. And even if he had remained a free peer of the realm, he would have regained neither of his prized possessions because Svetlana was resolute in her defiance, and as planned the Bentley Continental with the keys in the ignition had been stolen within hours of Mervyn having left it in the middle of a Wimbledon Common car park.

Nonetheless, the Devines were taking no chances. Instead, they stayed at Mervyn's tiny house and roamed the Common on a daily basis, regularly visiting the Hand in Hand where they'd made friends with landlord Sean O'Casey, and together venturing even further afield to Central London where they took in the tourist sights and happily joined in a "Fuck-off-back-to-Eton" screaming band of protesters at the gates of Downing Street where the prime minister was mumbling incoherently into a microphone at a bunch of media folk about the glories of Brexit and "the will of the people."

Buoyed by Leon's enthusiastic participation in this event, Mervyn reckoned the day after would be an apposite moment to fill him in on the details of the upcoming meet-up with Figov and Büchner; its background, purpose and so on, and was pleased with the outcome. Yes, as they sat in Mervyn's little study, Leon was astonished at the information but not once did he lose the new cool Mervyn took to be the hopefully re-emerging posture of the MI6 agent, the man had once been.

"Pretty weird," Leon said, scratching his head. "You're sure there's no catch?"

Which was when Mervyn admitted to the concerns he'd shared with Margery Middleton and outlined the strategy she'd proposed to ensure there were no unforeseen hiccups.

Leon laughed. "Like it," he said. "Spooks in the foreground and spooks in the background. Nice one. Just like the old days. And it's you and Sis who'll be going along."

"That's right. At noon the day after tomorrow in Regent's Park."

Leon left off scratching his head and rubbed at his two-day growth of bristle instead. "Don't suppose you'd like me to come along, too? Although I'd quite understand if you wouldn't," he said raising a palm. "On the other hand, it's *my* arsehole-ish behaviour that brought us to this pass."

Mervyn shrugged and nodded.

"So maybe I should help in clearing up some of the mess I left behind."

"You think you're up to it? This isn't some stage play we're looking at here, Leon. It's the real McCoy, so no theatricals."

Leon smiled. "How well you've come to know me."

"Sometimes I wonder if I know more about you than I know about myself."

"A textbook handler in The Circus's terms."

"You could put it that way."

"Well, I guess you'd just have to trust me on the thespian front. You reckon you could?"

Mervyn reached across the desk, took Leon's tentatively outstretched hand and shook it. "Actually yes, I think I could."

"Thanks for the faith."

"You're welcome. Just be yourself, your *real* self."

"That's a big ask, Mervyn. There are so many others to choose from."

"So pick the one *you* now most trust."

"I will. And you'll let Taya know I'll be joining the party?"

"No my friend, you will," said Mervyn, picking up his phone and tapping the Favourites option before handing over to Leon. "Meanwhile, I'll just pop downstairs and make us a cup of tea."

Twenty-five

After the unpredictable summer of one brief spell of blasting heat preceded and followed by cloud, rain, wind and general turbulence, the late September day of the Regent's Park meeting turned out sunny under an unbroken blue sky and with a temperature in the pleasant mid-twenties.

"It augurs well," Mervyn told Taya and Leon as they chugged north from Wimbledon in the ancient Morris Minor Traveller, Svetlana having been left at home in Mervyn's house to ensure Sir Montmorency couldn't find her, and to look after Suzie who'd never spent a day home alone in her life.

"Indeed it does," said Leon, sitting in the back seat with his sister. "Let's hope it ends that way too."

"Never lose faith in serendipity," said Mervyn, oblivious to the honking and hooting behind as he coaxed the old car from first to second gear with a double de-clutch after being stopped at the Warren Street traffic lights in Tottenham Court Road.

Taya laughed. "You're a hopeful man, Doctor Vincent."

"I try, my dear. Niggling little doubts there will always be, but without hope we are nothing."

"Doubts?" said Leon.

"Well, you know, whether the MI6 chaps and chapesses will be in place in case of any slip-ups, for example."

But Mervyn needed not have worried about that. Margery Middleton hadn't risen to her current position in The Circus had her CV contained evidence of slip-ups. Well prior to the high noon meet-up at Regent's Park, her agents were already in place at the Broad Walk Café, which they had bugged both inside and out. Two of them, Tullio and Anita (not their real names) were stationed at the counter as faux baristas, while several more—Harry, Norman, Norma, Angelica, Mildred, Barry, Ronaldo, Fritz, and Antoinette (also not their real names)—were distributed amidst regular customers in the outside area under the ancient trees disguised as passing cyclists in want of a caffeine hit, dog walkers, foreign tourists, or old folk passing the time of day over coffee, a blueberry muffin, and—being old-—a cigarette. To the uninitiated, the place appeared as regular as on any other day, which was just the way MM had planned it. Astonished *any*body would have been at the suggestion all of these "normal people" were expert shooters armed with their favoured weapons, or equally expert VDAs (Voice Detection Analysts) carrying in their trousers or skirts gizmos capable of listening in to any conversation within hundreds of yards.

No, no, Mervyn needn't have worried about any of that as his Morris Minor Traveller ground to a halt in Chester Road at the periphery of Regent's Park and Leon was invited to step out to satisfy the parking meter Mervyn couldn't understand because it no longer took money, only credit cards.

"Would you be so kind, old chap?" he asked Leon. "I've no bloody idea how these things work."

Despite this minor delay, however, Mervyn, Taya, and Leon were bang on time when they finally strolled up to the café and approached the seats in the covered area MM had designated for them. Sergei and Georg, unaware of any surveillance, were already sipping their coffees at the adjacent table, the very one from which Sergei had overheard Mervyn's and Taya's conversation all those weeks earlier.

Leon was first to spot them. "Shall I do the honours?" he said.

"Please," said Mervyn as, at picnic trestles in the outdoor area, the faux old folk, tourists, dog walkers, and cyclists immersed themselves in earnest, loud conversations punctuated by much gesticulation and laughter. What a jolly time they were all having as they covertly focused their various spy instruments in the direction of the two tables of interest.

And so it was that Leon Devine walked over to Sergei and Georg and, speaking his impeccable German, bade them welcome, then as they rose to their feet pumped their hands in the German custom. After that came the formal introductions to Mervyn and Taya, who also shook hands as Leon took to organizing five iron chairs around one of the tables.

"Shall we sit?" he said, at which everyone took their places and smiled awkwardly.

The first issue to be resolved was the matter of a lingua franca. Sergei, Georg, Leon and, at a push, Mervyn and Taya would have been happy enough to continue with German. But, as Mervyn quickly recognized, that might have caused translation problems for the MI6 team of old folk, tourists, cyclists and dog walkers with their recording equipment who might not have been so linguistically blessed. It was for this reason, despite his inbred dislike of such post-colonialism, that he was obliged to propose English.

"When in Rome and so on," he said.

Sergei was happy enough with that although, as he pointed out, it left Georg at something of a disadvantage. But Leon stepped into that breach by promising to interpret every word for him.

The next five or ten minutes were occupied by the three newcomers selecting their coffees of choice—flat whites, espressos, americanos, cappuccinos or whatever—Sergei and Georg being offered top-ups, and Mervyn going off to collect the orders from inside the café, which also gave him the opportunity to give baristas Tullio and Anita the heads-up with a secret password to verify the arrival of him, his friends, and their guests.

Once everyone was sipping and two or three were smoking—which caused some tutting and fingers under noses from the cyclists—the meeting proper started. Not promptly because there was no official agenda, meaning the opening exchanges were little more than uncomfortable sidelong glances. It was Mervyn who took again the initiative. He was, after all, the senior member of the group, *and* the one with the widest purview of the issues they were here to discuss.

"Friends," he kicked off with. "I am pleased we are able to come together in this way, but let me make no bones about the purpose of our meeting. Taya, Leon and I are here because of our shared belief in the potentially disastrous international consequences of the pernicious movement called Populism. Equally, we harbour a desire to make some, however small, contribution to its ultimate downfall in the UK, elsewhere in Europe and indeed, in the US. Russia, I suspect, we can do nothing to reform. Can I be assured this is also the case where Messrs Figov and Büchner are concerned?"

Leon muttered a quick translation for Georg's benefit and then both he and Sergei nodded affirmation.

"Jolly good, thank you. Equally I hope we are all minded to believe such an ideology has not sprung willy-nilly from nowhere, but is instead being orchestrated by malign powers in the White House and the Kremlin wishing the disintegration of decades of European collaboration for their own despotic purposes."

Words of assent around the table, including from Georg into whose ear Leon continued to whisper.

"I shall take that as unanimous agreement then," said Mervyn, raising his double-shot americano cup in the direction of the MI6 support team, which was the secret signal to the agents with LDLDs (Long Distance Lie Detectors) to alert him should they be receiving any negative or otherwise aberrant feedback from Sergei, Georg, and especially Leon.

And back came the secretly coded reply from a faux cyclist called Barry, who removed the tyre inflator from beneath his bike's crossbar and, as if demonstrating to colleagues its novel efficacy, stood up, pumped it three times in the air and shouted, "Blows my mind, it's so good."

Mervyn smiled. "For which I am most grateful," he continued once Barry's mind had stopped being blown, and he had sat down again with his pals. "As yet, although I am in contact with my old colleagues at The Circus, we on this side have no firm plan of action to offer, just a few loose ideas. But," he added turning to Sergei, "I gather from your email, Mister Figov, that you are in possession of information you think may be of help in this project."

Sergei nodded and asked if Mervyn had on his person a smartphone or any other computer device capable of receiving such info, which he intended to transmit only by super-encrypted email, the private key to which he would present on a green Rizla cigarette paper for swift commitment to memory before employing the paper for its intended purpose, namely smoking.

"Well, um, actually no..." said Mervyn, yet again experiencing the now familiar sinking feeling of belonging to some other century. "But," he added turning to Taya, "I know a woman who does. Don't you, my dear?"

Taya had thus far taken no part in the proceedings and was glad to be involved. "Indeed I do, Doctor Vincent, although I shall rely on your memory for the private key data. Mine is a sieve. Would that be okay with you, Mister Figov?"

"No problem. Any sister of Leon's I would be glad to trust."

Leon took Taya's hand and squeezed.

"Okay, then," said Mervyn, again raising his cup and sipping, this time in the direction of the faux dog walker responsible for hyper-recording the significant operation about to follow.

And back came her instant coded reply, which was loudly to praise her Labrador Basil for sitting on his bottom and politely begging for a sliver of turkey from her New Yorker panini.

"Good boy, *very* good boy," Antoinette whooped. Not that Basil gave much of a monkey's. The turkey sliver was already history, and he fancied another.

"But before we do, may I be privy to a least an *idea* of what it might contain?" Mervyn continued, once satisfied Antoinette was up to speed.

"A list of the names and contact addresses of those in the United States, Russia and elsewhere most closely involved with what you rightly termed 'despotic purposes,'" said Sergei. "There is little Georg or I can do with such intelligence. We are only small fry in the game, facilitators, you might say. But in the right hands…"

Mervyn nodded. "This is indeed a noble move and much appreciated. I shall, of course, do my utmost to see it reaches the hands you speak of. Now then, Taya, are we set to go?"

"Whenever you're ready, Mister Figov."

And so it was that some of the most sensitive data on Project Populism was transferred from Sergei's smartphone to Taya's while Mervyn's eidetic memory photographed the mixture of hieroglyphs and numbers of the green Rizla paper before Sergei used it for its intended purpose.

Thereafter, the meeting continued for a further hour fuelled largely by Leon with a frankness and humility he until recently wouldn't have believed himself capable. After all, this was the first time, even in conversation with Mervyn or Taya, he had openly disavowed his old political allegiances. As he spoke, both were relieved at the faith they'd put in him such that he was now able to.

"I was a fool playing some awful game," he admitted to Sergei and Georg in German. After all, this part of the meeting was for their ears only.

Georg slung an arm around Leon's shoulders. "Welcome to the club, brother, Sergei and I have spoken over the subject many times and now we are I think finally clear. Not so, Sergei?"

"As day. Hence today's occasion, which I hope will help us all to a new future, personally at least. God knows, the world around us may not change but *we* can."

"A strange alliance, but one for which I am so grateful. We must not lose touch, the three of us," said Leon.

"Like the three musketeers," Georg agreed, taking Sergei into the embrace with his free arm while, with spontaneity previously unknown to him, Leon joined in the hugfest with both new friends.

"Bagsy, me be Aramis," he said, at which Mervyn and Taya smiled and clapped.

"This is *some* new brother," Taya whispered in Mervyn's ear.

"Great to see," said Mervyn, who then stood and proposed a stroll in the park for all five of them. "Maybe a turn around Queen Mary's Gardens to see the late blossoming roses?" he suggested. "Good for the soul they are."

"With great pleasure," said Leon, breaking the huddle, rising from his chair, taking Taya's hand, and heading out into the sunshine followed by Sergei and Georg. "Lead on, Doctor Vincent, and we shall follow."

The only folk disappointed at this peaceful conclusion to the top-level, potentially fractious international meeting they'd been sent to supervise were Tullio, Anita, Harry, Norman, Norma, Angelica, Mildred, Barry, Ronaldo, Fritz, and Antoinette, all of whom had been hoping for something akin to the Gunfight at the O.K. Corral.

"A bit fucking bathetic," muttered Tullio to Antoinette, for example.

Barry agreed. "Might at least have had a punch-up or two."

"On the upside though, we got some top notch insider info," said Fritz, who had been the one responsible for sucking Sergei's hot list into his computer at the very moment it was being emailed to Taya's phone.

"Pity about the private key roll-up the Rusky smoked though," said Norma.

"Not to worry," said Norman. "It's on my hyper-zoom camera. Anyway, I'm sure Doc Vincent'll remember it for us, just in case. Mister Memory Man they used to call him in the Service."

Twenty-six

Connie Horowitz phoned Lizzie Leah before making the promised phone call to Leon.

"You figure around now would be a good time, hon?" she asked.

"Sure. He was on a real high the last time I saw him. Some big international spy deal he'd helped with. No more Mister Nazi for him, all that type of thing. Plus, he's squared stuff with his mum. Hadn't seen her for yonks but now they're best friends again, likewise him and his sister. No, now would be a great time to call. D'you still have his number?"

"Unless he's changed phones. Gimme the number you have and we'll check."

Lizzie did as asked and nothing had changed.

"You still don't reckon to make it over here for a face to face, though?" she said.

"Honey, I have asked myself that question over and over."

"And?"

"You're gonna think me crazy."

"Try me."

"Well, like, it's just I can't leave my life. Maybe it's middle age creeping up on me, menopause and all that."

"Already?"

"Not yet but I'm getting there, babe. Forty-three is...no...spring... chicken."

Lizzie laughed. "Snap! Same age as me. Leon must've had a taste for the oldies."

"The young-uns wouldn't be so dumb. *Any*how, like I was saying, I'm getting kinda set in my ways. The idea of getting on a big silver bird and flying all the way to Britland freaks me. Airports, hassle, twelve hours in the skies, and all to be in some foreign country. You ever been to the States?"

"Never."

"You wanna go?"

Lizzie had to admit she didn't and for similar reasons. Munich had been her only foreign trip in ten years, and she'd only taken it because she'd felt it her duty—and because Jürgen could come too.

"So I guess I'm preaching to the converted here."

"The girl you're preaching to is the preacher."

Connie chuckled. "So there's all that. *And*, like I said, there's my life here. I can't just up and leave my animals and my trees; *they're* my life too, and I don't want no dork messing with them while I'm gone."

Lizzie nodded. "I can understand that. I can understand all of it."

"You're a sweetheart, you know that?"

"It's not what everybody says."

"Well *I'm* saying it. Hey, and by the way, wadda you do when you ain't getting screwed over by gigolos?"

"I drive a bus."

"Wow! That...is...so...*neat*. A *bus*, huh?"

"Same route there and back every day."

"And you love it."

"And I love it. My dog Jürgen comes with me. The passengers love him."

"So we have animals in common. One day, *some*how, we have to meet."

"We will. Who knows where, and who knows when, but we will. *Any*how, that phone call to Leon?"

"Right, ookay, babe. We hang up and I'm gonna punch in his number. You take care now."

"Oh, hey, wait just one more minute before I forget."

"Forget what?"

Which was when Lizzie told Connie of the little plan she had thought up for Leon, and Connie fell about laughing before saying, "You...have...*got*...to...be...kidding me. Have you told him yet?"

"No, I thought I'd try it out on you first, and you're laughing now but let me know what you reckon after you've talked with him. Only *don't*, do *not*, say anything about it on the phone, okay?"

"No way José. Babe, whenever we talk I gotta keep my mouth shut about *some*thing. Last time it was the Mrs McGuires Society, now it's your little plan."

"Sorry about that, no really."

"It's okay, only joshing with you. You're right there on the front line, so you know what's going down. Only when you tell me will I tell anyone else. Now, hey, I'm gonna love you and leave you. Bye, bye, and kisses!"

Lizzie smiled. Some day maybe she would screw up the courage to fly out to California for a day or two. Just so long as Mervyn and Suzie would agree to look after Jürgen, which she was sure they would.

~ * ~

Hal Schornstein found himself in much the same intractable position as Yossarian in *Catch 22*. Just as Yossarian tried to escape flying more missions on the grounds of them driving him crazy only to be told craziness was the prerequisite for flying missions, Schornstein found madness to be no way out of *his* currently thorny situation. And Hal was no longer talking faux madness of the kind that had failed to impress the cops. What he *was* talking was full-on batshit. Like when in his life ever before had he muttered to himself in the mirror while shaving in the morning, or wept because he'd put the left shoe on the right foot and *still* tried to make it fit, or put his pants on back to front, or jumped up and down on his precious smartphone with all the key White House and Kremlin numbers? Or called his penis Pete? The list went on. No, no, in Hal Schornstein's view, he'd gone more bananas than even a regular banana.

And that was be*fore* he got into the nightmares. When he was still sane, Hal had dreamt a lot, but that was fine because in those dreams he always featured as the football hero making the winning touchdown in the last minute of a Super Bowl final, or he was Pat Garrett confronting Billy the Kid, or he was Neil Armstrong stepping out onto the moon, any fucking famous American lauded and applauded *that* was Hal Schornstein. But no longer, no siree. These nights he woke up bathed in sweat from *inter alia* having lost both legs to a marauding panther who'd broken into his Fifth Avenue apartment toting an AK47, hanging from Mars by a spider's thread spun around Pete the penis, and receiving the kiss of death from a trans ambulance driver called Basil(la) who'd run him down on purpose in order to practice giving the kiss of death to people s/he hated. That list went on, its common feature being Hal suffering humiliation, pain, and either real or forthcoming extermination—in other words failure.

But Hal met with no more sympathy than Yossarian did from Doc Daneeka when he took this growing catalogue of aberrant symptoms to a shrink called Doctor Heiner Schreiner and begged to be given the sick note that would keep him off work forever, or better still an introduction to some asylum in the Nevada desert where he could register under an alias.

Schreiner just listened stony-faced for the twenty minutes Hal blethered, then shrugged non-committally, diagnosed work stress even though Hal didn't dare tell him what his job *was* only that it was high-powered, prescribed a cocktail of Lexapro, Prozac and Propranolol to be taken in handfuls whenever Hal felt like it, told him to come back in six weeks and billed him a thousand dollars for the first consultation.

"But I'm fucking *crazy*," Hal protested. "How can I work when I'm fucking crazy?"

Schreiner shrugged again. "That's New York City for you. I signed off each and every guy who walks into my office saying he's gone nuts, there'd be nobody left to run the damn place. Most of 'em are only fooling anyhow. Looking for fat pay-off check and a nice vacation in Florida. Know what I saying?"

"No."

"Well, you'd better wise up, bro. We shrinks ain't so dumb. My advice? Remember the old saying: You don't *have* to be crazy to work here, but it helps."

That's when Hal stormed out of the office refusing to pay the thousand dollars and headed downstairs to the street, only to be met at the door by a receptionist gorilla called Seamus McCann who lifted him by his jacket lapels, slammed him against a wall, and shook him till his wallet squeaked.

"You wanna leave this building in one piece, bozo, you pay up Doc Schreiner's grand right now," said Seamus.

Hal paid up swearing never again to get involved with the shrink industry. He did use his Lexapro, Prozac and Propranolol prescription at a nearby pharmacist though, cramming two each of the little pills into his mouth as he left and hailing a cab to take him home. Of the unpaid cabbie Andreas Tolansky having the good heart to give Hal a fireman's lift out of the car across the street and into his building where he was turned over to the concierge who dragged him into the elevator and put him to bed in his apartment, Hal was to have no memory. He was to have no memory of the following seventy-two hours either.

What did for Hal Schornstein when he finally awoke, however, and caused him to leap from his bedroom window wasn't the repeated dose of Lexapro, Prozac and Propranolol swallowed with generous swigs from a bottle of Southern Comfort. That just had a happy numbing effect Hal quite liked as he stumbled to his computer. What freaked him was the "priority delivery" email from some Secret Service outfit in London that pinged into his in-box the moment he booted up.

"Dear Mr Schornstein," it read. "We have reason to believe you are intimately connected, with the approval of the White House and the Kremlin, to a plan designed through populist uprisings to destroy the democratically elected governments of Europe and would be obliged, at your earliest opportunity, to contact this office. Confidentiality guaranteed."

Not normal MI6 parlance of course, but Margery Middleton had broken protocol to rattle a few cages after Sergei Figov handed over the Schornstein name along with so many others. How could she have known it would lead to a crazy and practically comatose Hal leaping through his window to certain death all the way down on Fifth Avenue?

Not, as it happened, that Hal succeeded at even this goodbye-cruel-world bid for freedom. Nobody had told him, or he had been too doped or insane to notice, that the whole of his building had for two weeks been engulfed in scaffolding and walkways to enable a long overdue paint job. Surprised therefore was painter and decorator Magnus Adamik when suddenly from the window above him appeared a wildly arm-flapping man heading straight in his direction.

"Oh, for *fuck*," said Magnus, dodging out of Hal's flight path but leaning backwards against the railing in the hope of preventing any further fall. Which, magically, he succeeded in achieving with the result that Hal's descent resulted in nothing more serious than landing with a mega-splat in a thirty-litre trough of white paint.

On the equally fortuitous upside of this unexpected salvation, once he'd been hosed down, identified, and interrogated by police and medics, it was surmised that Hal was indeed several sandwiches short of a picnic and thus required long-term psychiatric investigation to prevent any further attempts at self-destruction, which was why, to his delight, he was whisked away to a special facility on Long Island.

Twenty-seven

None of the other agents provocateurs around the world to whom Margery Middleton sent the same message suffered anything like the same fate as Hal Schornstein, but with the British Secret Service on their trail, many were beginning to wonder about the wisdom of their current populist profiles, and a significant number quit their posts and disappeared to places like Ulaanbaatar.

Pleased at these fledgling signs of a fight-back, Margery decided to widen the scope of her activities and to this end summoned her trusted computer guru Arty Arthuro to her office.

"What say, Arty," she said after bringing him up to date on the apparent success of her previous tactic, "we up the ante a little here?"

"By, ma'am?"

"You know, using botties."

Arty smiled. "I think you mean bots, ma'am."

"Paff. Botties, bots, what's the difference?" said Margery, waving a dismissive hand.

Being of a pedantic nature, Arty explained "botties" to be the plural of the human bottom when childishly abbreviated to botty, while bots were robotic Internet devices able to repeat the same message ad infinitum if stimulated by a prescribed algorithm.

Margery giggled. "Well I s'pose it's the latter I mean. And less of the 'ma'am,' Arty."

"As you wish. And yes, it must be the latter meaning you're suggesting. Those bally things the Ruskies used to get the oik in the White House elected. And not only *that* oik, ma'am."

"No more *ma'ams*, Arty. You're sounding like a robot yourself."

"Apologies."

"Accepted. *So* if the Ruskies can do it, so can we. Am I right?"

"Spot on."

"And you reckon you and your chaps and chapesses could rustle up a few? We have the techie knowhow, don't we?"

"Indeed we do. And may I ask what you have in mind for content? We'll need something zippy, memorable, and with words of no more than one syllable. Anything too hard and our target audience will just switch off."

"And it would be?"

"The average Joe and Jane in the streets of Europe and the US. A message, or indeed mess*ages*, similar to the asininities that swung the twenty-sixteen referendum for the Brexiteers in the UK, something full of sound and fury."

"Signifying nothing?" said Arty, who'd read his Shakespeare.

"Very possibly, on face value at least. But, if repeated frequently enough to penetrate even the slowest of minds, sufficient to galvanize action by inspiring fear and misery."

"As in the Third Reich," said Arty who'd also read his Brecht.

Margery sighed. "Sadly, it is precisely to those depths of depravity one must sink, given the enemy we are up against. Any ideas for the zippy and memorable?"

"Which would be needed in translation too. For the Europeans."

"Of course. Plus a picture, if that's possible"

"No problemo. Of?"

"Your shout, Arty, you're the expert."

"How about the White House, Downing Street, and Kremlin psychos, red-eyed and rubbing their bellies while munching on national emblems, flags for example?"

Margery laughed. "Splendid, Arty. And the caption?"

"WATCH OUT, THE NAZIS ARE ABOUT. NEXT ON THEIR MENU WILL BE *YOU*."

"Yes, I like it. How soon would you be able to cobble together one of these bot thingies?"

"By this evening. How would that suit?"

Margery leaned back in her leather swivel and clapped. "You are a genius, Arty Arthuro."

"Just doing my job, ma'am."

"And circulation...?"

"Would be immediate once you've approved the final product. All it will need is the touch of a button and we'll be live all across the Internet."

"Whoop*ee*."

~ * ~

Ahead of his hearing at Bow Street Magistrates Court on charges of reckless driving and using threatening behaviour to police officers, at Paddington Green Police Station PCs Angus O'Connell and Jim "The Taser" Tomlinson did a check on the national police data bank into Sir Montmorency Devine's history to establish if he had any recent priors, which of course he did.

"Look at this," said Angus, pointing at what the Henley-on-Thames coppers had termed an "incident" that had occurred on the Devine estate.

"Mmm, busy little boy our peer's been," said Jim, scrolling through the report. "Shooting 'invaders' in their bums, eh? Only the local lads let him off. No reason given. Weird, eh?"

"Very. Mind you, you know how it is with toffs, how they can get away with anything they want. Wouldn't like to point any fingers, but who's to say he didn't have the local lads in his pocket?"

"True enough, Angus. Which we will never know."

"Not ever, my friend. Tell you what, though, why don't we have a little check in *Who's Who* to see if he's listed there. After all, you don't get to be a sir for nothing, do you?"

Jim laughed. "No, it normally costs a few thousand quid or being pals with Missus Queen or one of her screwball family."

Nonetheless, the pair checked *Who's Who* online and found there a glowing report of Sir Montmorency's diplomatic contribution along with his Russian wife Svetlana to American/Soviet relations back in the dark days prior to Gorbachev. It also mentioned the couple's two children, Leon and Taya.

Angus raised an eyebrow. "Impressive. But didn't he tell us he didn't *have* a family?"

"You're right, pal, he did. Otherwise, we'd have called them. Mind you, he *was* weeping a bit when he said it."

"True enough. Never stopped bleeding weeping since he's been here," said Angus, who took to rubbing his chin, then after a minute, added, "You reckon he might be more sad and mad than bad, Jim?"

The Taser nodded. "His past looks a whole lot different from his present, that's for sure. Shrink time before Bow Street, perhaps? If he has gone certifiably doolally in his old age, the charges aren't going to stand up anyway, are they? And we'd look like a pair of mutts who hadn't checked the Mental Health Act rules."

"Right. Plus, maybe we should try calling this family that doesn't exist. If they do, there must be numbers for them *some*where."

"First the shrink, *then* the family," said Jim, levering himself out of his chair. "No good stirring the pot till we know what's in it. Agreed?"

"Fair enough."

"I'll get on to the psych boys and ask them to send someone over."

That someone was Doctor Richard Duff, who turned up the following morning and spent two hours with Sir Montmorency behind closed doors running a series of tests to establish signs of Alzheimer's or outright insanity or both while Angus and Jim waited outside for results.

"Well?" asked Angus of Duff when the criminal/patient had been marched off back to his cell, again weeping. "What d'you reckon? Bonkers or bad?"

"It's a tricky case," said Duff, who had a reputation for arriving at this conclusion about all his cases unless the subject was openly admitting to being Boy George or a rabbit, hence the nickname Tricky Dicky.

"*Very* tricky," he added before listing in long and lugubrious detail the acronymed tests he'd run, thereby leaving Jim and Angus pretty much comatose.

It was Jim who finally interrupted. "And your conclusion from all this, Doctor? Do we keep him and charge him or do we send him to hospital?"

Duff scratched his head. "Hard to say. On the one hand yes, on the other hand no."

Angus sighed. "To which part of the question?"

"Both, although I would tend toward the latter."

"Meaning hospital?"

"Possibly, or maybe under strict supervision to his family. He needs care, no doubt about that."

"So you reckon the magistrates would throw out the charges?" said Jim.

"I am not a magistrate, Constable," said Duff huffily. "That's for you lot to wonder."

Both Angus and Jim shrugged and blew air through puffed-out cheeks.

"At least tell us what's wrong with him," said Angus.

Duff straightened his back and stuck out his neck like a turkey. "As far as I can deduce?"

"As...far...as...you...can...deduce," said Jim, at which Duff reeled off the acronym PRSD fuelled for many years, possibly a lifetime, by LTPAMHS.

"You must understand, however," he went on in what he thought of as clarification, "that there are many men out there suffering from the latter, if not yet, the former. Take our current prime minister, for example, or the deviant in the White House. Are they actually *crimi*nal, one asks oneself, or are they merely the worst manifestations of socially sanctioned nastiness? A moot point indeed, one feels, although in this case, the subject is at least showing remorse."

Angus checked out some wax in his left ear. "Mind telling us what the letters stand for?"

"Post Retirement Stress Disorder and Long-Term Psychotic Alpha Male Hubris Syndrome, both of which were conditions I explored in my doctoral thesis. You might say I in*vented* them," said Duff, preening.

Standing and showing Duff the door, Angus and Jim muttered, "Thanks so much, Doc," while choking back the "now piss off out of here" on the tips of their tongues.

"Fucking hell," said Angus when the show was over. "What...a... dork."

"You can say that again."

So Angus did. Then he said, "So what're we going to do now? Keep the old bastard here? Send him to the loony bin? What?"

Jim plucked a hair from his right eyebrow. "Call the family. That was one of our options in the first place, and the Duffer said it too, right? Just testing the ground before he turned up, I did a little research. There was no number listed for the son and the one for the mother just rang and rang and kept going to message, but I found one for the daughter, although I haven't tried yet. Want to give it a go?"

Angus nodded. "Do it, nothing to lose."

And that's how Taya heard of her father's parlous situation. Her phone had been blocked against *his* calls, but there was no way she could avoid one from the police. At first, she thought it was just another scam looking for money, but proper IDs were given and, from the description, there was no question of whom they had in their custody.

"Omi*god*," she wailed, employing a term she had long since foresworn.

Twenty-eight

Arty Arthuro's bots might have died the same swift death as many other lunatic fringe missives swirling around the World Wide Web had it not been for the English-speaking behind-the-scenes puppetmasters at the White House and Downing Street shooting themselves in the foot by vehemently railing against such accusations of nazism on Facebook, Twitter, Instagram, WhatsApp, Google etc, etc. Okay, the Kremlin, as usual when accused of nastiness of any kind, said nothing. It didn't need to, given the established absolutism of its psycho's power. But for the more recent autocrats controlling the US and the UK, the insult was just too much to bear. Plus, they feared, with its constant repetition, it might eventually trigger counter-productive memories in even the most cherished of their "left-behind working man" support base. Hence the manner in which their handlers waded into the debate by choreographing their puppets to deny absolutely, categorically, and beyond all reasonable doubt they were by any stretch of the imagination fascists, Nazis, or any other species of horrible anti-democratic sub-humans, quite the opposite, in fact. They were populists, defenders of the "people" against the arrogance of the Janus-faced intellectuals and parliamentarians and proud of it.

"Me? A Nasty? Good God and goodness gracious me, in the name of all that's blessed," blethered the Downing Street psycho whose continual proroguing of parliament was believed by many to be a criminal act for which he should be imprisoned. "By pursuing a successful conclusion of Brexit, I was simply enacting the will of working people. In me you can trust."

The White House psycho praised these words on Twitter saying his British counterpart was his kind of guy, one with whom he would surely do business, and reaffirming his own holier-than-thou belief that America was the greatest democracy the world had ever known and he would fight to the death to protect it. This in spite of facing yet another impeachment attempt and increasing unrest on both sides of Congress about his refusal to condemn racist, homophobic and other attacks by his core hillbilly and redneck supporters. The accusation of being a Nazi he ridiculed, saying he was the "sweetest guy on earth" and anyway, it was all a witch hunt and the usual fake news.

Which was when the story spread from a purely social-media bonanza to closer inspection by the international print, TV, and radio media. Not that the puppetmasters initially minded. In their inverted logic, such publicity would do no harm at all to their front men, would merely further fuel their popularity amongst the working saps who had bought their *Übermensch* narrative in the first place, who adored their heroes for breaking the very rules they too longed to break. And good fucking riddance to the "enemies of the people," media eejits who kept banging on in their girlie ways about democracy, ethics, and legality and telling them Populism was only the first step towards Nazism. Let them all rot in hell when the glory days came. So far, so very good for the psychos and their handlers.

Until small signs of the backlash began to appear, that was. To begin with, these were little more than isolated and easily dismissed skirmishes at populist rallies such as the Munich event, but that was only the start of things as Arty's bot continued relentlessly on, and on, and *on* to tell folk about the imminent menace of Nazism in their cities and towns, a menace they were no longer able to ignore or pretend was happening in someone's else's back yard. Even in the small and peaceable town of Lewes, East Sussex, windows were broken and anti-Semitic slogans daubed on homes. And similar atrocities were recorded in a number of European countries, most notably Germany.

All of which gave rise to the onset of the fledgling Save Democracy protest marches in cities across the United States and Europe that irritated the psychos and threatened to burst their bubble. They weren't *total* fools after all and, loathe it though they might, were fully aware of how the Extinction Rebellion had started. Small time, that was how, by some autistic kid from Sweden. But no matter how hard they'd tried to deride and rubbish her as a mentally deranged moron, she'd ended up in the same UN room as the White House psycho and made a fool of him. *Not* what they needed *this* time around. Not at all it wasn't, especially when this new bunch of kids, backed by their parents, took to school-striking, marching, and demanding the right to live their lives in the freedom of democratic dispensations.

What was particularly stupid of the proto-Nazis was to produce the counter to Arty's bot showing the same three psychos only this time smiling benignly while handing out candy to children above the caption: THESE GUYS NAZIS? YOU HAVE TO BE KIDDING."

Anyway, such was the extensive political fallout of Arty Arthuro's intervention and Margery Middleton was pleased.

"At least we've put a tiger amongst the pigeons," she told Mervyn Vincent on the phone. "A better result than one could ever have hoped for."

"Indeed," said Mervyn, who'd been following these events closely. "Which I assume means our initial plan of releasing a reformed Leon Devine onto the scene would be small beer in the circs."

"Quite. From what you've told me, the man has problems enough at the moment. Wish him well from me, would you?"

"With pleasure, Margery."

"Who knows, one day I might even welcome him back into the fold. On a trial basis, of course."

Mervyn smiled. "I'm sure he would appreciate the offer."

~ * ~

The man in question was currently back in the Devine family home in Henley-on-Thames where he, his mother, and his sister were awaiting the return of Sir Montmorency from Paddington Green cop shop to which Taya had given the family consent, but only after a critical exchange of views among herself, Svetlana, and Leon.

"We can't just leave him to rot in prison or some mental institution," Taya had argued, an opinion with which Svetlana had at first viscerally disagreed.

"Why not? Serve the old bastard right. I hope they throw the book at him and lock him up for a long time."

"That's the problem, they can't because he's gone bonkers, and the charges won't stick," explained Leon, who had insisted on taking part in the discussion despite Taya's advice to the contrary.

"It'll only upset you, darling. Leave it all to me and Mama," she'd said.

But Leon was having none of it. "Good of you, love. But if I'm going to be the new man I'm trying to be, this would be the toughest test."

Taya had squeezed his hand and kissed him. "True enough, darling. Good luck then."

"Leon's right, Mama," she said. "According to the cops, either we look after him or it's the loony bin."

Svetlana remained adamant. "Bah. The man ruined my life *and* yours, now we're supposed to take care of him all because the police can't lock him up? What's the matter with him anyway?"

Taya explained as best she could the PRSD diagnosis fuelled for many years, possibly a lifetime, by LTPAMHS.

"Tell me about it," said Svetlana. "The man's a monster. Charming for the first few years he was, then a...*monster*. You must know it, my poor Leonka."

Leon nodded. "He did me harm, no question."

"So why are you wanting to help him *now*?"

"Because, Mama, I too became a monster just like him."

"With*out* him you wouldn't have," Svetlana insisted.

"True enough. But I now understand his mindset, which may be useful when it comes to dealing with him. *I* am trying to change, and I may be able to help him through the process too. Not an easy road, but..."

Svetlana waved a dismissive hand. "And you think he *can* change? At *his* age?"

"The police say he was showing remorse," said Taya. "Weeping a lot."

Svetlana scowled. "Self-pity probably."

The conversation continued back and forth in this manner for a further hour until Taya tempted her mother with the plan for Sir Monty's future she and Leon had cooked up ahead of the meeting, the one that only allowed their father back onto the Devine estate on the strict understanding in future it would be Svetlana in control of every aspect of domestic arrangements. Any deviation from this volte-face and there would be hell to pay, including his immediate removal to the nearest psychiatric ward where they could give him all the brain-numbing pills they wanted for his PRSD/ LTPAMHS.

And, to their astonishment and pleasure, the ruse worked.

"Well, I suppose..." said Svetlana, firing up her fourth black Sobranie and sipping at her second glass of vodka. "And you children would help me in this new life?"

"All you'd have to do is call," said Leon with a smile. "And let us be clear, I shall be the one to present this deal to Father."

Svetlana laughed. "No disrespect, Leonka, but *that* will come as a big surprise to him."

"And about time too," said Taya. "Now are we finally agreed I should make that call and prepare the ground here till the police offload him?"

"Agreed," said Leon and, after a pause, Svetlana too.

"Okay then, I'll arrange a date and time," said Taya.

~ * ~

This was how it came to pass that some days later the trio was peering through the mega-lounge windows of the family home when the cop car pulled up outside the estate gates and asked to be buzzed through, a task Leon hurried downstairs to perform before idling at the front door to greet the parent who'd ruined his life.

And it was some shock he got when PCs Angus O'Connell and Jim "The Taser" Tomlinson stepped out of the suped-up Ford Focus and ushered from the back seat a wild white-haired, skeletal figure walking with some difficulty and the aid of a stick.

"Father?" said Leon, giving the thumbs up to Angus and Jim who, satisfied all was well, drove off.

"Son. Good to see you," Sir Montmorency managed to mutter as he crossed the threshold.

"Good to see you too. Mama and Taya are waiting indoors."

Sir Monty smiled. "That's nice, a proper welcome home party. Good of Mama to come too. I rather thought I might have lost her. Been a bit of a naughty boy, don't you know?"

"You're not the only one," said Leon. "Maybe one of these days we'll swap stories."

"With pleasure, son," Sir Monty was saying as Svetlana appeared in the hallway and took her husband in an awkward embrace.

"So you're back," she said as pleasantly as she was able.

"Not exactly in one piece, my dear, as you can see. But yes, I'm back."

Taya waved from behind her mother's shoulders. "Hi, Daddy."

"Hello, sweetheart. So here we are, all together again. I don't deserve it, but I hope it stays that way. Let us say lessons have been learnt, and I shall abide by them."

And, true to his word, Sir Monty did. Leon was to be pleased over the following weeks that his "new domestic arrangements" speech was deemed unnecessary even by Svetlana, and that common-ground understandings between him and his father were reached without recriminations. There were regrets, of course, but these were set to one side against the chance of a new future.

"One cannot bury the past, son," said Sir Monty on one occasion as the pair strolled the estate. "Like nuclear fuels, it has an unpredictable half-life. But at least one can learn from its mistakes."

Leon nodded. "True enough...Dad."

Twenty-nine

Having returned with Taya to her flat while Svetlana took charge of Sir Montmorency, Leon was still ruminating on buried pasts when he got the somewhat delayed call from Connie Horowitz. Delayed because, despite Lizzie Leah's reassurances, even the normally shoot-first-and-ask-questions-later Connie had debated with herself how to handle such a call to a guy two of whose toes she'd shot off. Okay, Lizzie had said he had new falsies, but still it could be kinda awkward. Okay too, he was now supposed to be Mister Nice Guy but how nice did a guy have to be to chat on the phone with the woman who'd maimed him? The nicest of *all* Mister Nice Guys, that was how nice. Twice more she had called Lizzie just to check and twice more she'd received the same answer, both times with the same message, plus confirmation she hadn't broken her word and called the other Mrs McGuires, to which she honestly replied no she hadn't. Also, she'd agreed to tell Leon nothing of her little plan for him. That she would leave to Lizzie.

"*Ookay* then, here goes," she muttered one sultry morning in Muir Woods after having patrolled her lands and found no poacher worthy of shooting.

"Who?" said Leon, understandably not recognizing a voice buried in the past.

"Um, Connie."

"Connie?"

"Horowitz? You mean the Muir Woods Missus McGuire?"

Hiatus while Leon's blood froze and he took to remembering nuclear fuels' half-lives, or in this case the potential dangers of being hunted down by the Mrs McGuire's Society against which Mervyn had warned him.

"You still there, honey?"

Honey?

"This *is* Leon Devine I'm talking with? Your friend Lizzie Leah told me that was your real name."

"Yuh-yes. Wuh-what d'you wuh-want?"

Connie took a deep breath. "To apologize."

"For?"

"Shooting your toes off. That was out of order."

Leon computed this as best he could. The woman was apologizing to *him*? Plus calling him 'honey'?

"Never mind," he said experimentally. "These things happen."

"Ain't that the truth?"

"Also," said Leon with a little more confidence, "I guess I should be the one apologizing to *you*. Back then, I was something of an arsehole."

"Yeah, well. We all have our ups and downs."

"More downs than ups in my case. Anyway, how're *you* doing?"

"I'm good."

"Still the Lone Ranger?"

Connie laughed. "You bet. Only, hey, Lizzie was telling me you ain't an asshole no more, so *some* upping must've been happening."

"She *said* that?"

"She sure did, several times. You should be thankful to that gal, Mister Devine."

Leon dodged that issue and instead, querulously, asked about the Mrs McGuire Society.

"You heard about that?"

"Yuh-yes."

"Well, no need to worry, honey. I ain't said nothing to them. Far as they know you could be in Honolulu. Also, it may be they're gonna let you off the hook."

Leon blew relieved air through his teeth. "Thanks."

"It was all Lizzie's idea. She's the gal you gotta thank."

"I will."

"Okay, so I've done apologizing and you were great with your accepting. Only other thing I called for was to wish you good luck with your life turnaround. Can't be easy."

"Thank you. It wasn't...*isn't*."

"I gotcha. I know how hard it can be. The woman you're talking with didn't even have the courage to fly over the Britland and say hello in person. Fear of flying. That was also a book, right?"

"By Erica Jong."

"That's the dame. *Any*how, all good wishes. Oh, and by the way, listen up when Lizzie tells you of the little plan she has for you. It's a humdinger."

"Plan?" said Leon, but the scratching of a sick raccoon at her door distracted Connie.

"Sorry hon...gotta run. Animals in need," was how she ended the call.

~ * ~

Alerted by Connie to her having hinted at—*not* described—her little plan for Leon, Lizzie struck while the iron was hot and called him too.

"Glad things are working out okay with your folks. Taya's been telling me all about it," she said after the initial hellos and how're you doings.

"Thanks. Yeah, pretty weird, but the old man seemed all set to be a better boy so I didn't have all that much work to do."

"Maybe the cops had something to do with that."

"Maybe, or maybe the situation just gave him the space he needed to take a good look at himself and not like what he saw."

"The same as you perhaps," Lizzie dared say.

Leon took it on the chin. "Like father, like son, eh?"

"Only it's normally like *mother* like son, like father like daughter."

"Well, well, anyway, *any*way. Listen, Lizzie, I just had Connie Horowitz on the phone. The Muir Woods Missus McGuire?"

"Oh yeah. Wow. That must've been a surprise, out of the blue like that," said Lizzie disingenuously.

"It *was*. Especially as she was calling to apologize for shooting my toes off."

"Golly gee."

"Yes. And she also said the Mrs McGuire Society might not be after my balls anymore."

"Great to hear."

"It was. Then she said you had some plan for me but wouldn't say what. You and she been talking?"

"A couple of times. I like her, Leon. She's a bit of a rough diamond, but she is an American frontier girl after all."

"True enough. Anyway, this plan?"

"Was the reason I was calling. Free this evening, are you?"

Leon laughed. "I'm always free, it's the new me. Sometimes I even watch TV— hey, that even rhymes."

Lizzie laughed too. "You're a poet and you didn't even know it. But about this evening, I was wondering if we could meet up for a chat."

"That would be nice."

"At The Hand in Hand, say around six?"

"Good with me. Should I ask Mervyn along too?"

"Not this time. Just you, me, and Jürgen."

"Okay, six it is."

~ * ~

And so it was that Lizzie Leah, Leon Devine, and Jürgen came together again on a torrentially raining evening at the pub that had played so much of a part in their story one way and another. And, as a special treat given the conditions, landlord Sean O'Casey welcomed them *all* inside, Jürgen included.

"Wouldn't want the poor doggie out there all on his own getting soaked," he said.

So, dripping, inside they went and, in the company of another Lurcher called Bill, a Retriever called Millie, two Heinz 57 mutts called John and Betsy and their nameless owners, found themselves a quiet table in a far corner by a genuine wood-burning fire. Jürgen wasn't best pleased, having preferred to sit closer to Bill, Millie, John, and Betsy but was quieted by a special lamb-flavoured Bonio provided by Sean while enquiring what Lizzie and Leon would like to drink.

"I could do you a couple of tasty rum and blacks to keep the cold out."

But no, as Lizzie had advised Mervyn on a blasting hot day in some other lifetime there was nothing a pint of Young's Special couldn't fix, so that's what they went for.

"Coming right up, my lovelies. Always the best choice," said Sean, who added, "And smoke if you want to. What's the point of laws when our self-titled 'prime' minister breaks them every day of the week?"

"So then," said Leon after the brimming sleevers had been set before them and Jürgen was chewing happily on his Bonio, "this plan of yours."

Which was when Lizzie Leah screwed up all her courage and asked Leon Devine how he would feel about becoming Vice-President of the Mrs McGuires Society, causing Leon to hold onto his chair to prevent himself from toppling onto the floor.

"*What*?" he spluttered. "Who, *me*? Something of an oxymoron *that* would be!"

Uncertain as to what an oxie moron was and thinking perhaps backward bullock, Lizzie just shrugged, smiled, and carried on with the speech she had been preparing in her head for some weeks, the one that championed Leon as a reformed macho male once versed in the ways of female exploitation to be *precisely* the sort of person to hold a torch for women's rights.

"Ever read *Fifty Shades of Grey*?" she asked.

Shamefully, Leon had to admit he had dipped into it. What he didn't admit was back then he'd pretty much modeled himself on the Grey character.

"Well, just imagine if Christian suddenly sees the error of his ways being Mister Dominator and apologizes to Anastasia for the harm he's done her."

"Wouldn't have been the same book that sold seventy trillion copies to sex-starved housewives all around the world."

"No, but just supposing."

"Okay."

"Think of how much more she might *really* have loved him if he'd come clean with her and admitted it was all a front to hide who he was deep down."

Leon nodded. "I see where you're going with this. For Christian Grey read Leo McGuire aka Leon Devine, right?"

"Spot on. And so, when we're talking about the Missus McGuire Society, think how much clout it would give the movement to be headed up by *both* Connie Horowitz *and* the bloke whose toes she shot off, the bloke—you—who's turned his life around and wants to make amends. How much insider advice you could give women around the world when it comes to recognizing the telltale signs *before* they get themselves into any shit. How they'd *believe* what you were telling them. How many miserable fantasies you could nip in the bud."

"You'd make a good lawyer, Lizzie Leah."

"Lawyer my arse, they're all liars looking out for a fast buck. I'm a bus driver and proud of it."

"Raaf, raaf," said Jürgen in a break from masticating his lamb-flavoured Bonio.

"*Any*way, Mister Devine, are you up for it or aren't you?"

"Do I have a choice?"

"Sure you do. Say no and I won't marry you. Say yes and I will."

Leon swallowed half his sleever of Young's Special in one gulp, took from a pocket a packet of Svetlana's Black Sobranies, selected one, with a shaking hand fired it up, and then collapsed into a faux coughing fit with much chest thumping.

"In your own time, love," said Lizzie. "But we haven't got all night."

"*Muh-marry* me?" Leon eventually managed to splutter.

"That's the deal I've got on offer, pal. Last time around it was Missus McGuire. *This* time it would be the real thing...Missus Devine. Your choice, take it or leave it."

"And this is *you* proposing to *me*?"

"You want an action replay?"

Which was when genuine tears came to the eyes of Leon Devine.

"I accept," he said.

"Being VP *and* marrying me?"

"Both."

"You're a good man, Leon Devine. Somehow, deep down, I always knew it. Kiss me to seal the deal."

It was while Leon was kissing Lizzie and Lizzie was kissing him right back that landlord Sean O'Casey reappeared asking about Young's Special refills and Leon told him the Young's had worked its usual wonders but, in the circs, perhaps a bottle of champers might be in order.

"Circs?" said Sean.

So, leaving out the *precise* details, Leon explained and Sean was delighted.

"Coming right up and on the house," he said. Never having experienced one himself, there was nothing Sean O'Casey liked better than the prospect of a good "welding," as he put it.

"And may God bless the both of you," he said hurrying off to uncork a bottle of The Hand in Hand's finest French bubbly.

"I'd rather be blessed by Russell's teapot," said Leon when Sean was out of earshot. "Far too many gods knocking around, faux human ones too, and all they ever cause is trouble. I live to tell the tale."

"It'll be a civil ceremony for us, love" said Lizzie. "John Lennon can play us out with 'Imagine.' All the people sharing all the world and like that?"

Leon shrugged. "Wasn't he a bit of a god, too?"

"Yeah, but he did his best to live it down. This is a Scouse girl you're marrying, Mister Devine, and trust me, we pick our heroes with care."

"And you picked me."

Lizzie laughed. "After a long and winding road, sweetheart, but with hope in my heart."

She was still singing extracts from the Liverpool FC anthem "Walk On" when Sean returned with the bubbly and two crystal glasses reserved for only special occasions. And once he'd set them down on the table, he joined in with the singing. Lizzie was delighted at the accompaniment as the two of them walked through tempests with confidence and pride and looked forward to a future in which they would never again have to walk alone.

"Didn't have you down as a footie fan, love," said Lizzie when the singing was over.

"It's not so much the football as the idea, darling. So much shit in the world at the moment, we need something...*anything*...to keep us smiling."

Looking on, Leon nodded. It was hard to argue with *that*.

Epilogue

Lizzie and Leon were married in a short service with no speeches at Merton Register Hall with only Mervyn, Taya, Svetlana, Sir Montmorency, Jürgen, Suzie, and—unexpectedly at the last minute Margery Middleton—as guests, and lived happily ever after. Well, as happily as any married couple. You know how it is with marriages, the little niggles that can surface unannounced, the need for forbearance, all that kind of thing, but generally speaking life was good. Lizzie carried on driving her bus and, from time to time, Leon took the ride to...partly, he said, to keep Jürgen company, although he also enjoyed the odd chat with other passengers.

Aside from the domestic scene, Leon was also enjoying his role as VP of the Mrs McGuires Society spending long hours on the phone and email to not only Connie Horowitz and its other members, but also endangered women across the globe. Within months, the service had gone viral and Leon was asked by Margery Middleton if he might consider a new and quite different role at MI6 with specific reference to protecting women in her organisation from such lures in exchange for state secrets, to which he agreed. A very busy but very contented man Leon Devine was to become.

Much the same could be said for his father and mother who, working in harmony for the first time in a long time, had at Sir Monty's behest reviewed their roles as lord and lady of the manor and established and funded a number of charitable initiatives in and around Henley-on-Thames. "About time I gave something back," was Sir Monty's new mantra and Svetlana loved him for it. Taya contributed full time, too, after quitting her post at the university on the grounds things weren't what they used to be, given how much it cared for money and how little for students.

Hal Schornstein too, after a year's intense treatment at the Long Island establishment, emerged a new man and, despite intense pressure from the White House, told the psycho who ran it where he could go shove his bullshit. "To a place where the sun don't shine," were Hal's actual words before, along with Sergei Figov and Georg Büchner, he relocated to the Indonesian island of Lombok where the trio set up an untraceable bot-and-troll facility dedicated to the extinction of populism. Not that it was a spectacular success, of course, as the Teflon psychos in The White House, Kremlin, and Downing Street steamed full on ahead with their hubris, but that's a familiar story, of whose disastrously rhizomatic nature you will be only too well aware wherever you live.

Which leaves Doctor Mervyn Vincent. Whatever happened to him?

Well, Mervyn turned down the offer from Margery Middleton of a return to MI6 with a generously enhanced salary, quit his private eyeing activities and became a novelist. Why? Not to recount lurid tales from his professional past, that was for sure. He'd sampled a few of those from ex-colleagues and didn't think much of them, or the movies they'd spawned. Too much surface glamour, too much reliance on genre fiction, and too little insight into the human species, Mervyn reckoned. No, no, if he were to write a book, it would have to come from his own heart and to hell with conventions. What he liked best about the process wasn't just the first draft in which some kind of a story emerged, but the later edits when he already knew what had happened but could add meat to the bones—new words, new insights, new twists. Every evening, as Suzie lay beside him, he devoted two or three hours to the process and enjoyed every minute of it.

Not that you will yet have seen the name Mervyn Vincent on a single spine in either your local bookstore or on the Internet, given publishers are so stuck on books they're sure will sell and unwilling to throw a lifeline to a person doing it differently. But who knew? Maybe someday, *some*body would put novelty before profit, Mervyn would muse. What should the novel *be* except new, after all? Not that the lack of recognition bothered him. What he took more pleasure from than being famous was constructing the world according to Mervyn, which was a much less crazy place than the real world. A shame fiction couldn't change that awkward fact, but you never knew. Maybe one day...

Meet Paddy Bostock

Paddy Bostock was born in Liverpool and holds a B.A. in Modern Languages and History, a PGDip TESL, and a PhD in English Literature. Down the years he has been a barman, a road worker, a songwriter, an educational researcher, a translator, a book reviewer, a university lecturer and Chair of Department, and a high school mentor. He lives in London with his wife, writer Dani Cavallaro, and likes animals and bicycles.

Works From The Pen Of Paddy Bostock

Mole Smith and The Diamond Studded Pistol - Tricked into believing he is to be accused of a murder he hasn't committed, PI gofer Mole Smith is inveigled into the search for an ancient order and its famous diamond-studded pistol. What Mole doesn't know, as he undertakes the quest with his partner Oksana, is what powers lurk behind the scenes.

La Joie de Vivre - To escape a floundering relationship and writer's block, Ambler leaves London for La Rochelle, where he stumbles into a tangle of corruption and revenge with a grisly murder at its centre: a crime which could cost Ambler his freedom — and his sanity.

Foot Soldiers - Outraged at the market economic policies adopted by their university, the Podiatry department kidnap a senior academic in protest. The chance coincidence of the interests of the gutter press, Welsh Freedom Fighters, and a Prime Minister struggling for re-election ensures a minor campus story escalates into cataclysmic national proportions.

Peace on Earth - Mankind profits from nothing more than war. Hence, rumours about the existence of a disk said to contain the formula to "peace on earth," obtained by a failed actor with a penchant for visions, pose a major threat to the planet. This unleashes a frantic hunt for the disk across continents, involving government agencies, master criminals, petty criminals, and would-be criminals, plus the local population of Pont-y-Pant: the tiny Welsh village on which disparate characters converge as the putative location of the errant disk

However, nobody has taken into account the role that will be played by the three-year-old Newfoundland acting as the disk's self-appointed custodian   .

Chosen - Jeremy Crawford has had enough of his life as a megawealthy banker and is prepared to give up all its privileges for the sake of freedom. The trigger of this drastic change of heart? The realization that, since childhood, he has made no choices of his own and only ever been 'chosen'.

Fubars - Tracing various meanings of the acronym "fubar," the story chronicles the adventures of an array of characters from diverse cultural, social and ethnic backgrounds, all of whom strive to leave their mark—at times in legitimate and at times in iniquitous ways. Among them are Fergus Ulysses Barr, the timid scion of Britain's selfish aristocracy, Dwayne Junior Zobinsky, the offspring of an unscrupulous New York tycoon and an iconoclastic abstract artist, Tosh, a half-caste renegade and troubadour, Tosh's loyal—and heroic—pooch, Mutt, and their respective girlfriends and assorted parents, as well as big-world politicians and their associates.

As the adventures unfold, one message emerges: whereas in the private sphere opportunities for harmony and reconciliation arise, mainly at the behest of the younger generations, in the public/political arena, strife reigns unabated.

The Jake Flintlock Series

Two Down - Failed crime-fiction writer, professional plagiarist and part-time private eye Dr. Jake Flintlock and his sidekick Dr. Bum Park are within a whisker of catching the killer of the Vice-Chancellor of the university that sacked Jake...But this is no ordinary murderer, as they are about to discover.

For The Love Of a Woman - Ravaged by sun, mosquitoes and his partner Claudia's extended family while on a summer holiday to seaside Italy, PI Jake Flintlock is keen—despite having been asked to stay to solve a local murder—to return to London for good. But then, after a second murder, he and his PI associate Bum Park are made an offer they can't refuse and once in Rome, discover a whole new meaning to the words la famiglia,

For The Love Of a Woman - Ravaged by sun, mosquitoes and his partner Claudia's extended family while on a summer holiday to seaside Italy, PI Jake Flintlock is keen—despite having been asked to stay to solve a local murder—to return to London for good. But then, after a second murder, he and his PI associate Bum Park are made an offer they can't refuse and once in Rome, discover a whole new meaning to the words la famiglia,

Hand In Glove - PI Dr Jake Flintlock and his sidekick Dr Bum Park are inveigled by American theater director Chuck Cinzano into the investigation of a severed hand in a baseball glove on Primrose Hill, London. The assignment morphs into a murder case as Chuck is "stabbed to death" in Jake's home. Having flown to Sausalito, CA, Jake and Bum begin to suspect they are being used as actors in a play. Yet, a real crime has been committed and somehow the culprit has to be found.

The Basque Head Case - Following the accidental discovery of a "head" afloat on the Regent Canal, London, PI Dr Jake Flintlock is seduced into taking on a case which draws him to Northern Spain and its darker history. There, in the company of his sidekick Dr Bum Park, Jake faces a mystery wherein an ancient Basque legacy of vengeance and strife intersects with a private vendetta - one with Jake himself as its unwitting target.

The *Magical Mystery Serie*s

Noddy In Wonderland - In his wildest dreams, Afghanistan war veteran Noddy Stoddart fantasised about becoming king of Liverpool, even though his brother, Knobby, told him he was crazy. But shooting government minister St John Jaunston in the bottom with an air rifle on a visit to the city leads bizarrely to Noddy's dream coming true--as president of the newly created People's Republic of Liverpool.

The Bore - Since birth, Professor Thaddeus Proctor has lacked any attractive qualities, his only asset being a formidable yawn capable of precipitating anyone who comes into contact with it into a state of soporific compliance. The yawn's power remains untapped until Thaddeus is offered the chance of competing in a TV game show, and becomes its champion.

Not even then, however, is the yawn deployed to the utmost of its capacities. It takes Thaddeus's removal to Fairyland, and involvement in the protection of its precarious peace, to test the yawn's true might, and reveal the professor is no mere "bore."

The Hanging - As the troll Vilius Vilutis hunts Cumbria in search of the magical onyx capable of revolutinizing smartphones and defeat his business foe Zingy Splitz, the elves Mordecai and Hazchem strive to keep the onyx safe. But then two hangings disrupt the peace, and darker forces begin to surface

What Ifs - The chance meeting with Gabi in Queen Mary's Garden, Regent's Park, is only the start of a series of unworldly events for aspiring writer James Cockburn, which will involve him first in a murder investigation and treasure hunt in St Ives, Cornwall, and then in the increasingly frenetic machinations of politicians and mobsters in both the human dimension and fairyland.

Letter to Our Readers

Enjoy this book?

You can make a difference

As an independent publisher, Wings ePress, Inc. does not have the financial clout of the large New York Publishers. We can't afford large magazine spreads or subway posters to tell people about our quality books.

But, we do have something much more effective and powerful than ads. We have a large base of loyal readers.

Honest Reviews help bring the attention of new readers to our books.

If you enjoyed this book, we would appreciate it if you would spend a few minutes posting a review on the site where you purchased this book or on the Wings ePress, Inc. webpages at: https://wingsepress. com/

Visit Our Website

For The Full Inventory
Of Quality Books:

Wings ePress.Inc
https://wingsepress.com/

Quality trade paperbacks and downloads
in multiple formats,
in genres ranging from light romantic comedy
to general fiction and horror.
Wings has something for every reader's taste.
Visit the website, then bookmark it.
We add new titles each month!

Wings ePress Inc.

3000 N. Rock Road

Newton, KS 67114

www.ingramcontent.com/pod-product-compliance
Lightning Source LLC
Chambersburg PA
CBHW070644100726
47907CB00007B/2100